Carson looked tired and a little bit sick.

Meg dropped her bantering tone. "What is it?" she asked with concern.

"Villa wants us to get married tonight," he blurted out.

Meg stared at him. He was definitely looking sick, and what's more, he wasn't making any sense. "What are you talking about, Carson?"

"A wedding, you and me. It seems that Villa's got marriage fever again, and he's decided that we're going to join him in matrimonial bliss."

"I've never heard anything so ridiculous in my life." Meg laughed.

Carson was surprised by her laughter—and a little miffed. After all, he'd had women begging to marry him in the past. They hadn't thought it was a ridiculous idea at all.

"Well, ridiculous or not, we'll have to humor him and go through with it."

"You're not serious!" Meg stopped laughing and her big eyes grew wider as she looked intently into his face. "You *are* serious."

Now it was Carson's turn to tease. "What's the matter? You have something better to do tonight?"

Dear Reader,

This month, Harlequin Historicals celebrates the arrival of spring with stories by four fabulous newcomers.

In *Steal the Stars* by Miranda Jarrett, the author uses her firsthand knowledge of the Rhode Island coast to weave a passionate tale set against the backdrop of America's struggle for independence.

Ana Seymour's delightful heroine finds herself the unwilling guest of an American *bandido* in the camp of the infamous Pancho Villa in *The Bandit's Bride*.

Arabesque by Kit Gardner, for those of you who like a touch of mystery, is the story of star-crossed lovers who discover the seamier side of London's upper class.

Set in medieval Wales, *A Warrior's Heart* by Margaret Moore is an unforgettable story of a soldier, wounded during the Crusades, and the spirited gentlewoman who turns his bitterness to love.

We hope you enjoy our March titles. And please be sure to look for more books by these four talented authors in the coming year.

Sincerely,
The Editors

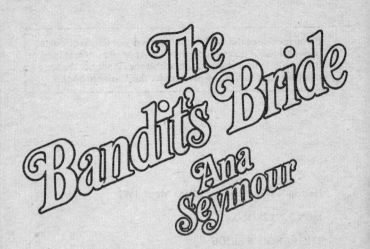

Harlequin Books

TORONTO • NEW YORK • LONDON
AMSTERDAM • PARIS • SYDNEY • HAMBURG
STOCKHOLM • ATHENS • TOKYO • MILAN
MADRID • WARSAW • BUDAPEST • AUCKLAND

Harlequin Historicals first edition March 1992

ISBN 0-373-28716-X

THE BANDIT'S BRIDE

ANA SEYMOUR

is a native Minnesotan of Scandinavian descent, but she has had a long-standing love affair with Mexico—and with a Mexican, her veterinarian husband from Mexico City, whose Latin exuberance has added zest to family gatherings. Ana and her husband live in a one-hundred-year-old house on the edge of one of Minnesota's ten thousand lakes with their two teenage daughters and a sled-dog reject named Aniak.

For my parents,
who taught me that history *is* romance;
and, of course, for M., K. and C.

Prologue

It was so rare to see something resembling a pout on Johnny's normally sunny face that Meg laughed out loud.

"I suppose you think Pancho Villa himself is going to ride right up to the Mendoza ranch and carry me off," she teased, tugging the brim of his Stetson down over his frowning face.

"I'm serious, Meg," the young cowboy said firmly. He took a step back from her and knocked down a hook full of harnesses that had been hanging on the wall in back of him.

"I can't understand your father letting you travel to Mexico at a time like this," he continued. "They've been at their revolution for so long now that it's gotten to the point that no one knows who's shooting at who anymore."

Meg dropped to her knees on the dusty floor of the stable and started to untangle the leather straps of the fallen harnesses. "Well, I'm sure no one's going to be doing any shooting in the middle of Rosa Maria's wedding."

Johnny looked down at Meg's slender back, which was outlined by the tight bolero jacket of her riding outfit. Her reddish-gold hair had come loose during their ride and tumbled in disheveled waves around her shoulders.

"How about I go with you, Meg?" he asked softly.

She turned her face up toward him and her smile lost some of its brightness at the expression in his eyes.

She hesitated a moment before answering. "I'm all grown-up now, Johnny. You don't have to watch over me like a mama polecat anymore."

She watched in silence as her friend heaved a great sigh and lowered himself to sit across from her, his back propped against the wall of the stall behind him.

"Don't ask me to stop watching over you, Meg. It's something that comes naturally, like breathing. I'll never stop."

A little furrow creased the smooth skin between Meg's eyebrows. Juan Carlos—or Johnny, as they all called him—was her very best friend in the world. They had grown up together on Los Alamos, her father's ranch, named for the broad cottonwood trees that shaded the sprawling wooden ranch house from the stark Texas sun. She didn't like to see him unhappy. But just lately it seemed harder at times to laugh together, harder to capture that feeling of devilish recklessness the two had always inspired in each other.

"I would never let Rosa Maria go through this wedding by herself, Johnny," she told him, serious now herself. "She doesn't even know the man, you know. Her family has arranged everything. And poor Rosa just goes meekly along."

Meg gave a rueful shake of her head as memories flooded back to her. She remembered the day she and Rosa had arrived together at the exclusive La Ascensión de los Santos school in El Paso, discovering immediately a common bond in their shared homesickness. That was more than five years ago now; they had both been fourteen and away from home for the first time.

Though they had stayed fast friends from that very first day, they soon discovered that in almost everything but their loneliness they could not be more different.

Rosa Maria had lived the sheltered life of the Spanish-bred Mexican aristocracy. Her family owned a good portion of the state of Chihuahua, and from birth Rosa Maria had been raised like royalty, pampered and protected into a state of absolute helplessness.

It was Meg who had shown her how to make her bed that first morning at school, who had even shown her how to dress herself. And it was Meg who had each day brushed Rosa Maria's long, lustrous black hair and swept it up into a demure bun, which was the only hairstyle the girls were allowed to wear. There had been no female vanities allowed at La Ascención, which had suited Meg fine.

Rosa Maria had always been fascinated and a little bit horrified by Meg's tales of growing up as the only girl on her father's Texas ranch. Meg's stories of cattle brandings, mustang breaking and quail hunts had left her Mexican friend wide-eyed.

"It's families like the Mendozas who have caused that whole mess down there," Johnny said, calling Meg back from her memories.

"From what I hear, things are settling down," Meg answered, her chin lifting slightly.

"Sure, tell that to the families of the eighteen American mining engineers Villa and his men pulled off a train and killed last month."

Meg gave a little shudder. "I know—I've heard all the stories. But I still can't imagine running into any trouble when I'll be miles from anywhere, tucked safely away at the Mendoza ranch."

Johnny reached a well-muscled arm toward her and curled his hand around the back of her slender neck. He shook his head, but for the first time since they had ridden in from their daily ride, his words were accompanied by a grin. "I've known you too long, Meg. Somehow trouble just manages to find you."

Relieved at the lightening of his expression, Meg jumped up and offered him her hands. "Not this time, Johnny. I couldn't get into trouble at the Mendozas if I wanted to. Rosa's father is too strict. Everything there is run in absolute order."

"Doesn't sound like your kind of place, *zorrita*." He used the nickname—little fox—the ranch hands had given her because of her quickness, cleverness and seemingly endless ability to be just one step ahead of them. The name also fit with her tawny red-gold hair, which flamed around her like a golden sunrise as she raced with them across her father's vast acres.

"I'm going for Rosa's sake, not to enjoy myself," she said primly.

"'Not to enjoy myself,'" Johnny mimicked, giving a mocking feminine wiggle. "You can't tell me you're not dying to see what mischief you can get into down there south of the border."

Meg gave a little giggle and shoved him backward into a convenient pile of hay.

"I'm a lady now, Johnny. I'm going to behave myself."

Johnny looked up at her with an exasperated smile. "Now that," he said under his breath, "would be something worth seeing."

Chapter One

Chihuahua, Mexico, 1915

The distinctive smell of rawhide jolted Meg awake, and for the first moments she thought she was out in the corral with a difficult mustang. She struggled at imaginary reins until her vision and sleep-fogged mind cleared and she realized with growing panic that her opponent was no horse.

Strange arms tugged at hers. Through the thin lawn of her nightdress the rawhide strips her assailant was wrapping around her bit sharply into her skin. In the darkness, the man seemed immense, a towering monster. Fear flooded through her, pounding past her ears and gathering in a painful knot at the base of her throat.

Her instinctive thrashing tore loose one end of the rawhide bonds, and the shadowy figure spit out a filthy oath in Spanish into the blackness of the room.

"You might help me out a bit here, *cabrones*," he said in the same language. Suddenly there were others, two—no, three—surrounding her bed.

A rough hand clamped down over her mouth, bruising her lips and pushing her head deep into the feathery mattress. She couldn't breathe. Without conscious thought she twisted her teeth around the fleshy part of the imposing hand and bit down with all her strength.

The intruder called Meg a name in Spanish that even the cowhands back at the ranch had never used—at least not within earshot of her. He pulled back his injured hand and whacked the side of her head, knocking her jaws together with a resounding crack.

The other man, the one with the rawhide, stopped tying her for a minute to whisper furiously, *"No seas imbécil,* Hernandez. You want this whole place down on us? Shut up and hold her still."

"The bitch bit me."

"Too much for you, eh?" The first man chuckled. He pulled something out of a pocket. "Here, stuff this in her mouth."

Her aching jaw was grasped by strong fingers as the man pulled open her mouth and crammed in a cloth that tasted faintly of gun oil. She gagged a couple times as the dry material hit the back of her throat. For a moment she forgot about breathing through her nose, and panic swelled in her again as she thought she was going to suffocate. Fortunately, her natural reflexes took over, and she collapsed in relief as a deep, full breath of air made its way into her lungs.

She closed her eyes. Steady there, Meg, she said to herself. With fierce determination she willed her fear-aroused body to calm itself.

If they were going to kill me, she reasoned, they wouldn't be tying me up. She strained her eyes in the darkness, trying to identify her tormentors, but all she could make out were menacing shadows.

"You shouldn't have hit her."

"I didn't plan to. I told you, she just about took off half my hand."

The gruff voices coming from the phantomlike figures added to the nightmare, though Meg had no trouble understanding their mumbled Spanish. It was all she had heard since arriving at the Mendoza *hacienda* three weeks ago. By now her ear was well attuned to the language's rhythmic cadence.

"Well, see if you can get this tied around her ankles without getting kicked in the gut." The disembodied voice was amused.

Bile rose again in her throat as she felt her nightdress being rudely pushed up and calloused hands grasping at her legs.

"*Muy buena, eh?* A little skinny, but nice," one of them said. "Do you think we get a chance at her after *el jefe* finishes with her?"

"Shut up. We don't even know why he wants her."

"I could make a pretty good guess, my friend." A hand slid up her thigh. Meg was afraid that she was going to be sick.

"Come on, let's get her out of here."

Two of them lifted her indifferently. Her head rolled backward and her sore cheek scraped against the cold metal of a *bandolera* full of bullets draped across the chest of the man who had tied her.

Within minutes they had her out the window of the first-floor guest bedroom of the Mendozas' sprawling ranch house and had boosted her up onto a huge horse into the waiting arms of yet another shadowy figure.

Her arms and legs were immobilized, her mouth had dried up completely around the dirty gag, and the side of her face throbbed. Nevertheless, she felt obliged to register some sort of protest and weakly attempted a struggle in this new captor's arms.

"Just relax, *señorita*," he told her brusquely in Spanish. "We've got a long ride ahead."

Ceasing all efforts at resistance, she let herself be pulled back against the rock-solid chest of the man. He held her easily, almost gently, with one strong arm.

She couldn't have said how long they rode through the night. Shock set in and numbed her senses. The voices of the other riders drifted in and out of her hearing, but the man who held her didn't say a word.

Eventually she became aware that they no longer were riding easily along maguey- and sagebrush-covered plains, but had instead taken a more arduous and steep trail that smelled of pine and was lined on both sides by rocky cliffs. She realized with a start that they were heading up into the harsh sierra. Her mouth twisted with irony. She had been begging Rosa Maria to take her on an excursion up into these haunting, barren mountains since her arrival in Chihuahua.

"It's not safe, Meg darling," her friend had told her earnestly. "The sierra is too full of dangerous people these days."

Meg had paid little attention to Rosa Maria's fears about the sierra. As they had sat each evening on the wide veranda of the Mendoza hacienda watching the sun set in the distance over the craggy peaks, Meg would bring up again and again her desire to explore them.

"We could take a picnic, Rosa," she cajoled her friend. "Just for the day—we'd be back by dark." At school she had been able to talk her unassertive friend into almost anything.

But Rosa Maria had for once held firm. "It is not possible, Meg. I'm sorry, but no one goes up into the sierra these days. There are *bandidos* everywhere."

Now the sierra was exactly where Meg was heading. And it appeared that she was being taken there by those very *bandidos* Rosa Maria had been so afraid of. For the first time since she had been so abruptly awakened she allowed herself to wonder who these men were, and, more important, what they intended to do with her.

It seemed they had been riding straight up for at least an hour. The inclined position of the horse kept her body flattened intimately against that of her captor. As she started to regain her reason, she became more aware of the indecency of the contact through the thin material of her nightdress. The man's hand rested casually against her stomach, his arm pressed against one unbound breast.

She attempted a sound of protest through the cloth in her mouth. By now the entire inside of her throat was so dry that the effort made her gag, and she gave a couple reflexive coughs.

The man holding her reached up and pulled on the end of the cloth. With blessed relief she felt it slip out of her mouth.

"I guess there's not much reason for this anymore," was all he said.

For a few moments Meg let the saliva pool back into her mouth. Finally, in her best schoolgirl Spanish she said indignantly, "I demand to know who you are and where you are taking me."

Her captor stiffened and pulled up his horse. "You're not Mexican," he said in disbelief.

"No, I'm not Mexican—I'm American. And I want to know the meaning of this outrage."

"Christ."

By now a couple of the other riders had caught up to them, blocked from going farther by the narrowness of the trail. Without loosening his grip on her, her captor turned around to them.

"I have news for you, Quiñones. Somehow you've managed to snatch the *wrong girl.*"

She heard several voices at once and could make out only part of the shouted Spanish.

"No es posible!"

"Who the hell is she, then?"

Her captor waved a hand at them and then spoke to her with thinly concealed irritation. "We might start with that question," he said, his voice deep. "Just who in the hell *are* you?"

She gave another useless twist against his steel-hard arm. "I don't have to tell you anything," she choked.

The men around her became somberly quiet as the reality of the situation began to sink in. Finally, one of them asked, "What are we going to do, go back?"

"No time for that now—it'll be dawn within the hour," her captor answered in a low-pitched voice. "We may as well ride on into camp and sort it out there." He shook his head in disgust and nudged his horse forward.

Meg's mind whirled. Who else at the Mendoza ranch could they have meant to take instead of her? The answer was already in her mind before she finished the question. It had to be Rosa Maria. But why? What could these ruffians possibly want with gentle Rosa, just days before her wedding?

But the more immediate question was, now that they had the wrong person, what would they do with *her?*

Lights in the distance told Meg that they were at last arriving at their destination—their camp, the man had called it. She expected some outlaw den in the mountainside and was surprised to see small wooden houses and neatly laid-out dirt streets. It appeared that the bandits' camp was just a small mountain village.

They stopped in front of one of the largest houses, and for the first time during the entire trip, her captor relaxed his hold on her. Without showing the slightest stiffness from his hours in the saddle, he swung easily to the ground and lifted her effortlessly down beside him.

He was tall, and even in the dark she could see how the broad shoulders and chest that had supported her during the ride tapered down into lean hips, around which a gun belt snugly rested. His face remained lost in the shadows.

For a moment, Meg lost her balance, trying to stay upright with her ankles bound. The man's arms were around her immediately, steadying her. With quick movements he untied the thongs around her legs, briskly and impersonally rubbing his hands over her calves and ankles as the circulation rushed back into them in a painful tingle.

"It appears things have gotten a little more complicated than intended, miss," he said to her politely. "I'll have to ask you to step inside and see if we can straighten this out."

He gently took her elbow, then stepped aside to allow her to precede him. Though her stomach was again jumping nervously as she wondered what would happen next, she allowed herself a moment's curiosity about the man who had been holding her. His voice and manners were as fine as any of the "approved" suitors who had been invited to the Sunday afternoon teas at La Ascensión. Yet, at the very least, he was a bandit and kidnapper, and probably a good deal worse, Meg thought.

She mounted the wooden steps to the unfinished door of the building and cautiously stepped inside. She blinked at the smoky, brightly lit interior of what looked to be a rough saloon. Two bronze-skinned, black-eyed men, bristling with bullets, guns and knives stashed over various parts of their bodies, looked toward her in surprise.

"You had good hunting, *amigos?*" one of them asked with a leer as the rest of the kidnapping group filed in behind Meg and her captor. But as he took in Meg's appearance, the speaker unsteadily straightened himself up from the bar.

"*El jefe* told us to wait for you and deal with the girl—but this is no Mendoza like I've ever seen." He weaved toward her and held out a hand to the reddish-gold hair that fell in disarray onto her nightdress.

Meg took a quick step backward. Once again the fear that had washed over her in those first few moments back at the ranch began to take hold. She felt her skin crawl, and the sour taste again rose in her throat. It was almost reassuring to feel the gentle pressure on her elbow of her captor standing behind her. Surely he couldn't be as bad as the horrifying man who was coming toward her.

She turned 'around to plead, to ask for help, but stopped when she saw the tall man who had been holding her. His skin was bronzed, almost like that of the other bandits who surrounded him, and his hair was black like theirs, but his eyes . . . his eyes were the most incredible glacial blue she had ever seen. They looked directly into hers and quite simply knocked the breath out of her.

Was there a slight warming of the icy blue, a slight crinkle at the corners of those eyes as she stood staring at him, speechless? For the first time all night, his voice held a trace of compassion. "Don't be afraid," he said softly, for her ears alone.

He took her arm more forcefully and led her to a table and chairs across the room. A low whistle followed her. Her captor removed the remaining rawhide that was binding her and she sat down. Suddenly conscious of being dressed only in her nightdress in a room full of men, she crossed her arms in front of herself nervously. Her captor, who had snapped a harsh "*¡cállate!*" to the man who had whistled, threw a rough wool *sarape* around her. She looked up at him in gratitude and found herself staring again at the frosty blue of his eyes.

"Who are you?" she managed finally, still speaking in Spanish.

He gave a long, almost regretful-sounding sigh, then answered, to her surprise, in perfect English. "More to the point, miss, who are *you?*"

"You're *American?*"

He pulled out a chair and sat opposite her. This time a definite hint of a smile deepened the creases along each side of his mouth. "We're not going to get anywhere if we do nothing more than sit and ask each other questions all night."

With his black hair falling carelessly over his forehead and a new twinkle in his cold blue eyes he looked suddenly younger, handsome—and like the very devil.

Meg tore her eyes away from his face and chanced another look around the room. The other men were staying back, evidently content to let her captor carry out the questioning. She looked back to him. For some reason she couldn't name, she decided to give him the information he asked for. "My name is Margaret Atherton. I'm from Texas and I'm here to attend the wedding of Rosa Maria Mendoza."

She watched as he ran a strong, bronzed hand back and forth across his chin in agitation. His movements drew her gaze to a small cleft that indented the middle of his solid jaw. It matched the deeper ones along each side of his mouth.

Meg gave herself a little shake underneath the heavy *sarape*. What in tarnation did she care about this outlaw's *face*, for pity's sake? She was in the middle of who knew what godforsaken mountain camp, being held, to all appearances, by a group of lawless cutthroats!

"And now it's your turn," she said with all the control she could muster. "Who are you, who are these men, and why have you brought me here?"

"My name is Carson," he said grimly, all trace of humor gone from his face. "It seems there has been, ah, an unfortunate mistake."

He turned to one of the grizzled men at the bar and spoke with an air of authority. "Someone's going to have to tell Villa about this. Is he awake?"

The man gave an uninterested shrug.

Carson shook his head once again in disgust. "Rafael was the one who supposedly scouted out the girl's room. Go find him and report what has happened to *el jefe* as soon as he wakes up."

Villa. Meg could not believe her ears. Of course she had heard of the exploits of the legendary bandit and revolutionary, but never in her wildest dreams had she expected to meet up with the man. If he was as bloodthirsty as she had read he was in the dime novels the ranch hands had hidden under their bunks back at the ranch, she was in serious trouble.

Carson pulled up his long frame from the chair and held out his hand to Meg. "Miss Atherton, perhaps you would try to sleep a little? We'll have to wait until morning to get this straightened out."

She thought briefly of resisting, but one look at the menacing group around her reminded her that she was in no position to argue. She reached out and felt her cold hand enveloped by her captor's warm one. Clutching the *sarape* around her defensively, she followed him out of the room.

The eastern sky had paled to a light gray. With Carson in the lead, they picked their way along the mud road until they came to an adobe building with a crudely hand-lettered sign, Posada de los Angeles.

"Inn of the Angels?" Meg translated, her mouth twisted with irony. She saw Carson's grin even in the dark.

"Somebody's idea of whimsy, no doubt," he answered, his voice deep and pleasant.

Who was this man? she thought to herself once again. And what was a man with a cultured voice and refined manners doing among the most ruthless band of cutthroats in the entire Southwest?

The interior of the building was set up like an old Spanish inn. The entrance opened onto a lovely little patio surrounded by a columned walkway, lined with large, solid-looking wooden doors. The place had an unreal atmosphere of peace after all she had been through this night.

"No one's up." Carson's voice was lowered. "There should be an empty guest room over here." He crossed to one of the massive doors and tried the handle slowly. It creaked open and a quick look showed it was unoccupied.

"In here," he said softly. "It will do you good to lie down for a while."

She walked slowly through the opened door, then turned, reluctant all at once to let him go. "Can't you tell me any more about what is happening?" she pleaded softly.

"Just rest." His voice was gentle. "We'll talk more in the morning."

The room's adobe walls seemed to give off a chill as Meg felt the big door close behind her. In the semi-darkness she heard a telltale clicking sound as her captor turned a key.

Almost unconsciously she beat her fists feebly against the massive door, then sagged against it in exhaustion as she heard the faint sound of her captor's footsteps retreating down the stone walkway.

It might have been several minutes that she leaned numbly against the cold wood, but, never one to give up completely, Meg eventually straightened up, pulled the *sarape* around her once more against the coolness of the room and took a deep breath.

"All right now, Meg. Get yourself together." The words echoed back at her from the thick stone walls. The bedroom was sparsely furnished. A small iron bed covered with a brightly colored Indian blanket was pushed against one wall, while a bulky wardrobe dominated another. A fragile-looking chair in one corner and a small table with a glass stovepipe lamp on it were the only other objects in sight.

Just to be sure the most obvious escape route was covered, she tugged once more on the heavy iron latch

of the door. It held tight. She was not going to get out
that way.

Directly across from the door a rectangular slit window was cut into the thick walls of the room. It seemed
to slant to an almost impossible narrowness at the outer
edge of the wall. Still, Meg thought, she'd squeezed
herself through tighter scrapes than that back at the
ranch. They had not called her *zorrita* for nothing.

A fox she would have to be tonight, she thought to
herself, if she were to get herself out of this predicament. Slowly she crossed over to the bed, her mind
working quickly. As she walked, her bare feet collected
splinters from the rough wood planks of the floor, reminding her of just exactly how ill-equipped she was to
make an escape in the middle of an outlaw camp, miles
from anywhere she knew, and without even shoes for
her feet!

She fingered the thick material of the Indian blanket. It would have to do. Working quickly now and with
determination, she lifted the shaft of the lamp out of its
base and broke it gently against the iron bed frame.
Using the sharp piece of glass, she cut strips of the
blanket and wound them around her feet. She bound
the *sarape* around her waist with a strip of the linen bed
sheet and with a smaller strip tied back her unruly mane
of hair. After a moment's thought, she tucked the jagged piece of glass into the bindings at her waist.

"I guess that's the best we can do," she said aloud.
With a resolute little shrug she turned to the window,
which now looked even narrower than before. She hesitated, but even the little bit of light coming into the
room was enough to tell her that it was already day-
break.

"Oh heck, if I get stuck, I get stuck," she murmured, and pulled herself up and into the smooth crevice.

Two years earlier she would have been through the opening like a lizard through a stone wall. At just about the time she had put her foot down and refused to go back for another year at La Ascensión, however, she had found herself developing cumbersome and unwanted curves—full breasts and rounded hips, which she now uncomfortably pushed through the tight crack.

With a soft thud she landed in the dirt just outside the window, her legs in a tangle of nightdress and *sarape* above her head. She lay there for just a minute before scrambling to her feet and looking around nervously for any witnesses to her escape. There was no one in sight, and it seemed that the back of this inn, or whatever it was, went right up to the edge of the woods. Without wasting any more time, she slipped quickly away in the dim dawn light.

Timothy Carson rejected the idea of trying for a couple hours' sleep himself. The girl had taken away the peace of mind he had fought so hard to gain these past few weeks working undercover at Villa's stronghold.

He had accepted the assignment reluctantly. He didn't particularly like spying, but ever since Villa's men had taken those mining engineers off the train at Santa Isabel and murdered them in cold blood, the United States army had known that something would have to be done about the marauding Mexican revolutionary.

"You're the best man I've got," his longtime friend and commander Colonel Sutherland had told him. "And to go up against Villa, we need the best."

In the weeks that followed Carson had, indeed, gotten closer to the notorious bandit than any agent ever before, but he had had to keep the reins on both his temper and his conscience to do so. His natural instincts to interfere in some of the more barbaric activities of Villa's group had to be curbed in deference to the greater importance of his overall mission. But so far he had only witnessed violence involving others who had chosen to be part of the fighting in the name of their so-called revolution. Until tonight.

From the first he had been uneasy about this special vendetta kidnapping. Villa had asked him to go along on the raid, almost as if this were a final test to ensure his loyalty. But it was hard to justify being part of an assault on an innocent girl, even if she represented the kind of aristocratic corruption that had torn this country apart. And now it turned out that the victim was not even one of the Mendozas.

Why did she have to be American? Probably some pampered rancher's daughter with not a brain in her head. She had no business being in Mexico at a time like this.

His eyes prickled from lack of sleep, and he unconsciously ran his hand back and forth over his jaw. And why did she have to be so damn gorgeous?

With a discipline born of years on the run, he had managed to ignore the way her soft curves had settled against him as they rode up to camp, but when he finally got a good look at her in the light, he had felt a hollow settle into the base of his stomach.

She had looked magnificent, her perfect face surrounded by a silken cloud of gold—or was it red?—hair. Could her eyes have been gold, too? He remembered them looking straight into his as her little chin tipped up in defiance.

Margaret Atherton—a mouthful of name for such a little sprite. He smiled to himself ruefully. Margaret Atherton. What in *hell* was he going to do about her?

Chapter Two

The most bothersome part of the walk up to now had been the stinging of her calves where the brambles had scratched them until she could feel rivulets of blood running down into her makeshift blanket shoes.

As for the rest, she was just fine, Meg told herself at regular intervals. The shoes were holding up well. She was plenty warm enough, almost too warm. It was a beautiful day, actually, with a slightly moist smell to the mountain air.

At least she was away from that camp... from those disturbing, incongruous light blue eyes. She found her mind continually wandering back to the man named Carson. He was American, she was sure of it. His English had been perfect, and his name was certainly not Spanish. Who was he? Why was he there amid a group of Mexican desperadoes?

"And why should I give a tinker's damn who he is?" she said aloud. Her hand came up reflexively to cover her mouth as the saucy phrase echoed out to the trees. It was the kind of language her father had despaired over as he tried to raise her as a lady without a mother's tender influence.

In this case the woods were the only audience to her indiscretion, and she lowered her hand with a smile, her first in several hours. With her natural good spirits beginning to take hold again, she even managed an off-key whistle as she picked her way down the mountainside. She was lucky it was downhill, she reflected, as she skidded in her blanket-bound feet down a particularly steep embankment.

Since before she could remember she had been able to find her way home from the farthest reaches of her father's ranch, her uncanny sense of direction surpassing even the most experienced cowboy's. Now, almost without thinking, she glanced briefly up at the sun. By her calculations, she should be reaching the flatlands in another hour or so. From there it would be an easy walk back to the Mendoza *hacienda*.

For the past few minutes she had been following the banks of a small mountain stream. Relaxed, certain now that the strange nightmare she had been pulled into was over, she let herself sink down beside it and cupped her hands for a cool drink. Her eyes closed involuntarily and exhaustion washed over her body in a great wave. Suddenly her thighs felt limp and shaky from the long descent.

The burning in her calves became intolerable. Lifting up the heavy blanket poncho, she saw that her nightdress was sticking to them in places, smeared with her blood. Carefully she picked the fabric away from her tender skin and splashed water over the wounds as best she could, gritting her teeth against the sting.

"I hope it hurts."

For a moment she thought the deep, determined voice was not real, a mere product of her exhaustion. But with recognition came a horrid, sick feeling that pounded through her and seemed to explode inside her stomach. She jumped back from the water and looked around wildly.

Though she had heard nothing of his approach, he was almost close enough to touch her. He leaned one broad shoulder nonchalantly against a tree, but his piercing blue eyes watched her carefully, and he seemed to be in total control of his body, like a bobcat ready to spring.

"Such an abrupt leave-taking, Miss Atherton. You didn't approve of the accommodations?" he inquired mildly.

Her eyes searched into the woods behind him, but to all appearances he was alone, and Meg willed her heart to slow to a dull thumping. She took a deep breath. Back at camp last night the man had seemed possessed of at least some decency.

"Please, Mr. Carson, just let me go. You yourself said they had brought the wrong person. What do you want to keep holding me for?"

With a curious, animal-like grace he pushed himself away from the tree and dropped beside her, one strong hand closing around her slender, scratched ankle. Belatedly she realized that her nightdress was up above her knees, leaving a goodly portion of her legs exposed to view. She bent over in confusion and tried to tug down the dirty, torn cloth to a more decent position. But he stopped both her hands with his one free one, and held her there a moment, his eyes coming up to hers with a smiling expression somewhere between admiration and exasperation.

"Not the time for modesty, Miss Atherton. I bet these cuts smart like the devil." He ran his finger gently along one of the deepest scratches and watched her flinch with pain.

He stood abruptly and gave a sharp whistle through two fingers. In a moment the looming figure of a huge chestnut stallion appeared through the trees and picked its way toward them, stopping within arm's reach. Carson gave the animal a familiar pat on its flank, then opened one of the leather saddlebags and dug inside until he came up with a small beaded pouch.

Without another word he sat down beside Meg again and began gingerly applying some sort of salve to her legs. Almost immediately the stinging stopped, and Meg looked at him in wonder.

"Aloe," he said curtly. "One of the reasons I'll take the Indian medicine man over the local sawbones any day."

"Thank you," Meg managed. "That feels much better."

He looked up at her and smiled, without reservation this time, and Meg felt a strange heat seeping into her. His smile deepened the creases around his mouth and lent a twinkle of warmth to his wintry eyes.

"You deserve this, you know, for the trouble you've caused." His voice was lazy with amusement. He smoothed his hands one last time down her well-shaped calves, then, somewhat reluctantly, pulled her night-dress around them. The good-natured smile slowly faded as he sat back on his haunches and regarded her gravely.

"I'll be frank, Miss Atherton. I would like nothing better than to let you go. However, your hasty departure has put me into a peck of trouble back at camp, and if I don't show up there soon with you safely in tow, it's worth my neck."

He stood up and offered her his hand. "I realize I can't expect you to share the sentiment on such short acquaintance, Miss Atherton, but it's rather a nice neck and I, at least, set some store by it. So let's get started back."

Meg felt the panic rising in her again. What could she do? She obviously couldn't outrun him in her clumsy garb. Anyway, he had a horse. Through her thin night-dress she could feel the hard outline of the piece of glass she had broken off back at the camp. He wouldn't be suspecting her to have any kind of weapon, so perhaps that gave her an edge. She would have to disable him, an idea she found not at all pleasant. But she couldn't go back. He had left her no other choice.

She let him pull her upright and followed him over to his horse, taking advantage of his turned back to quietly pull the jagged glass from her waistband. As he bent over to retrieve the reins that trailed on the ground, she struck as hard as she could and at the only vulnerable spot she could reach—his neck.

With nauseating ease she felt the sharp tip of the glass sink into his skin. Blood covered her hand in hot spurts as he turned halfway around, then fell heavily to the pine-needle-covered ground.

She drew back and watched with fascinated revulsion as a dark crimson stain spread slowly down the entire right side of his light buckskin jacket. The seeping red seemed to be draining him dry; his face was suddenly very white and still.

In shock she fell to her knees, the dripping glass still in her hand. "Holy Mother Mary," she breathed. She wasn't a Catholic, but in her direst moments she found herself falling back for comfort on the endlessly repeated prayers of the sisters back at La Ascensión. Up to now those prayers had mainly consisted of fervent pleas that her father not discover her latest escapade with Johnny. What she wouldn't give to have Johnny with her now.

She willed herself to look down once more to where Carson lay so still in front of her. Gently she reached out one arm and, cringing as her hand touched the sticky wetness of his leather jacket, rolled him over onto his back. Was he breathing?

"Are you dead?" she whispered to his motionless form. Her hand trembled as she brought it down toward his face.

In an instant she was flying through the air. Her head slammed into the ground and the breath left her in a great *whoosh* as she ended up flat on her back with Carson sitting heavily on her abdomen. His knees pressed painfully into her arms on either side of her. She tasted spatters of his blood on her lips.

"No, I'm not dead—no thanks to you, you little she-devil." Satisfied by a quick glance that she was immobilized, he whipped a brightly colored kerchief out of his pocket and pressed it hard against himself just above his right shoulder blade.

He grunted in disgust as he felt it begin to fill up with blood. "What in hell did you cut me with, an ax?" he asked her angrily.

She looked guiltily down at her trapped right arm. The bloody piece of glass was still clenched in her hand. With a hostile glance he reached down, plucked it from her nerveless fingers and flung it away into the middle of the stream.

He was furious with himself. It was almost beyond belief that after years and years of never letting down his guard, always being careful, suspecting everyone of everything, he had almost let this wet-behind-the-ears schoolgirl get the best of him. She had come darn close to slitting his throat, for God's sake.

His anger made his words even harsher than he intended. "You're becoming more trouble than you're worth, Miss Atherton. I expect it won't matter much to Villa whether I bring you back alive or dead. His theory is that dead people seldom make good witnesses."

Meg's head began to clear. His face was grim and pale as he looked down at her, but she somehow didn't believe his threats. She swallowed hard. "I—I didn't mean—" Her voice faltered. "Please don't take me back there."

Her wide, beautiful eyes looked up at him pleadingly. They *were* golden, he found himself thinking. And deep, surrounded by thick golden lashes. A man could drown in those eyes. Unbelievably, he felt himself swelling where his body pressed into her soft abdomen.

What is wrong with you, Carson? He just stopped himself from saying the words aloud. First you let her jump you like some kind of a greenhorn, and now you want to *bed* the chit?

Fortunately, she seemed to be either too agitated or too inexperienced to notice his body's untimely reaction. He eased himself off her and slowly got to his feet, still pressing the soaked kerchief to his neck. A wave of dizziness swept over him.

"Get up." He barked the command at her. Damn, but he had lost a lot of blood. It was going to take all his strength to get up on that horse and get himself and his prisoner back up the mountain to the camp. Now that he knew the trouble she could cause, he had no intention of letting her see just how weak he was feeling.

Meg scrambled to her feet and clutched at his arm, causing a painful wrench on his wound. "Listen to me," she started desperately, "my father can pay you—"

He reached around her with his good arm and jerked her back by her long hair. "No, you listen to *me*," he growled. "Your little attempt at neck surgery here hurts like hell, which means I'm not at my affable best. So you just sit yourself quietly up on that horse and shut up. If you so much as *sneeze* on the ride back, I swear I'll see that Villa has one more dead witness."

Her face was flushed, but those incredible gold eyes regarded him without fear. Her lips were just inches from his, full and moist and—God! He must be long overdue for a visit to Mama Lou's up in El Paso. Something about this girl made him as randy as a stripling.

He let her go and stepped back. His voice was softer now. "Go on, mount up."

He half pushed her up onto the horse, then, ill-concealing his discomfort, pulled himself up behind her. His neck felt as if it had been run through with a branding iron, and his stomach threatened to eject its contents any minute.

He settled into the saddle, then reached back and patted the big horse with a silent plea. It's up to you now, big boy. I hope you can figure out some way to get us home, 'cause I sure as hell won't be of much use.

As if in sympathy with its master, the giant stallion turned and started to make its way slowly up the mountainside.

He knew the signs. It was not the first time he had lost too much blood, nor would it probably be the last.

But it certainly was the most inconvenient. He felt cold all over, light-headed, and he clutched his prisoner like a lifeline in order to stay on the horse.

Sensing Carson's distress, Meg had not given him any trouble on the way up the mountain. She sat stiffly in front of him in the saddle, one knee tucked around the pommel, her *sarape* pulled tightly around her in spite of the strong mountain sun beating down at them from between the trees.

They would be back at the camp any moment. Carson didn't think he had the strength to so much as tug the reins, but at his soft "whoa" the big horse came to a gentle halt.

Meg looked back at Carson, appalled by the pallor of his face.

"Miss Atherton," he began, then stopped to reach up to the kerchief, which was now a crusted mass at his neck. At least it seemed that the bleeding had stopped. "What else do they call you? Miss Atherton is a bit too formal for my taste. Is it Margaret?"

"Meg." She answered him without thinking. Her flight from camp, a night and a day on horseback and no sleep had left her numb. At the moment she felt that if Carson had told her to take his horse and go back down the mountain, she wouldn't have had the strength left to do it, even to save her life.

"Meg." He nodded as though giving his approval. "Listen carefully, Meg, 'cause you have a choice to make. Thanks to your handiwork here—" he gestured weakly toward his neck "—I am extremely close to passing out. In fact, you could probably give me the very slightest of pushes right now and I would be on the ground."

Meg's lethargy disappeared as she realized the truth of his words. His skin was deathly gray; drops of sweat were beaded around the edges of his thick, dark hair. The arms that reached around her to grasp the reins trembled with weakness. Her mind clicked into action, considering the possibilities.

"But before you do," he continued, "I want you to consider this. We are not more than half a mile from a town full of very unfriendly fellows. Villa's men know every bush, every rock of these hills. They would track you down like a wounded deer, Meg darlin', and make just about as short work of you."

His eyes brushed significantly down from her bright eyes to where her nightdress and blanket rode up to reveal her shapely calves. "You'd make them quite a party."

An involuntary shudder ran through her. "Why should I think you're any different from the rest of them, Mr. Carson?"

He gave a weak grin. "Well, for one thing, when I have a party with a lady, I don't invite my friends."

He shifted in the saddle and dropped his hold on her as dizziness overtook him. Meg watched as he grimaced and muttered an expletive under his breath.

Gripping the saddle determinedly, all traces of a smile gone, he addressed her grimly. "Look, Meg, I wouldn't want to offend any of your maidenly sensibilities, but I may not have a lot of time here, so I will speak bluntly. If you don't want to be thoroughly and repeatedly raped by however many of Villa's men happen to be in the mood, you will trust me now and do exactly what I tell you."

Her stomach turned over at his words. She looked directly back into his extraordinary blue eyes and asked herself why she felt any safer with this man than with those she had seen back at the outlaws' camp. Perhaps it was because he was an American. Perhaps it was the gentle, almost tender way he had held her, had rubbed the feeling back into her numbed limbs last night, had smoothed the salve over her torn flesh today. But wasn't he one of them? Hadn't this group of cutthroats even treated him as some kind of leader? And hadn't he been about to turn her over to Pancho Villa, the worst of them all?

"What do you want me to do?" she whispered finally.

His glacier eyes warmed with relief—and maybe something more. "Meg darlin', if I had the strength I'd kiss you. I owe you for this, and I won't forget."

He made an imperceptible movement with his legs and the horse smoothly started forward. His left arm went back around her to take a token hold on the reins. Meg felt his hard chest leaning heavily against her.

"You're about all that's holding me on this horse at the moment, and I would just as soon my colleagues back at camp weren't aware of it. In the wild, predators attack the weakest animals in the herd, the sick and the wounded. They circle them and worry them until the unlucky creatures have no strength left, then they attack and tear them to bits. Villa's men are predators, Meg, never forget that."

Farther up the trail the outline of buildings was taking shape through the trees. "Just sit tight and let me hold on to you. Don't move, and *don't say anything.*" The urgency in his voice reflected the desperation of their situation. Suddenly Meg was very much afraid of what would happen if Carson's condition were discovered. What might they do to her when they found out that she had caused his wound?

Underneath the protective folds of her *sarape,* she grasped his arm, her firm grip trying to transmit some of her strength to him. Hold on, Carson, just a little bit more, she prayed to herself, her eyes closing briefly.

He responded with a weak, but definite, squeeze and seemed to sit up straighter in the saddle as the trail widened and they rode into the town.

Three swarthy *bandidos* were draped in various positions over a porch railing and hitching post in front of the first building they passed.

"*Hola, amigo* Carson," one of the group called out in a singsong Spanish. He made the name sound like *Carrr-song.*

"So you found the little *señorita,* eh? Did she give you much trouble, my friend?"

Carson answered with a grin, his voice surprisingly strong. "When have you ever known *me* to have trouble with a *señorita,* Chucho?"

He stopped his horse while they were still some distance from the group of men. Sweat was pouring down his face, and beneath her blanket Meg felt his hands clutch her waist in his desperate effort to stay upright. But his voice stayed steady and casual.

"Where's *el jefe?*"

"He's with his wife."

Carson gave something like a snort. "Which one?"

The man Carson had called Chucho straightened up from the wooden railing and started toward them, gesturing with his hands for Carson to be quiet.

"No, *amigo,* this is one of the real ones, Doña Luz. She's just come up from Chihuahua City. Looks like she's here to stay a while, too—brought a wagon full of stuff with her."

"Hallelujah," Carson said quietly into Meg's ear. "Our lucky stars are at work today, Meg m'girl."

To the little man approaching them across the dusty street he called in a louder voice, "Listen, Chucho. I'm as beat as a grandpappy coon dog after chasing this little filly through half the sierras. I'm going to go get some sleep."

By now all three men had fixed their eyes on Carson's bloodstained jacket. The two men back on the porch had straightened up and stood very still, watching them carefully.

"What happened to you, *hombre?*" Chucho had dropped the bantering tone. His voice was cautious.

Meg tightened her hold on Carson as he answered carefully. "Took a tumble down a riverbank trying to get hold of our visitor here. Nicked my neck and it bled like a son of a gun. But I'm fine."

Chucho looked warily from Carson to Meg. "What about the girl?"

"I thought I'd just take her along with me for the time being. I reckon my claim's as good as any." He paused to let his glance stab each of the three men in turn. Gritting his teeth against the pain in his neck, he half turned in the saddle and let his hand drift casually back to the polished stock of his rifle where it rested in his gun sheath.

Meg found herself holding her breath as a curious tension crackled among the four men. Finally, Chucho gave a little shrug and retreated a step, as if backing down from a fight.

"Villa sure as hell can't make much use of her with Luz here." He grinned. "Bad luck for him."

"Yeah, well, you can tell him I'm back and have the girl with me. But tell him I'll see him tomorrow. Right now I'm heading for bed."

Chucho lifted his eyebrows, his eyes going back to Meg. "That's exactly where I'd be heading if I were in your shoes, *amigo*." He accompanied his words with an obscene gesture that left no doubt as to their meaning.

Meg's face heated in a slow flush, but Carson's quick pressure around her waist kept her silent.

He forced his face into a lascivious smile. "I guess you understand why I'd just as soon not be disturbed till morning."

"Go on then, you lucky bastard." Chucho turned and walked back toward his friends on the porch, as Carson's big horse started slowly down the street. "Let us know if you need any help, Carson," he called after them, and the other two added their own crude suggestions for the proper servicing of his captive.

Meg's face burned and her doubts about her captor hammered again to the surface. "Where are you taking me?" she asked indignantly. She turned back toward him in the saddle, and the words died in her mouth at his deathly pallor. His head lolled crazily from side to side.

"Carson!" Panic lent sharpness to her voice. She glanced quickly around. There didn't seem to be anyone else watching them, but they were heading right into what appeared to be the main street of the town. After a slight hesitation she pulled the reins out of Carson's limp hand and urged the horse off the street and into a narrow passageway between two buildings.

"Carson, you've got to tell me where to go." His eyes were half-open as he made an effort to focus on her face.

With barely intelligible mumbles he told her to head down a side street to a small but neatly built wooden house, the only one on the street with a coat of whitewash and a cleanly swept brick walkway. She let the horse take them right up it, almost to the door, before she halted and turned back to Carson once more.

"Is this it? Can you make it inside?"

He nodded his head listlessly, but made no move to get off the horse.

With a sigh she straightened her cramped legs and jumped to the ground. Without her support Carson toppled off, too, practically landing on top of her. She caught him under his arms before he could collapse all the way to the ground and, heaving with all her strength, pulled him inside the little house.

As her eyes adjusted to the dim light she could see that the entire house seemed to comprise a single room. It was dominated by a large feather bed nestled into a wooden frame. With grunts and moans the two made their way over to the structure, collapsing on it together as their strength gave out at the same time.

For a moment they lay there, breathing heavily from the exertion. Gradually Meg became aware of the heat of his body against her bare thighs. She began to pull away.

"Don't go, sweetheart." Carson's voice sounded drunk and far away, and his grasp on her arms was feeble.

Meg's face flushed anew at the endearment. Regaining her breath, she sat up and answered him sharply. "I'm not your sweetheart, so just keep your hands off me."

Carson's eyes were closed and his only reply was a silly-looking grin. He certainly didn't appear to be very dangerous in this condition, Meg reflected. But that didn't change the fact that she was again a prisoner in Pancho Villa's outlaw camp, and that the only person who might be able to help her was acting like a drunk after an all-night binge.

She wondered again at his relationship with the outlaws. He didn't appear to be quite like the rest of them. Yet he had brought her back here. She had asked him to let her go back at the stream, and he had refused. What did he want from her? What were they going to do with her?

The sense of relief over having made it through the camp with Carson was now being replaced by renewed apprehension over her plight. Well, Carson had said he wouldn't forget her help. It was up to him now to find her some way out of this. She turned back to him on the bed.

"Carson," she called softly, then louder, shaking his uninjured shoulder, "Carson, what am I supposed to do now?"

But her question stretched unanswered into the dim light of the room. Carson was out cold.

Chapter Three

Meg awoke suddenly to find a pair of merry brown eyes no more than inches from hers. After a moment's orientation she remembered where she was. The events of the past two days came back to her with a sickening plunge in her stomach.

The previous evening she had tried to no avail to arouse Carson from his stupor. Several restless pacings across the room to the front window had revealed no traffic on the little street in front of the house. Carson's horse had evidently wandered off, and Meg was in no mood to go look for it.

She did consider once again the possibility of escape, but Carson's dire words about her fate if she were tracked down by Villa's men had dimmed her enthusiasm for any further attempts.

At last, as the room slowly darkened and she could see no lamps or candles about the place, she had settled into a chair near the big bed, pulled the *sarape* around her and nodded off into an exhausted sleep.

Now the sun was streaming in through the room's small windows and Meg could see that the brown eyes watching her belonged to a young Mexican woman, not much older than herself. The woman smiled pleasantly at her and reached out to give her a comforting pat on the shoulder.

"So you are awake at last, *linda*. I thought you might sleep through the day. You have had a very bad time, no?"

Meg responded gratefully to the woman's warmth. "It hasn't exactly been my idea of a pleasure excursion." She sat up and gave her cramped limbs an experimental stretch, at the same time becoming awake enough to realize that the big feather bed near her was empty. Carson—was he dead? But no, this woman wouldn't be smiling at her in such a friendly fashion if Meg had just killed one of their group.

"What happened to the man who brought me here?" Her voice was cautious.

"I don't think Carson felt the need to sleep all day like you, pretty one. He and some of the men have been out riding since morning."

"Out riding?" The last she had seen of him he had been unconscious, barely this side of dead.

The short, slightly plump woman plopped down companionably on the bed, causing mounds of feathers to puff up on each side of her. She nodded happily. "Hmm, riding. They went after some *soplones*—informers, men who would betray us to Carranza's *federales*."

Her arms were full and she opened them now to show Meg. "I have brought you clothes." She looked Meg up and down, visually measuring her. "They will fit around, but will be too short. Anyway, they will be better than what you are wearing."

Meg eyed the simple blue cotton shirtwaist thankfully. She would do anything to get rid of her grimy nightdress and the heavy *sarape* she had been wearing for almost two days.

"It will do very nicely, thank you. It is such a relief to find at least one kind person in this awful place, *señorita*."

"It's *señora*," the woman corrected her gently, "but you may call me Luz. My husband is Francisco Villa."

Meg flopped back in her chair, startled. How could this laughing, amiable young woman be the wife of the most notorious bandit in the Southwest?

Luz looked at her with an ironic smile. "You have heard of my husband, I see. But don't be afraid. Half of the stories they tell about him are not true."

She shrugged her round shoulders and gave a little giggle. "Unfortunately, the other half *are*. But you, *señorita*, are not to worry. I will try to help you, believe me."

Meg looked at the woman carefully. No matter who her husband was, there was no doubt that her eyes held nothing but friendship and sympathy for Meg's plight.

"I do believe you, Luz, and I do need help. I don't know the reason for this kidnapping in the first place, but I know that I am not even the person they meant to bring here. I have to get away, back to my friends. They will be frantic searching for me by now."

Once more she thought about the Mendoza family and what must be going on back at the ranch. Surely they wouldn't let her disappearance go by without taking action. Perhaps by now they had even telegraphed her father. He would be furious. Knowing Charles Atherton, she wouldn't be surprised if he had the entire Seventh Cavalry combing these hills before long. She had to get back.

Luz nodded to her patiently. "All in good time, dear. First things first. You need to eat something and get into some decent clothing."

Meg sighed. There must be some way to make this kindhearted woman see how desperate her situation was. But it wouldn't hurt to face the task more conveniently dressed. She stood and reached for the clothes Luz was holding out to her.

"I believe Carson brought in some water for you before he left this morning." She motioned to an old-fashioned washstand across the room. "I'll just leave you alone a minute to get yourself ready, then we'll go get something for you to eat and see if the men have returned."

The clean water felt wonderful against her skin, but Meg did not linger over her toilet. The blue dress fit snugly over her high breasts, sagged a bit at the waist and ended fully five inches above her ankles, but it was clean and smelled of sunshine.

Luz was waiting just outside the door of the little house, and motioned for Meg to follow her down the narrow side street up to the main avenue where Meg and Carson had entered yesterday afternoon.

At a large red building on one side of the street Luz stopped. "We'll see if Angelita has some food for you." She pushed her way through the wooden door of the building. Inside was a large room that resembled a dining hall.

"Most of the men eat here," Luz explained, then called loudly, "Angelita, *dónde andas?*"

From what was evidently the kitchen area of the building emerged the most roly-poly little woman Meg had ever seen, as broad as she was wide with huge arms hanging out of her loose embroidered blouse like two plucked turkeys trussed for smoking.

The round little woman grinned at them and nodded her head respectfully. *"Buenos días, señora,"* she addressed Luz.

"Angelita, Carson told me that this poor lamb here hasn't eaten in two days. Can you take care of her?"

Angelita was duly horrified at the thought of two days without eating, and within minutes she had Meg seated at a table loaded with more food than she could down in a month. The fare was simple but delicious, reminding Meg just how long it was since she had put anything in her stomach. She had been so determined to get away yesterday, then so upset at Carson's condition, that she had forgotten all about her hunger.

She was sopping up the last bit of rice and beans with a piece of tortilla when the door opened. Suddenly the room was filled with men, but Meg's eyes were fixed on the striking blue eyes of the tallest one in the forefront of the group. Carson's face had regained its normal tanned color, and he looked absolutely no worse for wear from their experiences yesterday.

She felt a perverse anger that all her guilt over his injury had been for nothing, and her expression turned into a glare as he approached her, one black eyebrow lifted and his mouth turned up in a devilish grin.

Before she knew what was happening, he had grabbed her around the middle and lifted her clear off the bench she'd been sitting on. He swung her around to the ground and, before Meg could utter a word of protest, his mouth came down on hers in a hot, demanding kiss. He opened her mouth with his tongue and expertly moved his lips over hers. Meg felt a liquid rush in her stomach and lower. Her breasts, crushed against his chest, hardened involuntarily.

After a long moment in which all will seemed to have left her, Meg pushed against him feebly. He lifted his head from her mouth but kept his hold on her, one hand going down to give her a familiar, caressing pat on her rear. "Did you miss me, *gringa?*" he asked her loudly.

Meg choked with indignation. With a mighty pull she wrenched her arm free of his grasp and started to bring it back to slap him. After growing up on a ranch full of men she was not completely without experience in defending herself from unwanted attentions, but never before had she been so shaken by an encounter. Even now her legs threatened to collapse under her.

In contrast to her agitated state, Carson appeared to be completely cool. He deftly batted her hand out of the way and in a trice had spun her around, holding both her arms easily with one of his.

"Now, Meg, darlin', don't let's show that nasty temper of yours to the gentlemen here. They're not as tolerant as I am of feisty females."

All at once Meg became aware of the room full of men in front of her. They looked as deadly as the group who had kidnapped her that first night, and their eyes were all on her.

By now Luz had gotten up and gone over to a middle-size man in the center of the group. He was handsome and dark-skinned with a bushy handlebar mustache and piercing black eyes, which were now filled with lazy amusement as he observed the two Americans.

"My friend Carson, when you asked me for the girl I did not know what a prize I was giving away." A wide-brimmed *sombrero* was pushed back on his head, and he was dressed richly in black wool trimmed with silver and high black leather boots that now clicked loudly against the floor as he stalked slowly toward Meg. He was about her height, so that his dark eyes looked straight into hers as he said very quietly, "Perhaps I will have to think again on this decision."

Meg retreated imperceptibly into Carson's arms. No matter how outrageously Carson was behaving, he at least was better than these grinning savages, than this dark-skinned outlaw whose eyes warmed so intently as they roamed up and down her body. Carson's grip on her tightened, but his voice was level, congenial.

"Have a heart, *Jefe*. After chasing through the sierra all day I was too bushed last night to do much more than sleep. I've hardly had time to get nicely acquainted with the lady." He ran his hands suggestively over Meg's waist and down the gentle slope of her abdomen as the men hooted their approval.

Meg restrained her impulse to put a sharp elbow into his ribs. She had trusted him before and it appeared she would have to once again. But just wait until she got Mr. Carson alone. She'd tell him a thing or two.

Villa's eyes burned hotly as they followed the progress of Carson's hands over Meg's curving hips, then went up to the red-gold cloud of hair framing her flushed face. A slight frown settled over his face.

"She is indeed a prize, this beautiful *gringa*," he said speculatively.

"But not *your* prize, *mi amor*." Luz's voice chimed sweetly behind Villa's back, startling him out of his perusal.

He turned back to her, his frown dissolving into a smile as he reached out to pull her to him in a big bear hug. "*You* are my prize, my Lucita. Never doubt that."

Meg felt Carson's arms relax around her and she thought he let out a long breath.

Villa was nuzzling Luz's neck and seemed to have regained his good humor. He paused a moment to look up at them. "So, go, my friend." He waved at Carson impatiently. "Go on and take her, and see if you have the strength to spend tonight doing something more than sleeping." He laughed heartily at his own joke and his men joined in with more joviality than the quip merited.

Carson wasted no more time. Pulling Meg roughly by the arm, he shouldered his way through the group of men and headed out of the dining hall.

They were no sooner out of the room than Meg squirmed out of his hold and faced him in a rage. "I'll thank you to let me go, Mr. Carson. I don't appreciate being dragged around like a maverick calf."

Carson's face remained calm, but his blue eyes glinted dangerously and his voice held carefully controlled anger. "My dear Miss Atherton, you'll be dragged wherever I care to drag you, and consider yourself lucky, unless you want me to wait another couple minutes for Villa to finish placating Luz and decide to come after you himself."

He started again down the street with long, determined strides that forced her into a little run to keep up with him. "Perhaps you would prefer Villa's tender ministrations to mine, but I rather doubt it."

Meg watched a muscle playing along the lean line of his jaw as he made an effort to rein his temper. He was furious, and recognizing the truth of his words, she decided to go along peacefully. For the time being.

Carson felt like hell. His neck wound ached and an entire reveille pounded inside his head. The last thing he had needed today was another bout in the saddle, but he had had no choice. His position with the outlaws was still too precarious to allow him to show weakness, particularly a weakness brought about by a wrangle with a female. He still could hardly believe it himself. The little witch! And now, when he was trying to save her pretty hide from being stretched out underneath an endless line of Villa's men, most likely starting with Villa himself, she had the nerve to argue with him.

He looked down at her lovely face, set in the stubborn expression he had already come to recognize. She did have nerve, that much was for sure. She'd been through more in the past two days than most of the overindulged ranchers' daughters he knew could even dream about. She'd managed to escape from the camp, had made her way alone all the way down the mountain and had practically killed him using not a weapon but a piece of glass, for God's sake.

He loosened his grip on her slender arm and slowed his pace a bit. She looked up at him and was surprised to see his face had softened into an unexpected grin.

He was remembering that kiss. He would wager three months' pay that Miss Meg Atherton had never been kissed like that before. Yet her mouth had softened, melted into his as though they were made to be together, forged for some kind of eternal existence. The kiss had started a slow fire deep in his gut that smoldered there still.

As he looked down at her, Meg felt the rosiness creep up again along her cheekbones. On the ranch the hands had teased her about her blushing, and Meg had cursed her fair skin and pale red-gold hair.

The flush heightened her beauty, and Carson's breath caught in his throat. She looked like a woman who had just been made love to—or was about to be. God! He'd been so busy protecting her from the *bandidos,* he hadn't spent any time wondering how he was going to manage to keep his hands off her himself.

They had almost reached his little house when he stopped abruptly, clearing his throat. "Look, Meg, I need to talk to a couple people and see if there's any way I can get you out of this place. I want you to go inside and *stay there.* Don't come out for anything, and don't open the door for anyone but me. No more tumbles out the back window, do you promise me?"

The concern in his eyes matched the earnest tone in his voice, and Meg decided almost immediately to trust him once more. She, too, had been more than disturbed by their kiss back at the dining hall. She was bright enough to understand why he had kissed her—it had been all an act for Villa's benefit. Carson had probably kissed dozens of women like that—hundreds, she told herself primly. Just because *she* had never known that a man's mouth could make her feel like that, make her melt away inside until she was ... well, anyway, it had all been an act, and now he was anxious to find a way to get rid of her.

"I promise, Carson. I'll stay inside."

"Good girl." His cool hand brushed gently along one of her still burning cheeks, then he was gone.

Meg could find absolutely nothing to occupy her in the little house. She fluffed up the feather bed and folded her discarded outfit from yesterday, but the rest of the room was already immaculately clean. The time passed slowly and it was late afternoon before she heard footsteps and Carson's low voice.

"Meg. Lift the latch."

He looked tired and discouraged and sat down heavily on the bed. His handsome face seemed shadowed, the lines alongside his mouth and in the middle of his chin etched more deeply than before. He rubbed the side of his neck absently.

"Does it bother you?" Meg asked.

He looked at her blankly.

"Your wound—does it hurt?"

"I guess."

Meg looked down at her hands. "Well, I—um—I wanted to say that I'm sorry. I didn't know it would go so deep."

Amusement lit his eyes. "You're a dangerous woman, Meg."

"No, I mean it," she went on seriously. "I've been sitting here thinking, trying to figure you out. You're not one of them, are you?"

The laughter in his expression faded, and he paused a moment before answering her with slow deliberation. "Yes, Meg, I *am* one of them. In fact, Villa has made me one of his lieutenants. I had the honor of saving his life a while back."

Meg's shoulders drooped in disappointment. During her time alone she had worked out a scenario where Carson was really someone else—anyone else—just not a member of the infamous Villa gang. He would come back and scoop her up onto his big horse and they would both ride out of these hills forever.

"But he's an outlaw," she protested weakly.

Carson shrugged. "Some call him an outlaw, some a hero. I guess it's a matter of where you're sitting."

"But even the Mexican government is hunting him down now, right?"

"That's just the problem—which government? It seems there's a new one every few months. Villa just happens to be on the wrong side of the current one."

Meg sighed. "So what is going to happen to me?"

He shook his head. "I haven't found a solution. Now that you've come to the notice of Villa himself, you can't just disappear. That would mean a neck injury for me slightly more permanent than the one you gave me."

"Just what does that mean?" she asked, growing more agitated. "I can't stay here—I have to get home. My father—"

Carson lifted a tired hand. "The best I can do for now is try to keep up the appearance that you are my woman. There are not many men in camp who would be willing to challenge me for your favors."

With a lightning-smooth motion he pulled a revolver from the holster that rested against his hip. He twirled the gun twice and had replaced it back in its leather sheath almost before Meg knew what it was. "I can be a dangerous man, too, Meg, darlin'," he said with a little-boy grin.

Meg gave a startled jump backward, then pulled herself up in her most dignified manner. "I'm not impressed, Mr. Carson. We have hands back on the ranch who can drill the eye out of an Indian-head nickel at fifty paces, but I've never known it to get them very far. They're still wrestling cows for a living."

Carson gave a hooting laugh. His face became less drawn and some of the color was coming back into it.

"Pardon *me*, Miss Atherton. Next time I want to impress you I'll try poetry and flowers. That's what your banker and lawyer beaux use, I presume?"

Meg began to feel slightly silly, but she didn't back down. "A little refinement never hurt a man, Mr. Carson. And if I were to have a beau, I would certainly choose a banker or a lawyer over someone who lives by his guns, like the horrible men in this camp.''

Her last comment brought them both back to the current situation. ''I don't know how a nice woman like Luz can stand to be here,'' Meg finished.

Carson's smile was gentle. ''Luz is a special lady. She's the only one I've ever seen keep Villa under some sort of control. He adores her.''

''What did they mean yesterday when they said she was *one* of his wives?''

Carson rubbed a hand across his chin in a rueful gesture. ''Villa seems to have several. At least three or four 'official' ones, and quite a few more who have gone through some sort of ceremony.''

''But that's awful!''

Carson made an effort to stifle his grin. ''Well, now, Villa's philosophy is that if it makes the woman happy, why not get married? And besides, he likes weddings.''

''But that's—well, it's against the law, for one thing.''

''Law has never been one of Villa's strong points.'' He slid a ways over on the bed to be closer to where she was standing, her little face a picture of indignation.

''Poor Luz . . . how can she put up with it?''

''Luz is his favorite, there's no doubt about it. She lives in his house in Chihuahua City.''

Meg shook her head in disgust. ''I can't believe it. What a terrible man.''

Carson reached out and took her hands. ''Meg, my little innocent. Marrying his ladyloves is one of the *good* things Villa does. It gives them protection in their villages, and special status.''

Meg felt her concentration wavering as his strong hands surrounded hers. His thumbs rubbed gently over

her wrists, just where her pulse was beginning to in-
crease its rhythm. With the slightest of tugs he pulled
her down beside him on the bed.

Even in the room's dim light the gold shone out of
her eyes, and Carson felt an overpowering desire to kiss
them shut and then bury his face into the billowing
softness of her hair.

"Meg." His voice was low and husky.

Meg suddenly felt an inability to move or even
breathe. Her mind no longer seemed to be part of her
body. It watched helplessly as Carson, his eyes narrowed with desire, bent his head down to her.

"Señor Carson!" The voice and a simultaneous rat-
tling of the room's wooden door abruptly snapped the
current between them.

Carson pulled himself up with an expletive and
crossed the room to open the door.

The youth who had called them looked to be barely
more than a boy, but he was dressed much as the other
outlaws and had a *bandolera* of bullets hanging from
one shoulder. His face held thinly suppressed excitement.

"You must come, Señor Carson, and bring the girl.
Everyone must come to the plaza."

"Slow down, Pepe. What's happening?"

The boy looked from Carson to Meg, his eyes dancing. "We're going to shoot the *soplones.*"

Chapter Four

The setting sun cast a burnished glow on the pink adobe of the buildings lining the small plaza. From all sides people were crowding in—women in brightly colored *huipiles* and poorly clad children with dusty bare feet. Nothing in the lively chatter reflected the grim cause that had brought them all together.

Carson's face was implacable. He had not said much since the summons had interrupted that strange, intense moment back at his house. He maintained a courteously loose hold on her arm as they were jostled along by the crowd.

Meg couldn't decide if the dryness in her throat was due to the fine powdery dust that billowed up as they walked along or to the slow horror that was developing inside her as the young boy's words echoed in her head.

In all her rough-and-tumble life at the ranch she had never seen anyone die. When her friend Johnny's father, Augusto—Old Gus—had been struck in the wrist by a rattler, her father had had to lock her in her room to keep her away from the bunkhouse as the gentle old man agonized through his last hours. She had wanted to be by Johnny's side, but in this her father had been adamant. He couldn't protect her from the sometimes down-and-dirty life on the Texas plains, but he could keep her from the stark ugliness of its deaths.

She couldn't afford to think about her father right now, or Johnny, or anything that meant home. She was the captive of desperate, cruel men, and she had to keep her wits about her. She looked up at Carson's finely chiseled face. His cold blue eyes held the aspect of carefully leashed power. She had the feeling that this man was every bit as dangerous as the sidewinder that had put an end to Old Gus.

The four prisoners huddled together miserably in the center of the plaza. Three were blindfolded and the fourth had a rough feed sack pulled down over his head and shoulders. A length of hemp was tied loosely around his neck.

One of the blindfolded prisoners looked to be little more than a boy, and clean streaks in the grime of his face bore witness to recent tears.

Meg's heart started beating faster and her stomach churned.

"Surely they don't really mean to shoot them?" She directed her words to no one in particular, but she spoke in English and was ignored by the excited people around her, whose eyes were on the four figures in the center of the plaza.

Carson's grip on her elbow tightened. He turned the full force of his gaze on her and spoke slowly. "If you have any sense at all you will keep that beautiful mouth of yours shut." His eyes flickered briefly to her full lips, and he swallowed with difficulty, feeling the movement all the way down to his nagging neck wound.

Behind his stony countenance his thoughts were whirling. Unlike Meg, he *had* seen men die—too many of them. He was not looking forward to adding four more to the count. But it was the presence of the feisty young girl at his side that made this scene different from several he had witnessed since he joined Villa's band weeks ago. She managed to bring out feelings in him—guilt, tenderness, protectiveness—that were totally uncharacteristic. He found himself worrying about the girl, feeling the need to take care of her.

First Lieutenant Timothy Carson had rarely had the opportunity to feel protective of anything or anybody. Not since the stormy day twenty years ago back at Fort Bliss, when the fort commander had come to inform him that his handsome, gay and ever-so-in-love parents had been lost in a deadly gully washer.

That day eight-year-old Timothy had become a man, Carson. An only child, mature for his age, Carson refused to accept the care and protection of the fort, which was the only home he had ever known, without earning his keep. By the age of twelve he could out-track the best man on the force.

Though the Indian problems had dwindled to the last few holdout renegades, Carson spent long days in the company of the Indian scouts still employed by the fort. Always a quick study, he soon matched them in horsemanship and excelled in their ancient weaponry.

From the drifters who filtered down from the Santa Fe Trail—drovers, prospectors, gamblers—he had learned to handle a side arm as if it were an extension of his hand.

From the whores who serviced the fort he had learned at an early age other, more pleasant uses for his whiplash-lean body. As he filled out into manhood, his handsome features and breathtaking eyes assured him the pick of the lot—whenever and wherever he liked. Still a quick study, his expertise soon earned him a rep-

utation for lovemaking as awesome as the one he had
for riding and shooting.

But still he was a loner, preferring to read every book
he could get his hands on rather than join in the fort's
good-natured social activities. Above all, he guarded
himself against any lasting attachments. He was not
about to risk the devastation of another loss such as he
had suffered with his parents.

Timothy Carson's education had been thorough in
everything that meant survival and nonexistent in everything that meant feelings. Those he had carefully
packed away with his toy train as the lethal storm had
continued to howl around the fort that day so long ago.

Now much of the chatter stopped as the crowd parted
and the stocky, powerful form of Villa walked briskly
into the plaza. Behind him was a big, swarthy man Meg
had not seen before. Carson's hand tightened painfully
around her arm. A cry of protest died in her mouth as
she looked up and saw his eyes ablaze with a hot blue
light, fastened on the newcomer.

"Who's that?" she asked Carson in an undertone.

"Aguirre, Villa's number-one henchman." He
dropped her arm and stepped casually in front of her,
blocking her view of the man. "He's not someone you
want to meet, Meg," he said to her softly over his
shoulder.

Villa, Aguirre and two other men appeared to be
conferring near the prisoners. From behind the shelter
of Carson's broad back Meg studied the crowd. The
young boy who had fetched them was now sitting directly in front of the prisoners with several friends. They
were laughing among themselves and passing around a
bag of pumpkin seeds to spit at the condemned men.

The first boy landed a stinging hit on the smallest prisoner's tear-streaked cheek.

The excited din of the crowd ceased altogether as Villa halfway raised one hand, palm out.

"*Compañeros.*" His voice was soft, but seemed to carry to the outer reaches of the square. "We have before us four traitors to the cause of liberty and justice for our country."

The snarling of two stray dogs down a dusty alleyway was the only sound to be heard.

"There is only one fate for such as they. We will show them no mercy—for to betray one's country is the greatest of all betrayals. As acting magistrate of Dos Cumbres, I hereby sentence them to death."

Something like a cheer went up from the crowd. The boys in the front pounded one another in excitement. Villa stepped back, and Aguirre motioned to two men with rifles to position themselves in front of the prisoner whose head was covered.

With the detached unreality of a nightmare, Meg saw them raise their rifles. Seconds later, two spots of red blossomed on the prisoner's loose-fitting shirt, and without a sound the man fell headfirst into the dust of the plaza.

There was a moment of silence. Still standing behind Carson, Meg was surprised to see that at some point she had taken hold of the firm muscles of his upper arms. They had tightened reflexively at the gunshots.

A smattering of applause and several cries of "*¡Muerte a los traidores!*" drifted over from the crowd. A wave of revulsion such as she had never felt before swept through her. Without thinking, she pushed Carson aside and stepped out into the plaza. Some of the crowd near her stepped aside, gazing curiously at the

American beauty with the golden eyes, which were at the moment blazing with fury.

"This is murder!" she cried in Spanish. More of the crowd turned to look at her, and from across the plaza, Villa and Aguirre craned their necks to identify the cause of the commotion.

From behind her came Carson's voice. "You damn little fool." He took her arm in a brutal grip and started pushing her through the crowd toward Villa. She turned on him indignantly.

"Can't you do anything to stop this? What kind of people are you, anyway?"

His lips tightened ominously. "One more word, *gringa,* and I swear I'll wash my hands of you. I won't even bother to pick up the pieces of what's left of you after they finish." He nodded toward a group of ten or so fully armed men who stood guarding the remaining prisoners.

The crowd parted to let them through as Carson almost dragged her forward. Villa waited for their approach, a half smile on his face.

"Your woman, Carson, does not approve of Dos Cumbres justice?" he asked mildly.

Carson halted when they reached Villa, leaving them standing only a couple steps away from where the dead prisoner lay facedown in the dust.

"I beg your pardon, *Jefe.* I've not yet had time to educate her on proper behavior for—" he stopped and surveyed the prisoners with a carefully casual glance "—for this type of thing."

"You can't just *shoot* people—" Meg was stopped by Carson's painful twist of her arm.

"You won't be interrupted again, I promise," he told Villa in a grim voice, his hold on her excruciating.

The small boys had stopped tormenting the prisoners long enough to watch this exchange, and it was being observed carefully, too, by Villa's lieutenant, Aguirre.

"I don't believe I've been introduced." His voice, though soft, carried an underlying menace that gave Meg a sudden chill.

"She's an American, Rodolfo. They took her instead of the Mendoza girl. Unfortunate mistake. She'll probably end up as one of the mysterious disappearances you hear about these days. But in the meantime, I've given her to Carson."

Meg was as horrified by Villa's nonchalant description of her situation as she was by the dead body lying not more than a yard away from her foot. She looked up in panic at Carson, but his eyes were locked with those of Rodolfo Aguirre.

"So. Quite a prize, amigo Carson." Aguirre shifted his eyes to Meg and took a quick but thorough, insulting inventory of her body. "Perhaps when you tire of the girl..."

He left the sentence dangling, his lips turned up in a lecherous smile as he turned back to Carson.

"You heard *el jefe,* Aguirre—the girl belongs to me. And I don't take lightly to my things being used by anyone else."

Of an equal height, the two faced each other with unremitting stares. The hostility between them throbbed through Meg along with the pain in her arm, still held fast by Carson. It was Villa who broke the silence.

"Carson, Rodolfo, we are not here to discuss the *gringa*. We have work to do."

Aguirre glanced once more toward Meg, then turned to Villa. "Allow me to do the honors, *Jefe*. We'll show our American visitor something about Mexican ingenuity."

He strode over to the prisoners and with brisk movements shoved them together so that the stomach of one was up against the back of another, leaving them lined up like the ivory dominoes Rosa Maria's father played incessantly at his big *hacienda*.

Then he turned to one of the men who had shot the first prisoner. *"Permíteme tu rifle, Juancho,"* he told the man, relieving him of his weapon.

Meg looked on in consternation. Villa watched his lieutenant's actions with a broad smile. Carson stood without moving, but finally relaxed his hold on her arm. Meg thought she saw a flicker of distaste in his eyes as he watched Villa's big lieutenant push around the much smaller prisoners.

The nearest prisoner was shaking badly and appeared to have wet the front of his trousers. Aguirre stood arrogantly in front of him and lifted the rifle. Turning slightly to meet Meg's eyes, he said in a taunting voice, "Watch, *gringa*. This is Villa-style efficiency."

With a hollow bang the gun sounded one single time, and first one, then the second, then the third prisoner crumpled slowly to the ground.

"Ha!" Aguirre's proud cry rang out over the gasp of the crowd. *"Three* kills with *one* bullet! Pretty good, eh?"

The young boys in front were cheering and pounding each other on the back. Aguirre turned to them and raised the rifle high in a mock salute.

Meg stood frozen in horror, and as she surveyed the crowd she saw the same revulsion reflected in many eyes, especially among the women. Villa continued to grin and walked over to slap Aguirre on the shoulder. "Rodolfo, my friend, I never know what you will think of next," he told his lieutenant.

Aguirre looked over to Meg and Carson. "We save ammunition this way. Very economical, no?"

He had addressed the question to Meg, but she was too appalled to do anything more than look up at Carson in mute appeal.

Carson's face was stony, but he seemed unmoved by the proceedings.

"Con permiso, Jefe," he said to Villa, ignoring Aguirre. "If that's all for now, I'll be taking my woman back to bed. *Hasta mañana."*

Without waiting for a reply, he turned sharply and once again started to pull Meg through the crowd. His hold on her was gentler this time, but by now her arm was badly bruised and she winced with pain.

With her final glance back the monstrous scene became imprinted on her brain. Villa and Aguirre were laughing over a shared joke, while the men who had been guarding the prisoners began pulling at the bodies, which lay jumbled together. The leg of one of them twitched slightly, and Meg's last glimpse of the plaza was the sight of one of the guards aiming a pistol at the twitching man's head.

Meg considered herself to be in good condition from all her activities at the ranch. Her father, of course, would have been happy to have her sitting quietly on the wide front porch in a crisp sprigged-muslin dress waiting for him with a cold glass of lemonade at the end of the day.

But that had never been Meg's style. And after her father had seen her throw a good-size calf to the ground and hog-tie it there, he had capitulated. Johnny had taught her the trick in secret—how to give that special twist of the neck, sweep the critter's feet out from under it and use her own body's weight to lever it down. Johnny had believed there was *nothing* that Meg couldn't do, and mostly she had proved him right.

But now it seemed that even the smallest of those well-conditioned muscles protested as Meg awoke slowly and tried to move. The climb down the mountain and all of the turmoil of the past two days had taken its toll.

Meg moaned aloud. Her eyes were still closed, but she knew she was on the big bed in Carson's room. She had slept poorly, a restless sleep full of grinning bandits and dead bodies. Her arm ached from Carson's rough treatment yesterday.

"You awake?" The deep voice seemed disembodied, coming from one of her nightmares.

With reluctance she opened her eyes. Carson towered over her, a steaming mug in each hand. He held one out to her.

"Coffee?"

She sat up with a groan and her right hand went involuntarily to her left shoulder. It felt as though it had been pulled out of its socket.

Carson looked down at her in surprise. "What's wrong with your arm?" he asked tersely.

Meg swung her feet off the bed and reached angrily for the cup of coffee. She took a scalding gulp.

"You ought to know what's wrong with it. You're the one who did it. But then, I suppose that's just all in a day's routine for you outlaws—murder, kidnapping, abuse of women. What's on the schedule for today?"

He scowled at her and put down his cup on the dresser next to the bed. "Let me see."

He none too gently grasped her left hand and tried to push up the sleeve of the dress Luz had given her. It only went up as far as her elbow, but the movement was enough to force another groan of protest.

"You really *are* hurt," he said, his scowl deepening. "Take off that dress."

"Just forget it," she said in irritation, pushing him away. She tried to rise from the bed but he insistently pushed her back down.

"Contrary to your opinion of me, Meg, I am not an abuser of women. Perhaps you should remember that you've slept in my bedroom for two nights now and so far have remained untouched. Now, stop acting foolish. If your arm is injured, let me see it."

As he spoke he began to unfasten the tiny buttons down the bodice of the dress. His big hands brushed lightly along the tops of her breasts, and a slow heat started up into Meg's cheeks.

Carson didn't notice her embarrassment. He was busy concentrating on keeping his own thoughts in line. The creamy white skin revealed underneath the rough cotton dress was creating in him a different kind of heat.

Carefully he pushed the dress off her shoulders and let it drop to her waist. The only undergarment Luz had provided was a crudely sewn shift. For a moment Carson couldn't move his eyes away from the sight of Meg's full breasts straining at the thin material. Dark shadows revealed clearly where her nipples had grown arousingly erect. The breath he was trying to take caught in his throat.

Meg noticed the change in him. His breathing seemed different suddenly and his eyes narrowed. In some way it both frightened and excited her. No man had ever looked at her like that. Indeed, no man had seen her so uncovered since her father had strictly forbidden her to swim anymore with Johnny unless she wore that ridiculous bathing dress he had bought for her in Austin.

There had been times when she had caught Johnny looking at her with a special sort of intensity. Sometimes after those moments he had been curt with her, even rude. But Johnny had never looked at her the way Carson was looking at her now. And Johnny's looks had never, ever caused this strange warmth to spread through her body. Why, she felt positively tipsy!

She pulled away in confusion, and the motion forced Carson to move his eyes away from her breasts to her left arm. The entire upper portion of it was a nasty reddish purple.

"God, Meg!" He ran his fingertips lightly over the bruises. "Are you telling me *I* did this to you yesterday?"

"Well, you didn't see anyone else dragging me around like a hog-tied heifer, did you?" she snapped at him.

She shifted away from him on the bed, but her anger softened a bit as she saw the horror in his face. She bruised easily, and the arm did look dreadful.

"I didn't realize—I didn't know—" he stammered, his eyes stricken with guilt.

"Well, now you do," she said primly. "It's done and there's nothing we can do about it. So if you would just help me back on with this sleeve."

She made a painful movement, trying to shrug back into her dress, but Carson stopped her by grasping her wrist again.

"No, wait. Are you sure nothing's broken? The shoulder—is it all right? It's not pulled out of place or anything?"

His solicitude restored her good humor and, more important, allowed that strange, intoxicating heat to dissipate. She began to feel enough in control to tease him a little.

"I don't know. I'm not sure I can move it." She molded her face into a grimace of pain.

Very carefully he put both hands on either side of her shoulder and pressed. It was tolerably sore, but Meg gave a cry of pain, which furthered deepened the creases alongside Carson's full mouth. He was very close to her, close enough for her to notice he had not yet shaved this morning.

"Where does it hurt?" he asked, his voice softly apologetic.

She hid a smile. "Right here," she said, placing a hand on her stomach.

He looked at her with puzzled concern.

"My stomach—that's what hurts. I'm starving! Don't you people know about three meals a day up here?"

She watched as his expression turned to one of undisguised relief, then anger, then amusement, all in a few seconds.

"It would seem the lady is also somewhat of an actress," he said dryly. "Still, this does look sore. Let me get you some liniment."

He rummaged through a drawer and came up with a can of Halsey's Liniment. Its pungent odor filled the room as he poured some into his hands.

"Mostly I use this on my horse," he told her with a grin. "Works every time."

"Whew, did you ever ask your horse how it liked the smell?" she asked with a little gasp.

"I think the smell is what does it, actually. It's so damn strong those muscles just give up. As soon as they stop acting up, you feel better."

They were both smiling now, in spite of the stench. Carson's hands smoothed the lotion over her arm and shoulder. Whether it was the liniment or his warm touch that eased the aching she didn't know, but she did feel a little better.

The bones of her arm and shoulder felt as fragile as a child's to Carson. He couldn't believe that he had been so brutal with her. He was trying to *protect* her, not hurt her.

Her skin was silky and warm. Long after he had covered the area with the liniment he continued to rub her gently, reluctant to break the contact. He looked over at her face. Her golden eyes were hidden from him by a thick fringe of dark lashes. A blush heightened the delicate line of her cheekbone. Finally she lifted her head and smiled at him. He had never seen anything so beautiful.

"I think that's probably enough," she said, suddenly shy.

Lost temporarily in her eyes, he had almost forgotten the continuing massage of her shoulder. With a final stroke down her arm he stopped and sat back on the bed.

"What in hell are you doing here, Meg?" he asked her softly. "You're just too damn beautiful. You ought to be—oh, I don't know—in Paris or some damn place like that." He sighed and ran his fingers through the dark waves of his hair. "Anywhere but in the middle of this godforsaken snake pit."

Meg's smile died abruptly. Carson's words had brought back to her all the terrible events of the previous day. What was she thinking of, teasing and smiling at this cold-blooded outlaw? A man who could stand calmly and watch four people shot down in cold blood. If she had had any doubts, the scene in the plaza had convinced her that he definitely was one of them. He was probably a murderer, too. And she had let herself feel pleasure over the touch of those murdering hands on her body.

A shiver of disgust ran through her, and she stood abruptly, pulling her dress around her as she moved.

"As I said before, Carson, I'm hungry. So unless you intend to starve me as well as manhandle me, I'd like something to eat."

He frowned, but stood and started helping her back into her dress. As if he had been reading her mind, he said in a subdued tone, "There was no way to stop it, you know."

"You didn't even try—you didn't even *protest.*" Her voice was cutting.

Carson shook his head and said more firmly, "There are certain things you simply can't change, Meg. I learned a long time ago to use my energies for the things I could change, and to make the best of the things I couldn't."

"I don't know how anyone can make the best of the murder of four innocent people."

"Innocence is a relative term, don't you think? You don't know what those men had done."

"Men? One of them was no more than a boy, Carson. What could he have done in his short life to deserve such an end?" The pitch of her voice rose as she felt again the horror of watching those bodies crumple like jackstraws into the dust.

Carson gave a deep sigh. "You would be surprised, Meg, at the atrocities committed by boys just like that one in this crazy so-called revolution. I'm not trying to defend the killing, I'm just saying there's nothing either you or I could have done about it, not unless we wanted to be Aguirre's next experiment."

Meg shuddered. "What a loathsome man. Who is he?"

"He's one of the few people Villa trusts, and he's a goddamned butcher. Stay away from him, Meg. Just stay clear the hell away from him."

When that grim mask settled over his features, it was easy for Meg to believe that he was every bit as lethal and lawless as the men she had seen carry out the executions yesterday. Yet something in her wanted to believe that there was more to him than that. Just moments ago his hands on her arm had been so gentle, warming her from without and within. She couldn't figure him out.

"Carson, tell me honestly. Are you going to help me out of this? Can I trust you?"

Carson looked down at her, watching as the golden flecks in her lovely eyes glazed over with unshed tears. His heart seemed to turn over inside his chest.

"Meg, I—" He turned away from her and walked over to the window, where he pounded once on the frame with the flat of his hand. "You can trust this—I don't want you to be hurt. I hope before long there will be some way to get you safely back to your family."

"But you won't go up against Villa for my sake— that's what you're really saying, right?" Her bottom lip quivered, but Meg bit down on it, determined not to cry.

Carson turned back to face her. He focused on the trembling of that full bottom lip and bit into his own, as if by doing so he could make the trembling stop.

"No one goes up against Villa, Meg. Not unless they want to end up exactly like those four in the plaza yesterday. But I will try to keep you safe until Villa gets involved with something else and forgets all about his aborted kidnap attempt."

Meg's head went up sharply at the reminder of how this had all started in the first place. "Well, if you won't help me, will you at least tell me why all this happened? Was it Rosa Maria you wanted?"

"If that's the Mendoza girl who's about to be married, yes. It was she we were supposed to bring back here that night. But that's all I can tell you, Meg, so no more questions. Now, let's go eat."

Meg's tears had completely disappeared as she quickly digested this piece of information. If these outlaws had been about to kidnap Rosa Maria, she had to find out why—and let her friend know.

"Rosa Maria is my best friend, Carson. If she is in danger, I intend to warn her."

Carson shook his head, but his expression had softened considerably. "Knowledge is a dangerous thing around here, Meg. The less you know about Villa's activities, the better."

He took Meg's good arm with a grip so careful he might have been holding an eggshell. "Don't think more about it." -

Meg let herself be gently pulled along, but her mind would not let the matter go. She had to learn the truth about the kidnapping, and she would waste no more time thinking about escaping from here until she did. If Carson would not tell her the truth, she would find it out for herself. There was at least one man in the camp who could definitely provide her with the answers. His name was Pancho Villa.

Chapter Five

The sun had become a bright red ball that skimmed the edge of one of the distant peaks as Meg made her way to the back of the squat adobe structure. It had not taken much subtlety to learn that this building was where Villa stayed when in Dos Cumbres. Luz was installed there now, too, and several of Villa's so-called lieutenants had quarters in the large house.

It had been a bit trickier getting off by herself to attempt this little mission. She had had to wait all day, until Carson finally became immersed in a heated poker game and she could casually tell him that she was going back to his house for the night.

She had agreed meekly that she would lock the door behind her and open only to his knock. Then she had hurried off, hoping to get her spying accomplished before it became too dark for her to see her way around.

Now as she approached the rear of Villa's headquarters, she began to have some doubts about the wisdom of her plan, but she stubbornly refused to give in to her fears.

Though she had seen two of Villa's men, rifles in hand, lounging carelessly in the front of the building, the back appeared to be deserted as she crept closer. Her hands touched the cold gray stone wall and she flattened herself against it. The spicy pork she had eaten for dinner did flip-flops in her stomach.

From up on the flat roof of the structure she could hear voices—male, laughing voices. And unmistakable among them was the authoritative timbre of Villa's own.

Perhaps this wasn't such a crazy idea after all, she told herself with growing excitement. In another few minutes it would be dark, and no one would see her then. She could stay here all evening if she had to, and certainly at some point there would be a discussion of the kidnapping.

At the moment they appeared to be discussing horses and livestock. She could very well be back at the ranch eavesdropping outside the bunkhouse. It had been one of her principal amusements when she was about the age when she first learned the real meaning of all those words the ranch hands bandied about so freely.

How horrified her poor father would have been if he knew the things she had learned from behind those bunkhouse walls. Meg smiled in the growing darkness.

"So, *gringa,* my friend Carson has tired of you so soon?" The Spanish words were softly sinister.

Meg whirled around with a gasp that was cut short by a large, thick hand covering her mouth and nose. A long arm clamped painfully around her middle. She struggled in panic as she recognized her assailant as Rodolfo Aguirre, the man even Carson had described as a butcher.

"Stop fighting me, *linda.* If you keep struggling, I'll have to hurt you." His voice was still quiet, but the threat caused a chill to run along Meg's limbs. She stopped moving and stood limply within his arms.

"That's better, pretty one." He removed his hand from her mouth and placed it lightly against her neck. "You want to be *nice* to Rodolfo. Otherwise, I'm going to have to take you upstairs and have you explain to *el jefe* just exactly what you were doing sneaking around the back of his house like some kind of dirty informer. You *saw* what we do to informers, didn't you, *gringa?*"

When she didn't reply, Aguirre pushed the heel of his hand against her neck, making her give a reflexive cough. "Didn't you?"

She glared at him and tried to spit out the words. "I saw you murder four men yesterday, if that's what you mean."

The defiance in her tone was mitigated by the cracking of her voice. Aguirre merely chuckled. His hand went up alongside her head to entwine itself in her hair. "That's good, *gringa*—I like my women with spirit."

Holding her head in place with his grasp on her hair, he smashed his hard, wet lips onto hers. A wave of revulsion hit Meg as his tongue invaded her mouth.

She squeezed her eyes tightly shut. *Blessed Mary, give me strength,* she silently prayed, and, tensing her entire body, brought her knee up as hard as she could into the huge outlaw's groin.

"Hijo de—" The oath was muffled by pain. At the sudden relaxing of his hold on her, Meg pushed herself away and raced for the nearby trees. The cooling evening air hit her lungs as she took deep, frightened breaths.

Before entering the woods she looked back to see Aguirre heading in her direction with long, determined strides. Suddenly she realized that the last place she wanted to be with him was in a dark forest. With a quick shift in direction she skirted around a nearby building and raced out into the street.

She hesitated just a moment as she thought quickly which way to go, but before she could start running again, Aguirre was behind her and had grasped a huge handful of her thick hair.

"You'll pay for that, *gringa*," he snarled in her ear.

Down the street a tall form separated himself from a group of men and started toward them at a lope. With incredible relief Meg recognized Carson. Sharply she called out his name.

"*¿Qué pasa?*" Carson slowed his run as he approached them.

With a slight shove, Aguirre released his hold on her hair. "I just caught your woman here spying on Villa's headquarters. I figure if you can't keep better control of her than that, it's probably time for someone else to take over her care."

Even in the gloom of the twilight, Meg could see the furious clenching of Carson's jaw. "That's not necessary," he said tersely. "I'll handle it."

The big man's voice took on a sneer. "I'm not so sure you've got the right anymore, Carson. Maybe we need to go talk to Villa about this."

Carson reached out and pulled Meg toward him. "The two of us have never needed Villa to settle our differences, Aguirre. I told you I'd handle this."

Carson's hand hovered around the six-shooter tied at his hip. Meg could see in his face the effort he was making to stay calm. "I'd count it as a favor if we could leave it at that."

The only sound was the rhythmic chirping of the *cigarras* out in the pines. Aguirre looked from Carson

to Meg and back again. Finally he shrugged. "Just remember—when you finish with her, she's mine."

He ran a thick finger along the edge of her cheek.
"We have a score to settle now, she and I."

He turned on the heel of his big boot and walked
away in the direction of Villa's headquarters.

Meg sagged in relief, letting out a deep breath, then
straightened, sucked it back in again and turned to face
an irate Carson.

Carson didn't trust himself to speak. Grabbing Meg's
hand, he angrily led her back to his house.

The damn fool girl just won't keep out of trouble, he
fumed silently. I relax my guard for just a few minutes,
and she's up to who knows what mischief at Villa's
headquarters and ends up head to head with Aguirre, of
all people.

Most of the females he'd been exposed to would have
been scared out of their minds to be a captive here in
Dos Cumbres. What did it take to intimidate this foolhardy girl? Perhaps it was time to teach her a lesson, to
show her what kind of fire she was playing with.

The mere thought of just exactly how he would go
about teaching her that lesson had Carson's blood racing as he quietly closed the door of his house behind
them and pulled the latch shut.

Meg stood miserably in the middle of the room while
he briskly lit the kerosene lamp. It flared brightly then
settled down to a steady light that cast a cozy yellow
glow over the small room.

She lifted her chin and looked bravely into his eyes as
he turned back to her. Her eyes looked huge and scared
in her pale face, and the slight quiver of her firm little
chin almost made him relent. Then she opened her
mouth.

"It's your fault, you know," she told him defensively. "If you had just told me what I need to know about Rosa Maria—"

Rage rose in him again. Where had his control gone? Carson wondered. He had always prided himself on his superb calm under any situation, but since this little vixen had been handed up into his arms just a few days ago, he seemed to be constantly losing it.

He took a couple deep breaths, trying to restore his equanimity, then decided to follow his original plan to teach the golden-eyed beauty a lesson.

"If I hadn't happened to be across the street, do you know what Aguirre would be doing to you right now, Meg?" His deep voice was calm, almost pleasant. Meg backed away from him a step, her eyes wary.

"He'd have you off in the woods somewhere, Meg, enjoying the delights of this lush body of yours." Like an animal stalking its prey he backed her up against one wall of the room, finally trapping her there between his outstretched arms.

"Carson—stop." Her face was no longer pale, and her breasts rose and fell in agitation.

His face hard, Carson reached a deliberate hand to the top of her dress and yanked downward, spraying buttons into the room. "Maybe I ought to just go ahead and take advantage of it myself, seeing as how you're so hell-bent on getting yourself raped."

Telling himself that it was all just to teach her a lesson, Carson did what he had been thinking about doing ever since he had pushed back her dress to tend her arm that morning—he slid one long, lean hand inside the top of her shift and let it close gently around the full curve of her breast. Her nipple sprang to life inside his palm, and he caressed it with a callused thumb.

Suddenly he forgot about Aguirre, forgot about teaching lessons. With irresistible urgency he lifted the white globe out of the thin shift and bent to fasten his mouth at its tip. His insides seemed to dissolve as he suckled and the pebbled nipple grew long and hard.

Meg leaned weakly back against the rough wooden wall. The scare she had just had, the worry over Carson's anger, everything faded as all her senses focused intensely on the feel of Carson's mouth around her sensitive breast.

Carson fell to one knee without loosening his hold on her. She looked down, and the sight of his curly dark head moving rhythmically against her sent a sweet, piercing pain all the way through the center of her body.

At last he pulled away and stood up against her, trailing soft kisses along the tender skin of her neck. Without conscious thought she twisted toward him, her mouth turning to his like a flower to the sun.

His awesome blue eyes were glazed, and he groaned as his lips desperately sought hers. For a moment it was liquid fire, then ice. Meg pulled away with a cry of distress.

Distractedly Carson tried to follow her movement with his mouth, but came back to his senses abruptly as his tongue tasted the salt of a solitary tear that was making its way down her cheek.

"What is it, sweetheart?" He sounded hoarse.

Meg put a trembling hand up to the side of her mouth where Aguirre's bruising had left her lip slightly torn. The area was beginning to discolor. She watched as the desire faded from Carson's eyes, replaced by a hardness that made her want to shiver.

"Aguirre?" he asked coldly.

"Yes." It was little more than a whisper.

"What else did he do to you, Meg?" His voice was harsh and urgent, but his finger rubbed feather-light along the edge of her sore lip.

"N—nothing. That is, he did this—" She reached up and put her hand gently over his where it rested near her mouth. "And then I—I jammed my knee into his—"

She stopped as bright scarlet flooded into her face. Carson looked down at her in disbelief. The icy hardness of his eyes gave way to relief and then a reluctant kind of amusement.

"Meg, you are the damnedest—" The words tripped over a strange lump that was building somewhere inside his throat. His body was still hard. In less than a heartbeat he could have had her back in his arms. But as he watched her proud attempts to repair the damage he had done to her clothes, the lump in his throat grew larger, bringing with it a sick feeling of guilt.

The flush had left her face as quickly as it had come. She looked unnaturally pale again, and the swelling of her lip was all too obvious. How could he not have noticed it before?

With a shake of his head Carson reached out and gathered her into his strong arms. There was no desire in him now, only an overwhelming sense of tenderness that was much more disturbing. He wanted to comfort her, to make things all right. It was the first time, he realized, that he had ever held a woman for purposes other than satisfying their mutual passion.

Meg snuggled into Carson's warm embrace. She didn't want to think about outlaws or Villa or kidnappings. She gave herself up to the wonderful feeling of strength and protection of his arms. She had been badly frightened tonight—was still afraid. But for just a moment, as she leaned her head against Carson's hard chest, it seemed that nothing in her life had ever felt so right.

Carson was the first to break the spell. Dropping a light kiss on the top of her red-gold hair, he pulled away from her and crossed the room to fetch a small flask of an amber liquid that had been sitting on his dresser.

Returning to her, he offered it with a rueful smile. "Maybe you could use a drink, Meg. I promise, no more ravishings. For tonight, at least."

Meg shook her head and, giving one last tug to the front of her dress, walked slowly over to sit on the bed. Carson sank into the room's only chair.

"Well, I sure could use one." He took a long swallow straight from the flask.

He sat regarding her in silence for several minutes as she finished tending to her ruined clothes. Finally he gave a deep sigh and said, "Meg, you're going to have to explain to me what you were doing outside Villa's headquarters tonight."

"I already told you. I mean to find out what he wants with Rosa Maria. She—she's not as strong as I am, Carson." She put her hand unconsciously to her swollen lip, and her voice quavered slightly. "I don't think she could survive an experience like this."

Carson looked intently at the perfect features of her face, marred only by the purplish smear at the corner of her lip. He took another pull of the fiery liquor.

"Go to sleep, Meg," he said softly. "You've had enough excitement for one day. Just lie back now and go to sleep."

Meg realized suddenly that she was bone tired. She barely had the strength to pull herself under the rough covers of the bed. As her head sank into the soft pillow her eyes closed of their own volition, and she was deep into a heavy, dreamless sleep.

Carson sat watching her, lost in thought. The flask was nearly empty by the time he roused himself enough to put out the light.

"How did you end up here, Angelina?" The fat little cook's sweet smiles seemed incongruous in this rough place.

"God love you, *niña,* I was born right here in Dos Cumbres. I've never known anywhere else." She finished scooping a thick, pasty mass of *avena* into a dish and pushed it at Meg. "You got to get some meat on those bones, girl."

"Doesn't it bother you to be cooking all day long for a bunch of outlaws?"

Angelina looked over at her in surprise. "There's some that'll call *General* Villa an outlaw, *hijita,* but I'm not one of them." Her normally sunny face became stubborn.

"After I lost my Manolo, it was *General* Villa who took care of us—came right to my house, he did. He says to me, 'Angelina, Manuel was a good man. We're gonna take care of you—you and the little ones. Anything you need, you let Pancho Villa know.'"

She sat down across from Meg, her ample posterior engulfing the small wooden bench. "For more than five years, now, *General* Villa has never forgotten his promise. He even visits the children—tells them to be good helpers to me and to grow up proud that their father was a *revolucionario.*"

Admiration and something like reverence shone from her dark eyes. "No one can tell me that Pancho Villa is a *bandido.*"

Meg digested this new information about the Mexican bandit leader in silence. She had now heard his praises sung by two good women, Angelina and Luz. What, she wondered, had these two thought about the murders in the plaza the other day?

Meg was not ready to be convinced of the man's virtues, especially when the matter of Rosa Maria's kidnapping was unresolved. And that was a mystery she intended to solve today.

When the men had ridden out this morning she had just barely managed to keep Carson from tying her up in their room all day. She had had to give her solemn promise not to get into trouble.

"I've never raised my hand to a woman, Meg," he had told her sternly, "but by God, I swear I'll blister your backside if you try anything today."

She had smiled up at him demurely and promised sweetly that she intended to seek out Luz and spend the day with her. Surely he couldn't object to that?

She smiled to herself at the breakfast table. She had already decided while lying in bed that morning that Luz was probably the only person who could give her the answers she needed about the kidnapping. Spending the day with her suited her plans exactly. First things first—she would find out the truth about Rosa Maria, and then, since Carson did not seem to be making any move to help her, she would figure out how to get away from him and all his outlaw pals.

"Have you seen Luz today, Angelina?"

"No, *niña*—she's probably over at their house. You need her for something?"

"Nothing in particular. I just want to talk to her."

The inside of Villa's house was surprisingly well furnished. Comfortable sofas and elegantly carved wooden chairs lined the large *sala*. Meg sank down into the luxurious feather pillows of a small love seat and waited for the gruff guard to fetch Luz.

The tiny Mexican woman entered the room with a smile. As Meg struggled to rise from the enveloping upholstery, Luz leaned over to give her a warm *abrazo*.

"Don't get up, *querida*. How nice of you to come and see me." She sat down next to Meg, leaving the two of them cozily ensconced together on the small seat.

"Now tell me," she said matter-of-factly, "have these ruffians been treating you all right?"

Luz's eyes were bright with intelligence. Instinctively Meg sensed that she could trust this woman, perhaps even find an ally.

"Mostly I've been treated fine, *señora*."

Luz reached over to take Meg's hand. "Just call me Luz, my dear. And I shall call you Margarita."

Meg smiled. "I would like that very much, Luz."

"So now that's settled, you can tell me why you have come here." She looked at Meg shrewdly. "I do not think it was to pass the time of day."

With scarcely a moment's hesitation, Meg began telling Luz the whole story of how she had come to be in Dos Cumbres. The kindly woman listened sympathetically and made no comment until Meg finished her tale with an account of her meeting with Rodolfo Aguirre the previous evening.

At this last Luz shook her head vehemently. "You must stay out of the way of that one, Margarita. Even *I* am afraid of him, though he would never dare touch me. That would be the one thing that would turn my husband against him."

"I've promised Carson I will stay away from him."

Luz smiled at the flush that rose in Meg's cheek as she spoke the name of the handsome American. "Carson is a very fine man, Margarita," she said softly. "I'm glad my husband gave you to him. I think you can trust him not to hurt you."

"He has been kind to me so far, Luz, but where I come from women aren't just given to men for their personal pleasure. I intend to do everything I can to get out of this camp. But first I have to find out the story behind my kidnapping."

Luz stared down at her lap and sighed. Meg looked over at her downcast eyes and urged, "Please, Luz, if you know anything, you must tell me."

Finally Luz looked up and her expression made her face look much older than her twenty-some years.

"You will not understand, *chiquita*. You will not understand because you have never been poor and you have never been persecuted. And because you come from a place where women, as you say, are more than playthings for their men."

She stood and wandered over to one of the fine lacquered chairs, rubbing her hand lovingly along the intricate carvings of its back.

"Francisco did not always have these things, Margarita. He grew up as a poor farm boy from an honorable family in Durango. They all worked very hard, but they stayed very poor, because that is the way of things in Mexico.

"But Francisco was happy, I think, and his family was happy, until the day when a neighboring *hacendado* with too much money and too much power decided to amuse himself by raping Francisco's sister, Mariana. He left her half-dead."

Luz's face was impassive as she told the tale, but Meg could sense a deep empathy in her that seemed to be part of her commitment to the outlaw leader.

"Francisco went to meet the man at his big *hacienda*. They say it was a fair fight, a duel, but anyway—" she shrugged "—he killed him. Poor, unimportant Pancho Villa killed the important son of an even more important father, and they would never forgive him, neither the law nor the *ricos*. In many ways my husband has been running ever since."

Both women were quiet for a few moments. It was hard to reconcile the picture of Villa as a poor farm boy with the powerful man she had met, a man who commanded murders with the wave of his hand. But though she was affected by Luz's story, Meg couldn't see how these events of almost twenty years ago were part of her current situation.

"I'm sorry, Luz, truly. But about the kidnapping—"

"Ah, yes. Please believe me, Margarita, when I tell you that I try very hard to encourage the good side of Francisco. Deep down he *is* a good man. But his bitterness against the great ranchers who have owned all of northern Mexico for so long is very strong. The years only seem to make it deeper."

Luz moved around the chair she had been holding and sat down in it. She leaned toward Meg earnestly. "Your friend, Rosa Maria, is marrying into the Lopez Negrete family, the ones who wronged my husband's family all those years ago. Evidently Francisco decided to seek some measure of revenge by sending them a—a deflowered bride."

Meg closed her eyes. She could picture gentle Rosa's face as it had looked when she met Meg's train in Chihuahua City, the childlike innocence of her big round eyes as she gave restrained little jumps of delight at seeing her friend again. It would have killed her, finding herself at the mercy of these men. For the first time, Meg felt grateful that it was she who had been snatched away from the Mendoza ranch that night.

She opened her eyes. "Are you sure about this, Luz? About—about Rosa Maria's fiancé?"

She tried to remember what Rosa had told her about her prospective in-laws. She knew that the marriage, as was the custom, had been arranged by the two families. Rosa scarcely knew the young Rodrigo Lopez Negrete who was soon to be her husband. Her shy young friend was not looking forward to the union, but had been raised to know that she had little choice in the matter. Meg hoped that Rodrigo would prove to be a more decent man than the kinsman who had so changed the life of Pancho Villa.

Luz was watching her with her gentle brown eyes filled with shame. "I was not here when Francisco made this plan. I am sorry, Margarita. I have had time now to make him see that it is unworthy of him to use a young innocent girl for his vengeance."

"You mean he no longer is planning this awful thing?"

Luz shook her head. "I have his promise that the Mendoza girl will not be harmed."

Meg looked at Luz with admiration. "You're amazing, Luz. How did you change his mind?" She couldn't imagine this tiny woman holding any sway over the decisions of the mighty Villa.

Luz's blush was clear even through her olive complexion. "I have my ways. We might not have quite the freedom of you American women, but we do have a certain amount of power."

Meg's laugh was partly for Luz and partly for the relief she was feeling. Rosa Maria was no longer in danger. There was now nothing to keep Meg here in the outlaw camp. In spite of Carson's warnings she was ready to try another escape. She had gotten away once, and she could do it again.

"I'm sorry I haven't yet been able to convince him to let you go, Margarita," Luz told her apologetically. Her face took on an impish look. "I'm still working on it, though."

Meg stood up. "I appreciate all your kindness, Luz. I may not share your sentiments about your husband, but he must be doing something right to have a woman like you behind him."

Luz gave her another embrace as they took leave of each other. Her voice was sad. "Perhaps some day soon, my dear, you, too, will know what it is to love someone—in spite of everything."

Meg gave her new friend a farewell smile, but shook her head slightly. She wasn't sure she understood that kind of love. The kind of man she wanted would *deserve* her love—she wouldn't have to make excuses and allowances for his behavior.

She hurried back to Carson's house, planning to pick up the *sarape* she had used the other day. She had no intention of awaiting the results of Luz's feminine wiles over her husband to determine her fate. Nor would she wait any longer for Carson's promises of help. She was going to get away—now, before the men returned.

She took a last look round the small room she had shared with Carson. It seemed more like a lifetime than just a few days. She remembered vividly the emotional turmoil of last night—first the frighteningly intense sensations of his mouth on her body, then the overwhelming protectiveness of his arms about her. She would never forget him, this blue-eyed bandit who had so rocked her emotions.

She sighed and reached for the door. It opened before she could touch it, startling her into taking a step backward into the room. Carson's broad shoulders filled the frame. He looked curiously at the *sarape* she had clasped in her arms.

"Going somewhere?"

Chapter Six

"I—yes—for a walk," Meg stammered.

Carson eyed her skeptically, but refrained from comment. Entering the room, he bent down to pull a canvas bag from under the bed.

"Well, there's not time now. We're leaving."

"What do you mean, leaving?"

"Leaving—riding out—you, me, Villa, some of the men. We're heading for San Felipe, about a day's ride from here."

Meg's heart sank to the bottom of her toes. "Why do I have to go with you? Couldn't you just leave me here?"

Carson threw the satchel on his bed and began pulling items out of the drawers of his dresser. He gave her a distracted smile. "Nope. Where I go, pretty Meg, you go. Villa gave you to me, remember?"

Meg turned away from him, tears of disappointment stinging her eyes. She might have the instincts of a *zorrita*, but even she would never be able to find her way back from a full day's ride farther into this rugged sierra.

Frustration heightened the anger in her voice. "Villa can't give me to you or anyone else. He has no right."

He went on with his packing. "Please, Carson, I want to go home," she ended despondently.

Carson felt one of those unfamiliar tugs at his heart. He straightened and turned around to her. "I know you do, Meg, but there's no way—not yet. You'll like San Felipe. It's a pretty little place."

Ignoring the fury in her lovely face, he reached for the heavy *sarape* that she was clutching to her as though she would strangle the life out of it. "You want to take this along?" he asked mildly.

It had been midafternoon before the group of twenty or so of them left, moving double file along the rough, narrow road. Meg rode silently at Carson's side. She had been surprised at the exceptional quality of the little chestnut mare they had given her. The feel of a fine horse underneath her had helped compensate for the disappointment of being taken yet farther away from her friends and family.

It was after dark when they stopped for the night. Chicken *tortas* wrapped in oiled paper were brought out for a quick supper, and then it seemed that most of the men were ready to bed down for the night.

Carson had already thrown his bedroll on a gentle grassy incline at the edge of the campsite. A large pine partitioned the area off a ways from where most of the men were settling down.

He was waiting for Meg as she came out of the woods after relieving herself. "Our blankets are over there, Meg. Are you ready to turn in?"

Meg took a quick survey of the camp. From what she could see in the dark, Villa and his closest associates had set up a rough shelter directly across the camp from where Carson was indicating. Most of the rest of the men were arranged in a circle around a large fire pit, though no one had bothered to gather wood and start a fire.

She turned back to Carson and said with a touch of this afternoon's anger, "I think I'll just stay here at the edge of the trees, thank you."

His body went very still, like a cougar waiting to pounce. She couldn't see his eyes in the dark, but something made her take a step back away from him.

The next minute she was flying through the air, hoisted to his shoulder like a sack of barley as he walked with long sure strides over to the hill where he had left their bedrolls.

He deposited her none too gently on top of the nearest mound of blankets, and before she could even gather her wits together to protest, had dropped down on top of her. His lean hardness pressed along the entire length of her body. She pushed against him in panic.

"What do you think you're doing—you great—*oaf!*" His broad chest imprisoned hers and made it hard for her to breathe.

"Scream," he said into her ear.

"Have you gone crazy?" She had managed to free one of her hands and pounded it against his back. She might as well have been pounding a brick wall.

"Scream, damn it," he repeated. This time he grasped her hair and pulled back sharply. Her cry was involuntary.

"Again." Another cruel tug.

Her shout was half pain, half rage, and she renewed her attack on his back.

Suddenly his hold loosened. He reached back to once again imprison the small fist that was mounting such an ineffectual assault, but his hold, though firm, was no longer brutal.

Meg relaxed. He had been playacting again, damn him, for the sake of his cutthroat colleagues.

"Oh, do get off me," she said impatiently. "You could have just *told* me to scream, you know. You didn't have to go through all this."

Carson let go of both her arms and moved his hands up to rub her head soothingly where he had yanked her hair. His body still lay intimately on top of hers. His hard thighs pushed down along the tender skin between her legs, and just above them, his rigid heat burned through her thin dress.

"It was more fun this way," he drawled lazily. His voice was low, amused, with a tone that Meg had not heard before. It was not the intensity of last night, but more like a lover's teasing, some private man-woman communication that Meg had never experienced. It sent a curling warmth throughout her body, but left her confused, feeling out of control.

He nuzzled her neck tenderly. "Mmm—how do you do it, Meg? All afternoon in the saddle and you still smell as sweet as sagebrush."

"Sagebrush?" She struggled to make her voice sound normal and tried to speak loud enough to be heard over the thunderous pounding of her heart. "Don't you mean as sweet as violets, or—or roses or something?"

His firm, full lips were taking tender little nips along the base of her neck. She could feel his silky hair move against her cheek as he shook his head slowly.

"I'm afraid my life has not been much of one for smelling posies, Meg, sweetheart. Ah, but sagebrush...that fresh smell of sagebrush just after a cloudburst. That's how you smell, Meg—fresh and wild and sweet."

His mouth was on hers before she could answer, wiping away any vestige of coherent thought. A thick bank of clouds had rolled over the moon, deepening the darkness around the camp. Meg's eyes closed tightly, and all the feeling in her body seemed to radiate from the gentle movement of Carson's mouth in and around hers.

She didn't know when she began to respond. It was just automatic—like breathing. Suddenly she wanted to do everything to him that he was doing to her. Her tongue rasped against the stubble of beard along his chin, then slid smoothly along the inside of his lower lip. Carson responded with a moan deep in his throat and pulled her tightened breasts more closely against his punishingly hard chest.

"God, Meg." When he pulled away after several moments, it was as if she had been plunged into icy water. Reflexively her arms reached out to urge him back. She could feel the shuddering of his chest as he took a deep breath of air.

He dropped his head so that his forehead rested between her breasts, muffling his voice. "Have you done this before, Meg?"

Confused and still feeling a strange sense of loss, Meg's voice was unsteady. "I...what do you mean?"

"Are you a virgin?" he asked bluntly, his voice stronger now, with frustration beginning to replace the huskiness of desire.

A puzzling mixture of guilt, anger and disappointment filled her as Carson's words brought Meg to the abrupt reality of where she was and just what she had been about to do—and with whom. She pushed against his chest, and this time he let her roll him off her. He propped himself up on one elbow and lay quietly looking down at her, but when she made a move to get up, he gently pushed her back against the blanket-covered ground.

"Don't run away and—damn it all, anyway—don't feel bad." Carson cursed himself under his breath. This was the one lesson in lovemaking that the girls back at the fort had not covered. He knew that if he made love to Meg he could make her happy—hell, he could make them *both* very happy. Even now his body was screaming in silent protest at the abrupt interruption of its pleasure.

But a virgin. He'd never messed with virgins. The only so-called "good" girls he'd ever slept with had been experienced and more than willing. And to tell the truth, he'd prefer a sassy, no-nonsense, worldly-wise whore any day. They made him laugh and they made him feel good, and the price was right. The "proper" girls were the ones who could turn out to be expensive in the long run. He'd sooner face an enraged bull in a cattle chute than a pretty filly with wedding bells in her eyes.

His body was cooling down fast, but a pang of regret filled him as he glanced over Meg's well-formed curves and up to her beautiful face. He winced at the uncertainty and shame in her wide eyes.

"Come on, Meg, just forget about it. We got carried away—it was natural," he said with gruff tenderness. "We've been together a lot, and we have two normal, healthy bodies, and this is what happens. But I'm not so crude that I would take you here for the first time outside, surrounded by other men."

Meg began to fume as Carson went on with his mat-
ter-of-fact explanation for what had just happened between them. Was the man crazy? Hadn't *he* felt all
that—that—even in her mind she couldn't put a name
to the intensity of those feelings. Had they all been one-
sided? Perhaps she was the foolish one. Carson had had
dozens of women—hundreds probably. He did this kind
of thing so often, it simply didn't mean much to him.
The thought fueled her anger.

"Mr. Carson," she said icily. "You will *take* me, as
you so crassly put it, over my dead body. I don't know
what happened to me just now, but I do know this.
When I make love for the first time it's going to be on
my wedding night, with my *husband.* And it's going to
be in an elegant bed with sweet-smelling linens, not on
top of a bunch of horse blankets."

With a final, indignant snort she reached over to pull
the edge of a blanket around her and turned over on her
side.

Carson settled back with an amused sigh. Even the
sauciest of the whores he had met would have to come
a ways to match the brass of little Meg Atherton. It was
a long time before he could sleep. There would be sweet-
smelling linens, no doubt, in San Felipe, he mused. But
a marriage bed? Now that was another story.

San Felipe was, indeed, a picturesque sight, the reddish adobe buildings contrasting nicely with the scrubby
green bushes that served as fences crisscrossing the
town. But Meg was not in a mood to appreciate the
view. Carson had been distant and distracted, and Meg
had spent the morning going over once again the reasons she could not possibly form an attachment to this

man who so freely admitted to being part of a gang of outlaw murderers.

Her behavior last night at the camp had been inexcusable. She couldn't imagine what had possessed her to respond like that to him. It didn't matter that for just a few moments she had never felt so wonderful. He was a *bandido*—ruthless and without morals—like Villa himself.

As if to confirm her thoughts, a nasty scene seemed to be taking place in front of her. Villa and Aguirre were stopped in front of a poor-looking house on the edge of the town and appeared to be berating a small boy no more than seven or eight years old, while a man who looked to be the boy's father cowered in the background. Indignantly, Meg spurred her horse ahead, determined to rescue the child.

"So, now you understand, Paquito? The only way the children of Mexico will not have to fight this revolution all over again in another fifty years is by going to *school.*" The boy's tiny shoulders shook as Villa's deep voice boomed over him.

The piercing brown eyes of the outlaw leader moved threateningly to the boy's father. "My men will return to check that the boy has begun to go to school—every day. I would not disappoint them if I were you, *amigo.*"

Meg's horse had stopped of its own accord just behind the group of men. Her mouth dropped open, her indignant words dying on her lips. Carson rode up beside her. Without so much as a glance at the scene in front of them, he rested back on his horse and watched Meg with a slight smile, as though he had read her intentions and now waited to see what she would do.

"Meg Atherton to the rescue?" he asked softly.

Meg ignored him and kept her eyes on the small child. The terror she thought she had seen in his eyes now seemed to resemble awe. Villa removed a money clip from inside his belt. With decisive movements he pulled a twenty-peso bill from the thick wad and motioned the boy forward. His slight frame still trembling, the child approached Villa's massive horse and reached up to take the bill the bandit was extending down to him.

"This is a present to you, Paquito." Without changing his stern countenance, Villa reached down and ruffled his hand through the boy's shaggy hair. "It is so you will study very hard. And so you will remember Pancho Villa—and that Pancho Villa said *you* are the future of Mexico."

The boy's big brown eyes grew impossibly wide.

"Will you remember?"

The tiny face bobbed up and down furiously.

"Good."

Without another word Villa wheeled his horse around and headed once again along the broad dirt road into town.

Carson's smile had turned into a broad grin. "Looks like you'll have to go rescue someone else, Meg darlin'."

Meg was too astonished by the scene she had just witnessed to take offense at his baiting. She stared into the cloud of dust that rose behind the riders. "One day Villa is ordering people to be shot down in cold blood and the next he is acting like the village saint. I don't understand the man, Carson."

Carson's grin died and he, too, stared thoughtfully after the fast-disappearing group of bandits. "You're not alone there, Meg. Trying to understand Villa has become an obsession in these parts. The man who can figure him out stands to gain a lot.''

Meg looked over at him sharply. Something in the way he had spoken made her feel that these words were of more than casual importance.

"What is it, Carson? What makes you say that?"

He shook his head impatiently as if clearing out unwelcome thoughts. "Nothing, Meg. Come on, let's catch up. Let's go see how San Felipe welcomes a hero."

Meg watched with mild disgust as Villa's head disappeared once more into the young *cantinera*'s ample bosom. The girl's giggles made it obvious to all in the smoky room that she was a willing victim, but a picture of the serene young-old face of Luz kept intruding upon Meg's mind as she witnessed the scene.

Quickly she finished supper—black beans and an unidentifiable *guiso*—and pushed her bench back from the table. They were eating inside the town's main cantina, La Flor del Oeste, which had been taken over as a dining hall for Villa's men, and Meg was not at all comfortable in the unusual surroundings. Back home she had sometimes wondered about what went on behind the frosted glass doors of the town saloon, but her father would have had her hide if she had ever thought of venturing inside.

It didn't help her uneasiness that Carson had been gone since before dawn. In the three days they had spent in San Felipe he had seemed unusually serious. He had managed to find them a small room to themselves that first night, and there had been no more shows of passion for the benefit of his colleagues—or for any other reason.

It appeared that Villa had come to San Felipe for a kind of war parley with other revolutionary leaders coming from Durango and Sonora. Carson had not been invited behind the closed doors of their meetings, but he had always seemed to be near at hand when the group took a break.

Meg was surprised to find herself piqued at his distraction. It wasn't that she *wanted* his attentions, she told herself, it was just that she was bored. She had attempted conversation with some of the townsfolk on several occasions, but the typical response was a frightened look and ducked head.

She let the cantina door slam shut as she made her way out into the pine-scented night. Across the street several of Villa's men were tossing dice in the glow of a kerosene lantern. She stepped back into the shadows, hoping they had not seen her, but a sudden silence among the group told her she had been too late.

"Señorita!" With a sinking heart she recognized the heavy voice of Rodolfo Aguirre. He pulled himself up out of the circle of men.

She gritted her teeth and took a step toward him.

"Where's your 'owner'?" Even in the dim light she could see his teeth gleaming in a sneering smile.

"If you are referring to Mr. Carson, he is around somewhere. I just now am heading for bed."

"Alone, *gringuita?* What a waste. Better you come and join our little party." With a couple long strides he had crossed the street to her and began pulling her back to the circle of lamplight, where all pretenses of a dice game had now ceased.

"How about it, *hombres?* Wouldn't you like Miss Gringa here to join our party?"

There were several loud shouts of assent as Aguirre lifted her by the waist and deposited her in the middle of the group. A large, dirt-encrusted hand covered hers and dumped a pair of dice into her palm. Someone in back of her grabbed at her skirt. She turned to pull it out of the offender's grasp when two more arms reached at her from the front. Off balance, she teetered a moment, then fell to her knees.

"You see, *amigos,* the *gringa* even knows how to shoot dice—on her knees."

"*Oye, mamacita,* you can play with my dice any time, eh?"

A swarthy round face appeared just inches in front of hers. The man was so close she could see the blackened stubs of his two remaining front teeth. She slid backward, trying to get away from the fetid smell of his breath, only to be clutched from behind by another rough pair of arms.

Pawing hands seemed to be everywhere, and she struggled against her rising panic. Controlling the quaver in her voice, she shouted, "Let me alone, you filthy—"

Suddenly a solid *crack* split loudly through the heckling voices. Next to her a man landed hard in the dirt, moaning and writhing with pain. Heads came up around the circle, and all eyes turned to the tall shadowy form standing quietly at the edge of the group.

"*Carajo,* Carson, what're you trying to do? You must've clean broke Contrera's jaw."

Several of the men stood up. "No need to get so riled, Carson. We were just having some fun."

Carson ignored them. "You all right, Meg?"

She nodded and untwisted her legs to get to her feet. With a last look at the man still groaning in agony on the ground, Meg took the hand Carson reached out to her and pulled herself up. "I'm fine, Carson, really. Just—let's get out of here."

Carson's blue eyes glinted almost black in the night as he slowly stabbed each member of the group with his gaze.

"Villa gave the girl to me," he said with deadly quiet. "If anyone disputes that, they can take it up with him." He stretched out the long fingers of the hand that had just wreaked such havoc on the face of the man still moaning at the edge of the circle. "Or with me."

When none of the men made a reply, he reached over and linked his hand with Meg's. Strength seemed to flow from his strong fingers into her shaky limbs. Her heartbeat slowed to normal and she let out a deep breath.

"Thank you," she said softly.

He tightened his grip on her hand as he led her away from the grumbling group of men. His mouth was set in a grim line, but this time his anger did not seem to be directed at her. "How long have they been hassling you, Meg—all day?"

"No, it just started—just now. I stayed in our room all day until I got hungry and came out for supper."

"I shouldn't have left you here alone."

Meg had had the exact same sentiments during the long, lonely day, but now she found she didn't like to hear him sound so furious with himself.

"It's all right, Carson. You came in time. Nothing happened. Let's just forget about it."

They had reached the four-room adobe house where they were staying. The half-blind old *señora* who owned the house was mashing some kind of chile seeds in her stone *molcajete*. Carson nodded to her but pushed Meg past her and into their room without stopping.

Once inside he swung the unfinished wood door shut and without a word encircled her tightly in his arms.

"I wanted to kill those men who were touching you, Meg. I hope I broke that bloody bastard's jaw."

Meg rested her head against his chest. It felt so right there. And the raw emotion in Carson's voice reached down inside her.

"We've got to get you out of here," he said finally, dropping his arms and pulling away.

He looked utterly tired, but he managed a smile and slid one finger gently down her smooth cheek. "I'm going to find a way to get you home, Meg. Get some sleep now, and don't fret about those men tonight. I promise you I won't leave you again until you're on your way back to your family."

Inexplicably, Carson's reassuring words made Meg feel like crying. She *had* been scared tonight—and disgusted. She *did* want to go home. But when Carson's deep voice went husky with that kind of rough tenderness she was coming to know, somehow the idea of leaving became unbearable.

She turned away to hide her emotion and walked quickly over to the lumpy little bed in the corner of the tiny room. Not bothering to undress, she threw herself down and pulled the heavy blanket up around her.

She cleared her throat. "I do appreciate all you've done for me, Carson. I might be dead now if it weren't for you."

"You might be safely back on Daddy's ranch now if it weren't for me, too," he muttered to himself.

His bedroll was a poor cushion against the hard wood floor. He tossed restlessly, frustrated with himself and his assignment. He had shot men down in cold blood and not felt nearly the pangs of remorse he had felt seeing Meg being manhandled by that group tonight.

At least today he had been able to get word of her whereabouts to his contact. He hoped that when word reached her father the man would have enough influence to get through to Villa and demand her release.

Unfortunately, his contact had been adamant about Carson's role in the matter.

"Protect the girl if you can, Carson, but don't endanger yourself or your mission to do so." The old army colonel had been an Indian scout in his prime, and some of his quarry's stoicism had obviously worn off on him through the years.

"Villa has become more unpredictable than ever," he had said with a shaggy shake of his head. "The *villistas* just raided a ranch outside of El Paso—killed the rancher and disappeared with the wife. People don't even want to speculate about how she ended up."

Carson had flinched. Since he had gotten himself close to Villa, he somehow felt responsible for the man's actions.

"There will be a lot more dead than one girl if we can't figure out what he's up to," the old colonel had gone on. "You're the closest we've ever been able to get to him. Just keep up the good work, and contact us again as soon as you know something more."

He had finally grown impatient when Carson insisted on bringing up Meg's plight.

"Forget about the damn girl, Carson. What's the matter, she got you itchin'? Look, I'll buy you a whole week at Mama Lou's when this thing's finished here. Hell, I'll get the *army* to buy it for you. That'll be a new one on the expense voucher!"

Carson had given the colonel no reply, but he spent the long ride back to San Felipe thinking that the old man was right. The beautiful American who had by such strange misfortune landed in his care *did* have him "itchin'." The problem was, it was an entirely new kind of itch for him. And he had the uncomfortable feeling that it would take a lot more than a week at Mama Lou's to cure him of it.

Chapter Seven

The shooting competition had been going on most of the afternoon, with the shots getting markedly more careless as the potent, locally brewed *mezcal* began to claim its victims.

It was the first of four days of *festival* in honor of the town's patron saint, though Meg wondered what old Brother Felipe would have thought of having his birthday celebrated by the likes of Villa and his men.

The early-morning mass had been well attended, since immediately following it, in the courtyard in front of the cathedral, cockfights had been scheduled. By the time Meg and Carson arrived, the wrought-iron railing around the church was spattered with blood. They had stayed to watch the action just long enough to leave her stomach in questionable condition for the rest of the day.

Carson had shown little interest in the gruesome festivities of the morning, but he had joined enthusiastically in the shooting. In fact, he and Aguirre seemed to be the only ones left who were taking the competition seriously.

Meg found herself watching him intently, comparing him to Johnny, who had several years back succeeded his father as the best shot on the ranch.

Johnny was shorter than Carson, his frame sturdier. His body type seemed to match the stability of his personality, and he shot as he did everything—rock steady and with deadly effectiveness.

Old Gus had taught both Johnny and Meg to shoot when they were barely big enough to hold the gun, but Johnny had possessed an extraordinary ability and, much to Meg's annoyance, had quickly surpassed her in both stamina and accuracy.

She had thought never to see a better shot, but as she watched the muscles tighten across Carson's back, she had to admit that the American renegade could give her friend a run for his money.

Carson was well aware of Meg's scrutiny, and it made him feel uncomfortably like a sixteen-year-old kid showing off for his girl. The so-called competition presented no real challenge. Aguirre was a fair shot, but Carson suspected that many of the rest of the men couldn't hit their own toes if they were to try.

At the beginning, when most of them were sober, he had purposely been careless with his shots, wanting to be one of the gang, but not wanting to stand out too much. Now, perversely, when he and Aguirre were the only serious contenders remaining, and with Meg watching him intently with her big golden eyes, he wanted not only to win, but to demolish his opponents.

The final set of targets had been set up—bottles at sixty paces. The first two men up had hit two apiece, and were lucky at that, to judge from the weave in their walk as they left the field.

Then it was Aguirre's turn. He gave a taunting salute to Meg before he took position. When he had finished his ten shots, six bottles were gone.

Carson was to be the last to shoot, and few spectators remained to see the end of the contest. That eased his conscience a bit for what he knew was dangerous showboating. With a quick glance back at Meg, he set to work, and with methodical precision neatly blew each of ten bottles to smithereens.

He couldn't resist a smug smile as he turned and caught Meg's admiring look.

"That was quite a performance, Carson," Aguirre said with a low whistle. "I wonder if *el jefe* knows that we have an expert marksman among us."

Carson silently berated himself for his lapse in judgment in showing off his skill, but he addressed the big bandit calmly. "My lucky day, I guess."

"I think that was more than luck, my friend," Aguirre said speculatively. "It seems, Carson, that there is a bit more to you than you have led us to believe."

An eager young lad of about eighteen interrupted to present Carson with the contest prize—a dusty bottle of French champagne. Villa had spotted it in the back of the cantina during the midday meal and had declared that it would go to today's winner. Then he and the little barmaid, Conchita, had disappeared up the stairs of the bar. He had not reappeared to witness the competition.

Some of the men who had finished earlier drifted back to offer Carson their congratulations, and it was several minutes before Carson took Meg's arm and led her off the field.

Aguirre watched with a new look in his eye as the tall American walked away. "I think, *gringo*," he said softly to himself, "that we had better keep our eyes open where you are concerned."

Carson studied the label on the bottle of champagne as he and Meg walked slowly back to their quarters. "I'll be damned if I know how this ever ended up in this godforsaken place."

Meg smiled at him. "However it got here, you certainly earned it. I've seldom seen better shooting."

"Seldom?"

"Well," she said teasingly, "I have a friend back at the ranch who could give you a hard time. I'd rate you about equal."

"What kind of friend?" He didn't know which irritated him more—her refusal to acknowledge his shooting superiority, or the idea that some other male was special to her.

Meg hid a smile. This kind of irritability she could deal with. Growing up on a ranch full of men, she was an expert on male vanity.

"Just a good friend," she said innocently.

Carson tightened his hand around the neck of the bottle. "A 'good' friend?" he mimicked.

"Juan Carlos—I call him Johnny. He's my father's chief stockman and our horse trainer, just as his father was when we were growing up together. There's nothing Johnny can't do with a gun or a horse," she finished, a note of pride creeping into her tone.

A little furrow between Carson's blue eyes marked his displeasure, and suddenly Meg wanted very much to make it disappear.

"Carson," she ventured, "I've told you a lot about my life on the ranch, but I know practically nothing about you or your family. Why don't you tell me something about your life?''

Instead of disappearing, the furrow seemed to grow deeper. His answer was slow in coming. ''In the past few years I haven't been in any one place long enough to have much of what you would call a life, Meg. And as to family—there's no one. My parents were both killed when I was a boy. I guess you could say I was raised by the army.''

This last slipped out before Carson thought to guard his tongue.

''By the army? But how—I mean—'' Meg hesitated for a painful moment. ''Well, how did you get to be an outlaw?''

Carson ran his hand back through his hair. ''Look, Meg, my life is my own business, understand? I've never shared it with anyone, and I like it that way.''

She could see the beginning of that coldness, that distance that came over him and completely shut her off from him. It happened any time he seemed to be about to open up to her. This time she was determined not to let it.

''I'm sorry about your parents, Carson,'' she said softly, not pushing any harder for the moment. They walked along in silence for a few moments.

''When you say you've never shared your life, does that mean there's never been anyone special—'' she stumbled a bit on these words she had wanted to ask him almost from their first day together ''—a—a woman, I mean?''

Carson looked over at her with an exasperated expression, but Meg could see a glint of humor in his eyes. ''I'm not a virgin, if that's what concerns you, Meg.''

Much to her annoyance, Meg felt the familiar flush creeping up her face. "No, of course not—I *assumed*—"

She stopped in embarrassment as Carson raised one eyebrow, the corners of his mouth now smirking into a smile.

"Oh, you're impossible," she finished in an angry burst.

"You're the one who changed the subject," he observed mildly. "You were starting to tell me about this *friend,* Johnny."

A tensing of the lean line of his jaw belied the casual tone of his statement.

"There's nothing more to tell," Meg told him a little impatiently. "It's just that seeing your shooting reminded me of Johnny. We used to do a lot of it together."

"You, shooting?" His dark brow went up with the question.

"Yes, Mr. Carson. I'm a pretty good shot, if I do say so myself. I certainly could have done better than most of those drunken louts out there today," she added.

Carson looked down at her slight form with a skeptical eye. They had reached the woods that skirted the back of the small house where they were staying.

"Rifle or six-shooter?"

"Either," she said with studied nonchalance.

Carson stopped walking, whirled his revolver out of his gun belt and, putting the champagne down on the ground, quickly loaded the weapon with six bullets.

"Let's see you do your stuff, Annie Oakley," he said, his voice lazy with male indulgence.

Meg smiled to herself. She might not be equal to the famous markswoman of the Buffalo Bill's Wild West shows, but her skill with a gun was impressive.

"What's the target?"

"Do you think you could hit the knot on that tree?" Carson asked her.

She whirled the gun once in her hand in imitation of Carson's actions, then shot six times in rapid succession.

"Nice shooting, Meg," he told her with just the slightest hint of condescension. "It looks like you got a couple right on target."

"Let's check it out." The arrogant so-and-so, she thought to herself. He thinks he's the only one who can shoot a gun.

Carson sauntered over to the gnarled old tree that they had chosen as the target. He straightened abruptly as he reached it with Meg right behind him.

When he didn't say anything she reached around him and casually counted the tiny holes, which were so close together that from a distance they had been indistinguishable.

"Four, five, and that makes six," she counted evenly.

Carson's face had taken on a look of shock. He supposed he should have suspected that in addition to being too damn foolhardy for her own good, she was also a crack shock. What more did he have to learn about little Meg Atherton?

He reached over and deftly took the revolver out of Meg's hands. "I think I'd better take this back," he told her with a boyish grin that took years off his face and made Meg's heart crack.

But if she had expected more of a compliment on her impressive performance, she was to be disappointed.

"Come on, Annie. Let's put this stuff in our room and get back uptown. There's going to be *barbacoa* tonight—I saw them bring in two fat goats earlier today. Have you ever eaten *tacos de cabrito?* I swear it's the most mouth-watering food this side of mother's milk."

He gave her an outrageous wink, then his strong hand wrapped around her slender one, and he pulled her toward their house.

Carson looked wearily around the smoky cantina. He didn't want to be there. He would have preferred to stay with Meg when he escorted her back to their room a couple hours ago. But it was time he put some thought into his work. He had neglected it too often since Meg had arrived on the scene. Reluctant to leave her alone, he had spent more time with her than with the *villistas* whose confidence he had worked so hard to earn. Now they were beginning to cut him out of their conversations again. And he hadn't at all liked the look in Aguirre's eyes after the shooting today.

He let out a long sigh and tilted back in his chair. Maybe he should turn in. Hell, everyone was too drunk to do any serious talking tonight anyway. Except Villa. Carson swung his eyes over to the corner, where the magnetic leader was, as usual, surrounded by his followers. He had never seen Villa drunk, nor out of control in any way. And when he was with Villa there was always the chance that he could learn something, perhaps enough to complete his assignment and head back to the States.

He let his thoughts drift. If he finished here, he could take Meg back himself. He envisioned riding with her up to her father's big ranch house. *"I've rescued your daughter, sir, from the hands of those dastardly out-laws. Here she is, safe and sound.''*

The scene continued with the grateful father praising his daughter's heroic savior, and Meg with that telltale flush over her cheeks, gazing up at him with eyes full of love....

A derisive smile hovered around his lips. Once she got out of here he would be the *last* person Meg would want to see. And when her father heard the full story he would most likely welcome Carson with a load of buckshot, or worse.

Stop dreaming, he told himself scornfully, and get to work. He took a final gulp of the *mezcal* he had been nursing all night. The sour taste burned all the way down to his stomach. He pushed himself away from the table and sauntered over to the group around Villa.

Villa saw him approaching and called out to him. "Eh, *amigo*—you're just in time to congratulate me.''

Carson grabbed a flimsy wooden chair and straddled it backward facing the outlaw leader. His heart picked up its beat. Had a major decision been made during Villa's meetings with the other rebel leaders? Were they finally going to cross the border in open defiance of the U.S. army?

He kept his voice carefully casual. "*Felicidades, mi jefe.* Now, just what am I congratulating you for?''

Villa's booming laugh stretched out over the room. "I'm going to get married!''

For the first time Carson noticed—hidden by the big bodies of Villa's men—the tiny form of Conchita sitting on the floor next to Villa's chair. The pretty, dusky-faced girl was hanging on to Villa's leg and looking up at him with the devotion of a lovesick puppy dog.

Carson forced a smile. "Well—good news. When is the happy event?"

"Tomorrow night. Friday is a good day for weddings, no?"

You should know, Carson thought to himself, but he only nodded in agreement.

Villa reached down to pet Conchita's silky black hair. "Won't my little flower make a beautiful bride?" he asked with a wide grin.

The girl beamed, and several of the men rushed to agree with their leader. Carson gritted his teeth in frustration. It appeared that Villa's mind was definitely not on his military campaigns. At this rate, Carson reflected, he would never be able to leave the bandit's camp.

Normally content to float along wherever the next gust of fortune took him, he was feeling a strange urgency to have this job over with. Maybe he was getting old, he thought sourly. Or maybe it was the feeling of having some money for the first time in his life. The bonuses from his last three assignments were safely deposited in a bank in El Paso. With the sizable one he had been promised for this job, it would make a nice nest egg. That is, if he ever got out of here.

"How long will we be staying in San Felipe, *Jefe?*" he asked Villa nonchalantly.

Villa's sharp brown eyes shifted quickly from the girl at his feet to the American. He didn't like questions, but his answer was good-humored. "Why, until after my honeymoon, of course."

He turned his attention back to the giggling girl. "She is as pretty as your *gringa*, eh, Carson?" He leaned over and gave her a smacking kiss.

Villa regarded his American recruit thoughtfully. "Carson, I've just had an excellent idea. Tomorrow is my wedding day, and I will be a very happy man. I would wish *everyone* could be so happy on this day."

With a broad sweep of his hand he encompassed all the men in the room. "And you, my American friend, you should be so happy, too. So this is what we will do. Tomorrow we will have not *one* wedding, but *two!*"

Carson felt his stomach sink below his leather gun belt. "Um—whose will be the second wedding?" he asked feebly, already anticipating the answer.

"Yours, my friend, yours! Tomorrow when I marry my little Mexican buttercup, you will marry your American beauty rose. Ah—" he glanced around the group seeking appreciation "—I make poetry, no?"

Meg was awake when Carson came back from washing up the next morning. He had been relieved to find her asleep when he returned the night before. He had been too tired and not quite sober enough to tell her of the evening's developments.

Villa had ordered a bottle of whiskey in honor of the upcoming nuptials, growing more and more enthusiastic about the plan to have his American friend join him in wedded bliss. All of Carson's protestations had been waved aside as unimportant. Villa was not one to change his mind.

Carson had stayed until the bottle was empty, having finished a good portion of it himself. This morning he wished he hadn't. He suspected that his head should be a whole lot clearer than it was to deal with Meg's reaction to his news.

"Good morning," Meg said brightly as he entered the room. She was in one of her cheerful moods. Well, that would end soon enough, he thought grimly.

"Morning."

"I waited for you last night—you must have come back late."

"Um-hmm."

"We're not very talkative today."

Carson sat down next to her on the narrow bed. "We've got a problem, Meg."

He looked tired and a little bit sick. Meg dropped her bantering tone. "What is it?" she asked with concern.

"Villa wants us to get married tonight," he blurted out.

Meg stared at him. He was definitely looking sick, and what was more, he wasn't making any sense.

"What are you talking about, Carson?"

"A—a wedding—you and me. It seems that Villa's got marriage fever again, and he's decided that we're to join him in matrimonial bliss."

"I've never heard anything so ridiculous in my life." Meg laughed.

Carson was surprised by her laughter—and a little miffed. After all, he'd had women *begging* to marry him in the past. They hadn't thought it was a ridiculous idea at all.

"Well, ridiculous or not, we'll have to humor him and go through with it."

"You're not serious!" Meg stopped laughing, and her big eyes grew wider as she looked intently into his face. "You *are* serious."

Now it was Carson's turn to tease. "What's the matter? You have something better to do tonight?"

Meg sputtered with anger. "Don't you make jokes about this, Carson. There's no way we can get married. It's crazy!"

He flopped back on the bed, his head reverberating with circles of pain as it hit the mattress. "I don't know about that. There have been some in the past who considered me what they call a good catch."

"But you're an outlaw—you're on the run with a band of murderers." Meg's voice reflected her growing horror. "Men like that don't get married."

"Villa does, regularly." He sat up again, trying to find the position of least agony. "Listen, Meg, we don't have any choice. In case you haven't noticed, what Villa says is law. You don't argue with him."

Meg jumped up and began pacing agitatedly across the room. "There must be something you can do, Carson. Tell him—tell him I'm already engaged. Or—I don't know—tell him *something*."

Her pacing footsteps pounded in his head, and his irritation grew at her vehemence against marrying him. In reality, last night—after the initial shock—the idea had started to sound not so bad to him. After all, she had wanted a wedding night—now he would give her one. The very thought of it had joined the whiskey in sending a pleasant warmth through his blood.

And beyond the wedding night, what the hell. Maybe he would even like being married and having a bunch of little red-gold-haired kids running around.

Of course, in the cold light of day he knew she was right—the idea was ridiculous. Except for the wedding night part of it. That prospect still set him tingling.

"I tried, Meg. I did everything I could think of to talk him out of it, but Villa's a stubborn man. Once he gets a notion in his head—"

She turned on him furiously. "I'll just *bet* you tried! Just like you said you would try to get me out of here. The truth is you're afraid to go up against him. He says 'jump' and you say 'how high?'. It's disgusting!"

She was thoroughly enraged now, and Carson decided that it would be expedient to leave her to herself for a while. Perhaps she would not be so opposed to the idea once she got used to it. Even she couldn't deny the attraction between them. People had gotten married for a lot worse reasons than that.

He stood and put an arm around her shoulders. "Why don't you just take your time getting ready this morning? I'll come back in a half hour or so to take you to breakfast."

He took one last look at her before walking out the door, and her thunderous face made him try an attempt at humor. "Things could be worse, you know. Villa could have decided to marry you himself."

He was able to get the door slammed before her shoe reached him.

Chapter Eight

If little Conchita giggles one more time, Meg thought to herself, I'm going to smack her.

Nothing had gone right in this nightmare of a day, and the girl's incessant twittering was about to drive Meg mad.

She had not waited for Carson's return that morning. Instead, as soon as he was out of the house, she'd stomped out of her room, determined to straighten out the mess he had so cavalierly dumped in her lap.

The very idea of the two of them marrying was preposterous. He was an outlaw—he had *kidnapped* her. If her father were here, he would probably hang him from the nearest tree.

But her determination had worn down as the day progressed. She seemed to be the only one outraged by the forced marriage. In desperation, she had even tried to get in to see Villa himself, only to be rudely stopped by Aguirre and informed that *el jefe* was busy preparing for his wedding.

If only Luz were here, she thought miserably. Villa's gallant little wife—*real* wife—had been her only ally throughout this whole ordeal.

By midafternoon she had ended up sitting forlornly on the tiny bed in her room, tears running unheeded down her cheeks.

"¿Señorita?" It was the old lady who owned the house. The woman had been kind to them during their stay here, and Meg gave her a teary smile, not wanting to upset her.

She had come to offer Meg her own wedding dress, an intricately embroidered garment whose colors were still brilliant even after all these years. It fell loosely to the floor, every fold covered with exquisite designs.

Though touched by the woman's kindness, Meg's first reaction was to refuse. She didn't want to dignify these farcical proceedings by any special adornment. But the misty look in the old one's nearly sightless eyes as she tenderly stroked the treasured costume had changed Meg's mind.

"I'd be honored to wear it, *señora. Muchas gracias.*"

When Carson arrived to fetch her for the ceremony, she'd been almost glad she was wearing something so special. The piece of tin that served for a mirror in their room had reflected a strange image back at her. The vivid colors of the dress made her look exotic, foreign. It was as though she were leaving behind the old Meg, devoted daughter of Charles Atherton, forever.

For a moment she had let herself wonder what it would be like if all this were real—if she were really about to become Carson's wife, not as the result of the crazy whim of an outlaw leader, but because they truly loved each other and wanted to be together for the rest of their lives.

It was a foolish thought. She quickly snapped back to reality, noting that Carson, while he had somehow managed to find a freshly laundered suit of clothes, was still wearing his gun belt.

Even now she couldn't believe she was standing calmly reciting wedding vows to a man with a gun strapped to his hip. The ceremony was solemn and quiet—except for Conchita's giggles.

The town priest stumbled over his words a couple times, though Meg couldn't tell whether it was in nervousness over his illustrious guest or in fear for their souls. He had to know that Villa's marriage, at least, was beyond all bounds of the teachings of the church.

The poor little man had duly blessed the rented rings and the *arras*—thirteen pieces of silver that Carson sardonically slipped into her hands, promising to endow her with all his worldly goods. His mouth had quirked a little at her exasperated expression, but neither one had interrupted the proceedings to voice any objection over the old ritual.

Villa had decked himself out regally for the occasion in tight-fitting gray pants literally covered in silver embroidery. Conchita wore, over a plain full skirt, a shorter version of Meg's dress with fewer designs. Her jet-black hair was plaited into two intricate braids that wound delicately around her head, accented by bright red flowers. Meg had to admit that the girl looked beautiful.

"I should have gotten you some flowers for your hair," Carson had whispered to her when they arrived. Meg ran her fingers uneasily through her loose hair. She had left it down, perhaps in some subconscious effort to look more bridelike. Now she regretted not having put it up in one of her more customary styles.

Carson knew immediately that he had said the wrong thing—as if Meg's glorious mane of hair could be improved by mere flowers. He was having trouble know-ing *what* to say. He'd never been married before, never even been close, and the situation had him more than a little rattled.

He had thought he was handling the whole thing pretty well until he had seen her in that dress, fascinat-ingly beautiful with her red-gold hair falling around her shoulders and down her back like a wild and wondrous cloud. She had taken his breath away—knocked clean out of him all the words he had rehearsed. They had walked to the church in silence.

To Meg's mind Carson appeared completely re-laxed. The warm contact of his hand with her ice-cold fingers was her only touch with reality during the long nuptial mass.

The rest was a dream. The musky incense smell of the old cathedral brought back flashes of memories of the long, hypnotic hours of chapel during her days at La Ascensión. Candles surrounding the uniquely native votive offerings—colorful depictions of saints and birds and flowers made from china paper—all along the sides of the church sent eerie flickers dancing around the im-mense sanctuary.

Finally, the traditional *lazo* of white silk was being draped around her shoulders and Carson's, symboli-cally uniting them until death and beyond, and then his firm lips were on hers for a brief but startling kiss that she felt all the way down through her legs.

The home of the *alcalde,* San Felipe's mayor, had been chosen for the honor of Villa's wedding recep-tion. There the jovial leader accepted the congratula-tions of both his men and prominent townspeople. Everyone seemed absolutely oblivious to the fact that

Villa had gone through this "till death do us part" ceremony several times before.

Conchita's family was fully represented. Little brothers and sisters appeared to be everywhere, all in fine new clothes that Villa had secured for them. No one seemed worried that their sister had just married a bigamist.

Since the dancing was yet to start, a number of men from the town were singing revolutionary songs. One played a guitar while another accompanied the lively beat by hitting with drumsticks a long piece of wood wired to his belt.

Meg recognized the peculiarly Mexican philosophy of the popular ballad "Valentina": *"Si me han de matar mañana—que me maten de una vez"*—"If they're going to kill me tomorrow—they might as well kill me right away."

She and Carson listened to the music in silence, mostly ignored by the rest of the wedding party.

"It's simply incredible," Meg said finally, watching Villa engulfed in still another *abrazo* of congratulations. "What is the power he has over these people?"

Carson had been watching Meg, not the celebration, but his eyes shifted now to the other side of the room, where Villa stood surrounded by fawning admirers.

His words were soft, pensive. "I think it's because he truly is one of them. Or he was, and then he made it big—power, money, even his own army. The people here feel that if he can do it, anyone can. Suddenly, in a land without hope, there is hope. Villa represents their hope—*su esperanza.*"

His voice trailed off, and Meg sat without comment for a few moments. She was surprised to hear him so serious—and so insightful. Finally, she said, "Sometimes I think you're even harder to understand than Villa, Carson."

He grinned then. "I guess you'd better start learning to understand me if I'm going to be your husband."

Over to one side of the room the furniture had been cleared away. Two fiddle players appeared and began wailing out with dubious success the whining strains of "Adelita." Several couples joined in with a dance that looked to Meg to be somewhere between a waltz and a schottische. Carson jumped up from the sofa they'd been sharing and pulled Meg with him.

He bent over to say in her ear, "We might as well enjoy ourselves. It's not every day one gets married."

Meg found the rambunctious dance impossible in her long dress. She would have fallen if it hadn't been for Carson's strong arm across her back. But when the music slowed in a haunting rendition of a tragic folk song, Carson tightened his hold on her and they seemed to flow as one across the polished wooden floor.

She could feel the hardness of his flat stomach against hers. His thighs brushed hers with every sway of the music. He put his hands into the soft fullness of her hair and brought her head closer to his chest.

Meg let herself relax for the first time all day. It felt so right to move slowly, eyes closed, enveloped by all of Carson's masculine strength. He smelled fresh, like the fragrant wood of the *ocote* torch pines that covered the surrounding sierra.

"Are you hungry, Meg?"

The question snapped her eyes open. "I beg your pardon?"

His voice was husky. "I asked if you're hungry. If you don't want any supper, let's get out of here."

She looked around the room. Liquor was flowing freely, and the ribald jokes had started where Villa now sat with Conchita on his lap. The girl's dark face was red with embarrassment.

"By all means, let's leave." She pulled herself out of Carson's arms, trying to ignore the empty feeling she was left with when the contact was broken.

Once outside, Meg started heading in the direction of their temporary home, but Carson gently took her arm and turned her in the opposite direction. "Let's walk," he said simply.

The fast twilight of the mountains was over, and a sliver of moon provided the only light on the dark street. Meg shivered slightly in the thin cotton dress.

"Cold, sweetheart?" Carson slipped a long arm around her shoulders. They walked that way peacefully for several minutes. They had left the last buildings of the town behind and were heading uphill into the sierra when Meg finally asked, "Where are we going, Carson?"

He stopped and pulled her around to face him. "Just a little farther, Meg." He bent his head and kissed her very gently on the mouth. His tongue whispered silkily against her lips, then was gone. She felt the coolness of the evening air replace his mouth.

He led her to a small cabin, nestled among nut trees and pines on the side of a hill. There was light coming from the little windows, and when he pushed open the door Meg saw that it was coming from a big stone fireplace that covered an entire wall of the room.

At the other end of the room was a bed—a big bed, covered with a snowy-white feather tick. On a nightstand next to the bed was a careless arrangement of pine boughs and wildflowers in an overcrowded vase. Next to it was a rough basket filled with fruit, the bottle of champagne Carson had won at the shooting and two long-stemmed glasses.

"You did this?" Meg asked him in amazement.

He grinned sheepishly. "You wanted sweet-smelling linens, if I remember correctly."

The sudden memory of that night on the trail made her cheeks burn. He had asked her then if she was a virgin, and she had been furious with him. She still should be. What was happening to her?

"But, Carson," she managed finally, "surely you don't think—I mean, we're not *really* married."

He came up behind her and stretched his arms around her, smoothing his big hands slowly down her rib cage and over her abdomen.

He spoke softly. "Where I come from, a priest says you're married, and you're married. That's all there is to it."

"But this marriage was a sham. We don't love each other. We have nothing in common." Her voice cracked in desperation.

He turned her gently in his arms and nuzzled her neck with his lips. "I can think of a very important thing we have in common right now, sweetheart. We both want each other. I feel like I've been wanting you for a lifetime, Meg."

His arms pulled her to him forcefully, and he half kissed, half bit a sensitive spot between her neck and her shoulder. The contact seemed to ignite something inside him, and suddenly his mouth came hungrily over hers, deep and arousing. His hard body molded itself against hers.

The room whirled around her, and for the first time in her life Meg felt as if she might faint. She pushed

herself out of Carson's arms, confused and over-
whelmed by the force of her feelings, by the power the
two of them generated when they were together this
way.

"I can't do this, Carson," she said, close to tears.

He took a deep breath and stepped back from her. He
stood for a moment watching the long sweep of her
golden lashes over her downcast eyes.

"Let's have some champagne," he said finally.

He opened the bottle with his back turned to her and
did a swift losing battle with his conscience. Though he
had had ample experience with the relaxing effects of
liquor in the art of seduction, he had never before used
the technique to seduce a virgin. But didn't the rules
change when the virgin happened to be your lawfully
wedded wife?

"Try some, Meg—it will soothe your nerves."

The lukewarm drink bubbled all the way down to her
stomach and stretched itself out along her limbs. It *was*
soothing, she decided.

By the fourth swallow she had accustomed herself to
the drink's dry, fruity flavor. It actually was quite delicious, she said to herself, finishing up the glass.

Carson was watching her with wry amusement.

"It's good," she said somewhat defensively, lifting
the glass toward him. Obligingly, he refilled it, then set
the bottle down and lifted his own, still untouched glass.

"A toast, Meg. What shall it be? To wedded bliss? To
Pancho Villa's matchmaking skill?"

He clinked his glass gently against hers and said very
softly, his hand reaching up to her cheek, "How about
'to us'? You and me, Meg. Let's drink a toast to us."

His steel-blue eyes looked down mesmerizingly into hers, and Meg suddenly found it impossible to swallow the mouthful of bubbles. She swayed on her feet.

Carson quickly took her arm and eased her back into the downy softness of the bed. He put both her glass and his own on the little table.

"Maybe we don't need a toast," he said hoarsely.

Putting both his hands under her arms, he lifted her farther up into the middle of the bed, then followed her down into the feather mattress.

The planes of his ruggedly handsome face looked suddenly foreign in the firelight. His icy eyes glinted hot with desire. A thrill of excitement and fear shivered through Meg's body.

"This is so crazy, Carson," she murmured as his mouth sought hers. "I don't think—"

"Shh, that's right, sweetheart, don't think," he said in a throaty whisper.

Now his mouth was gentling hers, opening it, then searing it with liquid heat. Meg felt a great wave of desire surge low in her stomach. Her body rippled under him, and he moaned deep in his throat and clutched at her hair.

"I want you, Meg. I'll be careful, darling. I won't hurt you, I swear."

The words came out in a rush as he urgently began pulling the Indian dress up over her head. With her limbs numb, Meg let him undress her until she lay naked, her satin-smooth skin strangely sensitive against the wool of his trousers.

"Meg." His mouth was on her breasts—first one, then the other—laving them in rhythmic circles that were building up a new, intolerable pressure inside of her. Now it was *her* hands clutching *his* hair. She would die if he didn't stop—she would die if he did.

Carson had never felt such overwhelming, demanding desire in his life.

He took one last pull at Meg's perfect, pink-tipped breast, then rolled to one side and began undressing. His hands shook from raw need.

He held one up in front of her. "I'm shaking like a schoolboy, Meg."

She didn't answer, only looked up at him, her eyes luminous. Her hair was spread out around her, flaming red from the glow of the fire, and contrasted starkly with the white of the bed covering and the pale rosy flesh of her skin.

Carson ran his hand from her neck across the velvet smoothness of her stomach and down into the mass of golden curls between her legs. He closed his eyes in desire and relief as he felt the moisture that was already there, waiting for him.

"You're all ready for me, Meg—can you feel it?" He moved himself over her. "We're going to be so good."

The last word was lost as his mouth once again consumed hers, leaving her unable to breathe, to think, unable to do anything but surrender to the devastating feelings that had overtaken her.

In the midst of those sensations was pain—but briefly—and then she was back to terrifyingly intense pleasure that seemed to be building, building, until she didn't know if she could bear it. Then everything burst through her all at once with tremendous force, like the nitro sticks they used to clear rocks at the ranch. She sank farther back onto the bed. Carson was still on top of her—still inside her—but unmoving now, his body heavy.

He was the first to stir. He eased himself partially off her and softly kissed her parched lips. "Are you all right, sweetheart?"

She moved her head vaguely in a motion that was neither affirmative nor negative.

Carson rubbed his thumbs up her cheeks, which had gone from bright red to ghostly pale, becoming concerned at her stillness in the aftermath of their lovemaking. He had never, ever felt a climax to equal the one they had just shared.

"Meg?" His intense satisfaction was rapidly dissipating as fear began to set in. He gently shook her shoulders.

Her long lashes fluttered open.

"Does this mean we really *are* married, Carson?" she asked with a weak smile.

He gave a relieved chuckle. "If I'd known marriage would be like that, I'd have gotten myself hitched a long time ago."

She reached out to give him a swat but couldn't make her arm rise high enough. "What have you done to me?" she said feebly.

"I think we did it to each other, darlin'." He flopped down on his back beside her. "Don't ask me to fight any battles just now, though."

They lay together in quiet peace, letting their breathing return to normal. The fire crackled cheerfully and sent warm flickers of light dancing across the wood-beamed ceiling of the room.

"Carson?"

"Mmm?"

"Do you have another name, besides just Carson?"

He laughed. His strength was returning rapidly, and he felt completely wonderful. He propped himself up on one elbow in order to have an easy view of Meg's delectable body.

"My parents called me Timothy. Since they died it's pretty much just been Carson."

"Timothy?" A little giggle escaped her.

"What's wrong with that?" he asked mildly, too happy to be indignant.

"It sounds so civilized."

"I can be a pretty civilized fellow when I want to be."

"You had me fooled."

His blood was racing again just from looking at her. He grabbed both her wrists and pulled them above her head, stretching her out helplessly underneath him as he shifted his body over hers once again.

"I forgot, you wanted a husband who was a banker or—what was it—an accountant? Someone civilized? Well, I'll tell you something, Meg. There's nothing civilized about what just happened between the two of us. It's purely primitive, wild. And it's about to happen again." He rubbed his already hardened body against her, then released her wrists and reached over her for the basket of fruit on the bedstand.

He picked a plump red grape and, with warm fingers that still smelled of their bodies, pushed it into her mouth. The sweet, watery fruit felt good inside her dry mouth. She savored it a moment before swallowing as Carson studied the basket and picked out a fat peach.

"A red-gold beauty," he said to her softly, turning the fruit in the firelight. "And ripe, just like you."

He took a big, dripping bite, and some of the juice dropped onto her naked breast. She reached up to wipe it away, but he caught her wrist and moved it aside. Slowly he bent and licked the spots with his tongue. It left a trail of tingling sensation all along the sensitive curves of her breasts.

When he had finished licking away the last of the sweet drops from her silky skin, he offered the still dripping peach to her.

"Have a bite, Meg," he urged.

She bit down generously, filling her mouth with succulent sweetness. The taste lingered as his mouth came down on hers.

By the time he pulled away she was again fully, throbbingly aroused. His grin gleamed at her devilishly in the firelight. "I'm going to teach you how to eat in bed," he said softly.

She was stiff the next morning—and embarrassingly sore. Carson was nowhere to be seen, but the upset basket of fruit beside the bed brought vivid and mortifying memories of the long night they had spent together.

She stretched herself out along the cozy feather bed. It was the first time in her life that she had ever awakened in a bed naked. It felt naughty and luxurious.

Where was Carson? All at once she desperately felt the need to see him, to hear his voice. She needed to reassure herself that last night had not been part of some kind of mad dream that she had been in since the night back on Rosa Maria's *hacienda*.

Was it all true? Was she, indeed, *married?* Were they real, those incredible, wild feelings she had experienced last night? Or would she wake up suddenly to the booming sound of her father's voice?

"Good morning, sweetheart." The rich deep tones definitely did not belong to her father. She pulled the covers up around her as Carson came through the door, awkwardly balancing a straw bag, a large earthenware jar and an already sagging bunch of flowers.

His smile was boyishly exuberant, and unlike her, he appeared not the least bit worn out by his vigorous activity the night before.

He dropped the flowers into her lap, then set down the bag and jar and leaned over to give her a light kiss. "Breakfast for my bride," he said cheerily. "Unless you would prefer fruit?" One eyebrow went up wickedly as he moved his bright blue eyes suggestively from Meg to the spilled basket.

Meg flushed. "Breakfast would be nice," she said softly. Inside, her heart swelled. He looked so handsome this morning, his black hair tousled in careless waves.

He might be an outlaw, she thought to herself, but he makes me happy. I've never felt this way before.

She didn't try to put words to the feeling. It was still just too absurd to think that she could have fallen in love with him. There could never be a future for them together. But for right now...

She sat ensconced in the middle of the big bed as Carson pulled sausages, a round of cheese and freshly baked *bolillos* out of his bag and tossed them in her lap right on top of his crumpled flowers. Soon they were both laughing, and Meg resolved to set aside all thoughts of anything but how very happy she was. The future would take care of itself.

Carson was more light-hearted than she had ever seen him as they demolished the food he had brought, both ravenously hungry after considerable exercise and no supper the night before. They washed it all down with sweet apple cider from the earthenware jar.

When the last crumb had disappeared, Carson reached out and took her tenderly in his arms. "How's my wild, most-definitely-not-civilized girl doing this morning?" he asked gently.

Her accursed blush betrayed her once again. "I'm doing just fine, Carson. No, better than fine—I feel wonderful." She rested her head contentedly on his shoulder.

He looked at the heightened rose of her cheek, then down to where the covers had slipped enough to reveal the lush curves of her breasts. His body stirred.

"You look wonderful, too, sweetheart. I could start in all over again." He lifted her chin and gave her a soft, chaste kiss. "But we'll take it easy today. I don't want to wear out my welcome."

He held her a moment more until he finally realized that his body was not receiving the sensible messages being sent by his mind. He was determined to be more careful of Meg today. He didn't know much about virgins, but he knew that their passionate night would be daunting for even many experienced lovers.

With a sigh he lifted her to one side and got up off the bed. "I guess you'll have to put your wedding dress on to walk back to town."

He glanced appreciatively along the trim lines of her body as she leaned over the side of the bed and retrieved her Indian dress. "Not that you're not beautiful just the way you are."

She smiled up at him, the warmth of his gaze ridding her of all shyness.

Meg had kept her resolution throughout the day. She pushed all thoughts of the future—her father, anything but Carson—out of her mind.

The central plaza was brightly decorated for the *festival,* with streamers cut with images of birds and flowers and other colorful designs. In one corner of the square an old woman sat on a striped blanket selling delicate silver *milagros.* The townspeople bought them as tributes for their patron saints to ensure good fortune and health.

The parade honoring San Felipe wound slowly around the festive square. The procession was led by a statue of the patron saint, carefully tied onto the middle of a broad farm wagon. Its paint was faded and badly chipped, but the townspeople seemed not to mind, and many threw flowers onto the wagon as it passed by.

Several children not much more than five or six years old followed the cart dressed as angels. Grubby little bare feet stuck out beneath the robes, but the faces were truly angelic, except for two of the cherubs who had dropped over to one side to engage in a wrestling match.

Meg and Carson had seen nothing all day of the other newlyweds, and most of Villa's men also seemed to be taking the day off to recuperate from the wedding festivities.

After the parade, Meg and Carson meandered aimlessly along the cobblestone and dirt streets of the town. They talked about their childhood—they had both suffered the loss of a mother's love. They talked about horses and Mexico and their favorite foods, anything but the bizarre circumstances of their wedding, and the impossibility of a future together.

It was as if each of them wanted to believe—for this day, at least—that they could go on forever like this, walking hand in hand in quiet contentment in the crisp mountain air of the Mexican sierra, far away from the rest of the world.

They wandered through the marketplace of the town, with its colorful pyramids of fruits and vegetables, and stopped for a while to talk with the *yerbero,* a wizened little man with long gray hair whose impressive assortment of native herbs offered cures for most of the world's ills.

The still-bright eyes of the old man shifted knowingly from Carson to Meg.

"This one," he said, addressing Carson. He pointed a bony finger at a pile of brown leaves in front of him. "You take as a tea, every morning before you get out of bed, and you will always have much sexual power."

Meg restrained a giggle, and Carson turned his blue eyes on her.

"I don't know, Meg, what do you think?" His tone was serious. "Should I try some of that stuff?"

The old man vigorously nodded his agreement. "You will like. It will make you *muy macho,* eh?"

Carson leaned toward Meg and whispered close to her ear. "How about it, sweetheart? Would you like me to be *muy macho?*" As he finished the words his lips gently pulled at her earlobe, then he ran his tongue along the sensitive skin of her neck.

She pulled away with an embarrassed glance at the old herb seller, who was beaming up at them with a nearly toothless smile.

"If you were any more *macho,* Carson, they'd have to put you in a cage," she said testily.

She had spoken in English, but at the tone of her voice the *yerbero*'s smile faded.

Carson looked down at the man and shrugged. "Sorry, *mi viejo*. It seems the lady is sufficiently satisfied."

A blush heated Meg's cheeks as they turned to continue walking along the narrow *mercado* aisles.

"I also have a very good blood purifier for bad-humored wives," the old man called after them.

They waited until they had turned the corner to start down the next pungent row of food stands before they both dissolved with laughter.

Some of the older children had begun shooting *cohetes* at dusk, but the main display was to start when true blackness descended. It seemed that the entire town had crowded into the plaza.

Meg had never seen anything like it. They had shot off fireworks on the Fourth of July back at the ranch, but they were nothing like this.

"The townsfolk work on these *castillos* for weeks before the celebration," Carson told her.

She watched in awe as the first huge, intricately built wood castle was ignited. Starting with one slowly revolving circle, little by little the structure exploded with brilliant spirals and shooting stars.

Now more of the *castillos* were being lit. Across the plaza two of them took the form of fiery battleships, spitting sparks at each other in a glittering mock war. Near them a gigantic ten-foot clown moved its burning arms up and down in a blazing dance. Across the way an exploding *torero* gave the death lunge to his last bull.

"It's unbelievable." Meg laughed. Carson's arm was around her shoulders and he gave her a little squeeze.

He looked at her. Her hair had pulled loose from its neat chignon and formed delicate tendrils around her radiant face. She looked heartbreakingly happy.

"I think I'm falling in love with you, Meg," he said softly, as the rockets cracked and sparkled around them.

Chapter Nine

For a moment the entire world seemed to be exploding around them. A shower of red, white and green sparks cascaded down a wooden wall forming a glowing Mexican flag.

Meg's breathing had stopped. "What did you say?"

Carson shook his head and pulled her up against him, tucking her head under his chin. His throat was too full to speak. He hadn't meant for the words to come out, but in that instant he had realized that it was true. He was falling in love with her. Now just what in the hell was he supposed to do about that?

It felt so right to be here with her, her firm young body tight up against his, watching her eyes widen with wonder as one bright starburst after another filled the sky.

But she was a kidnap victim, here against her will. And he reckoned that as soon as he found a way to get her out of this place she would never want to see him again.

One by one the whirling, shooting sparks began dying out. Here and there a final dying flare brightened the night sky, then plunged into darkness.

Carson started walking slowly with Meg toward the little street that would lead to their cabin. They had already moved their things there, deciding to take as much advantage as they could of their cozy honeymoon lair.

The excited shouts of the children faded in the distance as they reached the edge of town. They walked in silence.

Had she heard him right? Meg wondered. She could swear he had said he was falling in love with her, but it seemed utterly impossible. She was just another conquest—by now she understood that he must have had many. She was his captive, and an amusement for a time. Renegades like Carson didn't fall in love.

Her own feelings were too confusing, too new to analyze. She only knew that she could never tell Carson in words how deeply he had affected her. She was already his prisoner—she couldn't give him that additional power over her.

But though she wouldn't say the words, she knew she wouldn't be able to hide the intensity of her feelings when they were together in their big bed. And she resolved to put aside her doubts and enjoy her first experiences of true womanhood. She had promised herself a few days of happiness, without worries about what any of this would lead to.

So she let Carson pull her head onto his shoulder and walked dreamily along with him up the path to their tiny cabin in the hills.

By the time they reached their destination, the wave of uncharacteristic emotion that had overtaken him during the fireworks display was receding, and baser instincts were starting to take over. But he was still determined to keep his good resolutions of the morning and let her recover for a day from her rather thorough initiation into lovemaking.

"You go on ahead inside and turn in," he said a bit rigidly. "I'll be along in a little while."

His words startled Meg out of her dreamy haze. "Where are you going, Carson?" she asked him in distress.

Carson sighed at the pleading tone of her voice. "There's a little creek behind the cabin. I'm just going to go for a quick swim, then I'll be along directly."

She felt bereft as his warm arm pulled away from her shoulders. After the long, wonderful day they had spent together, she felt a terrible reluctance to be separated from him.

She thought for a moment. "A swim sounds grand," she said finally. "Am I invited?"

Carson looked down at her in surprise. "Meg, I'm talking about a mountain stream. The water will be colder than a son of a gun."

She grinned up at him. "Last one in is a billy goat."

This wasn't working out the way he had planned, Carson thought ruefully as he watched the moonlight gleam on Meg's slender white arms. Without a moment's hesitation she had shed her clothes as they reached the rushing waters of the stream, retaining only her thin cotton shift.

His eyes went to her shapely legs as she hoisted the garment up and waded a little ways into the stream. The icy water made her toes curl around the smooth rocks of the bottom.

"Come on, Carson," she called gaily. "I guess you're going to be the goat."

"I guess I am," he muttered to himself. He had not yet removed his clothes, but he did so quickly and plunged headfirst into the water. He came up sputtering, the cold shocking an oath from his lips.

Meg had bit her lip at the brief glimpse of his magnificent naked body, but now she stood laughing at his reaction to his icy plunge.

He moved toward her like a stalking animal. "Laughing at me, are you?" he asked in mock anger.

Suddenly his big arms reached around her waist, and she was pulled on top of him into the frigid stream. The rushing cold numbed her body everywhere except where it was in contact with his, and she clung to him a moment in stunned surprise.

As her skin became more accustomed to the water temperature, she wriggled out of his arms and, with the natural skill she had had since she was a child, swiftly swam around behind him. Before he could even turn to see where she had gone, she had jumped up on his back, submerging him again in the icy depths.

This time when he surfaced he had regained control, and spotting her across the stream, swam in smooth, strong strokes to her side.

"So you want to play?" he asked her softly. He stood and the upper half of his body glistened with drops of water. As she floated in front of him, her eyes were level with his narrow waist, which tapered down from his powerful shoulders and chest looming above her. Under the water she could see the shadow of the thick triangle that surrounded his manhood.

With two hands he lifted her out of the water and up against him. Her dripping shift clung to her body, hiding none of its lush secrets.

"You want to play?" he repeated huskily.

The cold water turned to warm where their skin pressed together. Meg's body was a delicious combination of shivers and heat as Carson's arms enfolded her and his mouth met hers in a slow, hot kiss.

"I wasn't going to do this tonight," he said finally. He pulled the soaked shift up and over her head.

"Why not?" Her voice was hazy.

"Damned if I know," he whispered, lifting her legs around him and entering her right there in the water.

"We're going to catch pneumonia," he murmured. She felt impossibly tight around him as he moved expertly inside her.

"It's worth it," she answered him on a deep breath that ended like a sob.

Then both were silent. Their mouths and bodies played each other in passionate harmony as the moon-frosted waters swirled around them.

Villa was not happy. The Sonoran leader, Rafael Villareal, was to have arrived with his men two days ago, and there was still no sign of him. Now Villa was beginning to fear a trap. It wouldn't be the first time. During the bloody years of the internecine Mexican revolution, he had been betrayed more than once by some of his closest followers. A few months back he had ended up in a jail cell in Mexico City and had come a hairbreadth from execution.

"Contrera, Lopez, Leon—and you, Carson. Get to the telegraph at El Aguila and find out what the devil is going on," he barked. "Seldano, you and Garcia ride down into Chihuahua City and let Beltran know where we are. Tell him to have my men there ready for immediate action if necessary."

Carson winced. If this was the beginning of a rebellion against Villa, it was coming at the worst possible time.

He needed to think. He was sated and lethargic after a second long, erotic night with Meg. With their bodies quickly growing rigid with cold, they had not tarried at the stream, but instead had sought once again the deep softness of their big bed. In spite of her inexperience, Meg's body had been as eager as his to explore further the incredible sensations they produced in each other.

How could he leave her? Especially now. And yet, if a major split was developing in Villa's ranks, it was something the U.S. army needed to know about.

He ran a hand across his tired eyes, and when he opened them, Villa stood in front of him.

"What's the matter, Carson? Not sleeping so good these days? Could your new wife have anything to do with that?" The outlaw leader was shorter than Carson, but solidly built, and the clap he gave Carson on his shoulder almost knocked him off balance.

Carson smiled coldly. "Thank you for the concern, *mi jefe,* but I'm just fine."

"Good, it's a long ride to El Aguila. I'm counting on you to watch out for these others—you have more sense than the rest of them put together. Find out the truth for me, what Villareal is up to. You will do this, *amigo?*"

"I'll do what I can." He took a step back from the outlaw leader, whose face was just inches away from his. "If you'll excuse me, I'll go get my things together."

Fury and frustration combined to give him a thunderstorm appearance when he entered the small cabin. Meg had still been asleep when Villa sent for him to attend the early-morning meeting.

She was awake now, tidying the room and singing a cheerful cowboy ditty. Her hair was pulled back from her face with a bright ribbon one of the villagers had given her as a wedding present.

He caught her around the waist and swung her around for a long, half-angry kiss.

She pulled away, her bright smile fading. "What's wrong?"

"Villa's sending me and a crew of men to a town north of here to hook up with the telegraph line. There may be trouble with one of his men—the Sonoran leader."

One look at his face told her that he was worried. Of course, she thought to herself, he would be worried about Villa. He had, after all, thrown in his fortune with the Mexican leader's. It never even occurred to her that his worry might be for her.

All she knew was that he was leaving—she didn't know for how long, or if she would ever see him again. So much for her idyllic honeymoon. A lump rose in her throat.

"When do you leave?"

"Right away." He ran his fingers through his hair. "I'm damned sorry, Meg, believe me."

"That's all right." She smiled wanly. "We both knew that all this—" she moved her hand to indicate the cabin and the big bed they had shared "—was just pretend."

He grabbed her roughly and pulled her against him. "There's nothing pretend about it, Meg," he said fiercely. "Everything else here may be pretend, but we're not, and *this* is not."

His mouth took hers in a feverish kiss that left Meg weak in his arms, the room spinning around her.

Abruptly, he let her go and crossed the room to snatch up his saddlebags.

"Stay inside the cabin as much as you can." He attempted a smile. "I'll be back as soon as possible. Then we're going to do some serious talking about what's real and what's pretend."

Without so much as a goodbye, he turned on his heel and left, the cabin door slamming shut behind him with a startling bang.

Meg stood limply in the middle of the room. He was gone. He had said he would be back, but a strange sense of emptiness settled over her as she walked in a daze to the soft bed they had shared. The strong, dynamic man who had come into her life with such abrupt cruelty, changing her irrevocably, appeared to be leaving it in much the same fashion.

At first it wasn't hard to follow Carson's advice to stay inside the cabin. She simply didn't have the spirit to do much else. She spent most of the first morning lying on their bed, intermittent tears streaming down her face.

What was to become of her? She had fallen in love with not only a ruthless outlaw, but one caught up in a revolution in a country that wasn't even his. What could possibly result from that?

She closed her eyes so tightly that ribbons of color began to dance behind them. She had the bizarre notion that if she could just somehow drive herself far enough into the blackness of her mind, she would open her eyes and be safely back in her bed on the ranch, with Johnny sneaking in through the side window as he had done since they were children.

But when she finally opened them, it was not the lace-curtained canopy of her bedstead that met them, but the rough log beams of the mountain cabin. They were cold and stark now, not dancing with magic firelight as they had been those two wonderful nights, which already were beginning to seem to Meg like a dream.

By afternoon she felt better. Her eyes were puffy and prickled slightly, but her natural optimism was returning. Carson hadn't given her any indication of when he would be back; perhaps it would even be by tonight. She cheered herself with the thought. He would come riding in and sweep her into his strong arms and carry her all the way up the path until they tumbled together into their big bed.

I think I read that in a fairy tale somewhere, she giggled to herself.

She spent the rest of the day wandering through the town, chatting occasionally with the women along the way. She showed up at the cantina at supper time, hoping somebody would remember that she had to eat.

Many of Villa's men were gone, but several of those remaining hovered around watching her and bringing her choice bits of food to eat. It seemed that now she was a married woman they were beginning to accept her presence.

A few of them ventured a question or two, and before long she was at the center of a nostalgic discussion about their own women they had had to leave at home. One after another they softly spoke the names of their loved ones with faraway looks and an occasional tear in their eyes. They looked shy and homesick and not at all the fierce desperadoes she had first thought them to be.

She was almost sorry to leave the gathering, but she heeded Carson's warning and hurried to get back up to the cabin before dark, bolting the wooden door behind her.

As she climbed despondently into the big, cold bed, she wondered if she would ever completely sort out her feelings about this strange Mexican adventure.

The next day promised to be equally uneventful, until the monotony was broken by the arrival of an unexpected visitor—Luz Villa.

Meg was just leaving the cantina after midday dinner when Luz's wagon pulled up, piled high, as usual, with trunks and parcels. It appeared that Luz did not know the meaning of traveling light.

Meg's first reaction was pleasure. She was so happy to see the little woman's friendly face that she forgot for a moment the events that had taken place since she last saw her in Dos Cumbres. But after the greetings and a warm *abrazo,* it suddenly occurred to Meg that this time Villa might not be so happy to see his wife. For the past few days he and Conchita had descended only rarely from their love nest on the upper floor of the cantina. As far as Meg knew, they were there together now.

"How's your handsome *Americano?*" Luz asked her in an affectionately teasing tone.

"Um—" Meg's mind was whirring. "He's ridden out for a few days, Luz, and I've been *so* lonely. Why don't you come up to my cabin for a nice long chat?"

"My dear Margarita, that's very kind of you, but I really should go find my husband."

Meg looked helplessly around the mostly deserted street. "Well, first let's get someone to help you with your things. Why don't you wait right here while I see who's available inside?"

She headed nervously back into the cantina, hoping to find someone who could help her handle the delicate situation, but Luz followed right along behind her.

There were a few men lounging around the bar tables. Luz took a moment to look around, then addressed one of them in an authoritative voice. *"¿Cómo estás,* Hugo?"

The man had been playing cards with three others, but he jumped up immediately on seeing Luz. One by one the others at his table joined him on their feet.

"I'm fine, thank you, Doña Luz. How—how are you?" He shifted uncomfortably from one foot to the other.

"I'm very well, Hugo. I've come to be with my husband. Could you tell me where I can find him?"

A look of resignation came over the man's face, as if perhaps it was not the first time he had been in the middle between these two.

"He's upstairs, *señora,* but I think he is *muy ocupado* just now. Why don't you let me tell him that you are down here?"

He started edging his way toward the staircase, but before he could reach it, the dauntless Luz had pushed past him and was determinedly making her way up the stairs.

"Dios nos libre," Hugo muttered under his breath, then went back to his card table.

Meg wondered if she should try even now to stop Luz from going upstairs, but before she could gather together her thoughts, the sturdy little woman had disappeared down the hall at the top of the stairs.

There was no sign of Luz, Villa or Conchita at supper, and Meg again went back to her cabin for a long, lonely night.

· When she returned to the cantina the next morning, much to her surprise, the first two people she saw were Luz and Villa, sitting peacefully side by side.

Luz called out to her cheerfully. "Come sit with us, Margarita."

Warily, Meg walked over to their table. Villa was energetically working on the huge plate of breakfast in front of him. He smiled at her with his boyish charm in full force.

"*Señorita,* I have not had the chance to ask you how you are enjoying our—" he waved his hand indicating the crudely decorated bar around him "—hospitality?"

Meg bit back a rude retort as she looked over at the serene face of her friend Luz. "Fine, thank you," she said curtly.

"That's good," Villa continued, stuffing a *tortilla* into his mouth, "because I like my guests to be happy."

He smiled over at Luz, and she smiled placidly in return.

Meg was mystified. Of course Conchita was nowhere in sight, but what had happened yesterday? Didn't Luz care that her husband had taken another wife in her absence?

"Are you all right, Luz?" she asked the woman delicately.

"Of course, Margarita," Luz answered her calmly. "You are the one who must be lonely, with your man away."

"He is a brave one, that American of yours," Villa interrupted heartily. "You must thank me sometime for giving you to him."

Again Meg held back her comment, but she was beginning to be amused rather than angered. Villa was so sure he knew exactly what was right for everyone else. It was a kind of supreme confidence that she had never before witnessed. Perhaps this was part of the secret of his leadership.

After the initial awkwardness, she found that she actually enjoyed their company during the meal. Villa was even more jovial than usual and did his best to entertain both women with humorous stories of his long campaign for control of this part of the country.

Another long day stretched ahead of Meg when Villa and Luz finally left her alone at the table. She left the cantina slowly and walked through the now familiar streets of San Felipe. The mountain sun was strong and by midmorning she began to feel its effects.

A sudden inspiration hit her. She would go back to the little stream where she and Carson had swum the other night. With the entire underside of her arms now soaked with sweat, a dip in the refreshingly cold water sounded glorious.

In a few minutes she had made her way up the little path to their cabin. She had nothing to wear while swimming. Her shift would again have to do, but she had never seen anyone else on this path, so she didn't really need to worry about being disturbed.

Mountain jays cackled warnings to one another as she approached the rushing water. It looked crystal clear and inviting, and it took Meg no more than a few seconds to discard her shoes, stockings and soggy dress and take the first plunge in.

The frigid water hit her with the force of a blow. Fortunately, the stream was shallow enough for her feet to hit bottom before she could be carried away by the shock. She stood for a minute catching her breath, then began to move in slow, flowing movements through the chilly water. After the startling initial entry, the water began to feel quite good, and she continued to luxuriate in it until her skin was solid goose bumps.

When the cold turned into shivers, she pulled herself up on the grassy bank. The sun was now directly overhead and she could feel its rays warming her cold limbs. She lay back, closed her eyes and sighed with pleasure.

"Are you dreaming of your American lover, *gringa*?"

The coldness that had nearly dissipated from her body came back in a rush. She sat up abruptly and turned in the direction of the voice, though she had instantly identified its owner. There was only one man in camp whose voice never failed to project deadly menace.

"Aguirre!"

"What's wrong, *gringa*? You are not happy to see me?" He took a step closer and towered directly over her. "I, however, am *very* happy to see you. Especially like this."

Her shift was soaking wet—very nearly transparent—and his beady eyes raked up and down her body with undisguised lust.

Meg made a desperate grab for her dress a few feet away. As she pulled one end of it, Aguirre calmly moved his big leg and planted his boot firmly in the middle of it.

"It would be a shame to cover up such beauty," he said softly.

"Get out of here," Meg spit at him. "If Carson were here—"

Aguirre dropped on one knee beside her and grabbed a handful of her wet hair.

and come back here with the entire U.S. army if she had to.

She had never felt more humiliated and dirty. With an exclamation of disgust she stood and dived back into the stream. She let the freezing waters rush by her for several minutes, hoping that they would wash away the touch of that stinking animal from her body and from her mind.

She didn't know how long she stayed there in the water. Her feet were so numb when she finally pulled herself out that she could hardly stand up on them. She pulled her muddy dress—with Aguirre's footprint in the middle of it—over her wet shift, but her fingers were too cold to fasten it.

She wanted to be numb—it was better than having feeling come back into her body, allowing her to remember the sensation of those huge rough hands mauling her.

Hardly knowing where she went, she found her way back to the little cabin. Her teeth were chattering and her body began shaking all over from cold and shock. She sank deep down into the feathery tick and pulled it around her. It smelled of *ocote* pine, like Carson. Little by little the warmth of the bed lulled her and she fell asleep.

It must have been late afternoon when she heard the knocking on her door. She had slept soundly and awoke as if out of a heavy dream. A moment passed before the memories of what had happened to her earlier came flooding back with horrifying clarity.

"Who is it?" she called out sharply, the sick feeling of fear back in her stomach.

"It's Luz, Meg. Are you all right?"

Meg sat up in bed and buttoned her dress. "Come in, Luz—I'm so glad to see you."

It was reassuring to see a friendly face. With bustling efficiency, Luz entered the room and crossed over to light the kerosene lamp against the deepening shadows of the afternoon. She had a jug of water in one hand and a clean dress in the other.

"Now tell me, Margarita, what is it that happened to you?"

Meg gave her a straightforward account of what Aguirre had done to her—and what he would have done to her if Villa had not appeared.

Luz nodded gravely. "I saw Rodolfo following you after breakfast this morning. I told Francisco that he was up to no good." She gave a grim smile. "And I told him that if he didn't want to see his top lieutenant ground into mincemeat by the tall American, he had better do something about it."

Meg closed her eyes and took a deep breath. "You may have saved my life, Luz, my friend."

Luz disregarded Meg's thanks. "Sometimes men are pigs, no?"

Meg was amazed to find that she was sufficiently recovered to give an involuntary laugh at Luz's blunt summation.

"Now, the question is, Margarita, are you hurt? Are you strong enough to travel?"

"Travel?" Meg asked in confusion.

Luz faced Meg, her legs spread in a stubborn stance that seemed to puff out her already ample bosom. "Travel," she said firmly. "I'm taking you out of here—home—or at least to Chihuahua City, where we can contact your Mexican friends."

Meg's eyes widened. "Is Villa letting me go?" she asked.

Luz smiled like a cat. "Francisco will know nothing about this until we are far away from here. Then, when he finds out it is I who have taken you, he will do nothing."

"Are you sure about this, Luz? You could be putting yourself in danger."

Luz crossed the room and sat next to Meg on the bed. "I will try to explain it to you, my friend. It is not always so easy to be the wife of Francisco Villa. You already know that he had another woman here in this town." She gave a deep sigh. "It is not the first time."

Meg made a murmur of sympathy, but Luz only waved it away. "You do not need to feel sorry for me. It is a very great thing to be the wife of Pancho Villa— I, of all people, know that. But it is not always an easy life. He must know my displeasure when he has hurt me. So it is like a game we play—he does something bad to me, then I do something bad to him. It is only fair."

She grinned mischievously. "Stealing you away will be the thing I do to him this time. He will be very angry. But he will know *why* I did this thing, and I promise you, he will not come after us."

She cocked her head to one side. "And maybe next time before he looks at another woman he will think twice—maybe," she ended with a sigh.

Meg had listened to Luz in wonder at her tidy sense of justice. It was not an arrangement she would ever want to be a part of, but it seemed to suit the outlaw and his little wife, so who was she to argue its absurdities? Especially when it meant her freedom.

She was beginning to feel good again. There appeared to be no lasting effects from her attack, except for a slight soreness in her side where Aguirre had shoved at her with his boot at the end. She stretched and swung her feet off the bed.

Freedom! She would go home to her father and Rosa Maria and Johnny. There had been times during her long ordeal when she thought she would never see their faces again.

A sobering thought struck her. Did this mean she would never see Carson's face again? The idea left a hollow in the pit of her stomach. How could she leave him after everything they had shared in the past few days? But what else could she do? Luz was offering to free her from a nightmare. And, as she had seen clearly that day, what she had already experienced could prove to be only the beginning. If Aguirre got his hands on her again...

Luz had been watching her closely while she struggled with the conflicting feelings inside her.

"You are thinking of your handsome American, no?" she asked her gently.

Tears welled up and threatened to spill out of Meg's eyes, but she blinked them furiously away. "I'm not thinking of anything but getting home," she told her friend firmly.

She had made up her mind. She really had no other choice. Luz reached out a comforting hand to her, and she grasped it warmly.

"When do we leave, *mi amiga?*"

Chapter Ten

Southwestern Texas, January, 1916

Rosa Maria and Johnny had gotten off on the wrong foot from the very start, Meg reflected to herself ruefully as she watched her two best friends in the world exchange insults.

"If the royal entourage is ready to go," Johnny was telling the slim, black-haired Mexican girl, "I'll go get three or four freight wagons to load up your baggage."

He said it with a good-natured smile, but Rosa's aristocratic nose turned up a tad as she answered him haughtily. "If you had stayed in your native country, Juan Carlos, you would have learned better manners."

"Sorry to disappoint you, princess," he answered undaunted, "but this *is* my native country."

He had given Rosa Maria the nickname *princess* from the first day she and Meg had arrived back on Los Alamos.

At the insistence of Señor Mendoza, they had been accompanied to Texas from Mexico by three men from the Mendoza *hacienda,* as well as Rosa Maria's ever present *dueña.*

"We will take no chances that you could fall again into the hands of those desperadoes," he told Meg kindly. "My family will forever bear the shame of the grief we have brought to you."

She had, indeed, been treated like someone in mourning since the Mendozas had taken her back to their home from Villa's house in Chihuahua City. People lowered their voices around her, and she was offered food at every opportunity, as though she had spent the past few weeks starving in the middle of a desert.

Her initial reunion with the Mendoza family had been joyful, but things had become more and more difficult since then.

"I was generally treated very well," she kept repeating to anyone who would listen, but she heard the whispers and saw the sideways glances. Meg knew that Mexican society operated under a strict code of morality. Rosa Maria would be ostracized if she were to spend an evening without her *dueña,* much less several weeks alone with a band of outlaws. Meg just hoped things would be different when she got home.

The worst moment was when Señor Mendoza had insisted that she be seen by the family doctor. She knew that everyone suspected that she had been "badly used" by the *bandidos,* and she had shared with no one the true story of her outlaw marriage. Could doctors tell about things like that? she wondered.

Fortunately, the amiable old gentleman merely listened to her heart and asked her a few general questions. He pronounced her completely fit, much to the relief of the entire Mendoza clan.

The reunion at Los Alamos had been wonderful. Their old cook, Henrietta, had burst into tears every time she looked at Meg and engulfed her in copious hugs regularly throughout the afternoon.

Her father had been uncharacteristically emotional, folding her tenderly in his arms for several long moments.

But it was Johnny who had been the most exuberant, sweeping her up in a great bear hug that nearly crushed the life out of her. "I knew those big bad bandits couldn't keep you for long, *zorrita*," he had told her proudly. "I told your father that, knowing you, it wouldn't be long before you'd have the cutthroats begging for mercy."

His infectious grin had made her feel that she was truly, finally home, and she laughed wholeheartedly for the first time in days.

When she introduced him to Rosa Maria he had been courteous and friendly to Meg's old school friend, but later had secretly scoffed at her close chaperonage and excessive luggage. In the days that followed, he continued to be amused over what he considered the antiquated customs of "the princess." Though of Mexican origin, Johnny was thoroughly American in his thinking.

Watching them wrangle over Rosa's baggage, Meg reflected that it was too bad that their cultures clashed. They might have made a good pair.

Though not tall, Johnny was solidly built—his work outdoors had conditioned him to perfection. When he worked with his shirt off, his golden-bronze skin rippled with muscles. His face was handsome, with high cheekbones and liquid brown eyes. He wore his reddish-brown hair unfashionably long.

Rosa, on the other hand, was all delicate femininity. Her skin was translucently pale, giving added emphasis to her huge, striking black eyes.

Ignoring Meg's protests, she had insisted on accompanying her back to her father's ranch. Meg's usually docile friend had been uncharacteristically firm in her decision.

"It's my fault that this terrible thing happened to you, *mi querida* Meg, and I am going to see that you are delivered safely back to your father."

Meg secretly suspected that one of the reasons her friend wanted to travel with her was that it forced an additional postponement of her wedding to someone she didn't even know. The union with the Lopez Negrete family was strictly political, and poor Rosa was just the pawn.

In their talks together during the days before the kidnapping, Meg had tried to convince Rosa that such marriages of convenience shouldn't be happening in this day and age, but her friend had been raised too firmly to be willing to speak up against her stern, authoritarian father.

What a shame it was that Rosa would never have a true love match, Meg thought once again, seeing the handsome pair her two friends made. Johnny's skill with horses had made him well respected in the area, and her father paid him good money. But Meg knew that even so, the Mendozas would never have considered him as suitable for their daughter.

It didn't make much difference anyway, Meg decided, since the two couldn't seem to get along.

The bags were all loaded—in one wagon, not three or four—and Johnny stepped away to allow the two girls a moment alone. Meg was dreading the goodbye. She clasped her slender friend to her warmly.

"Remember, you promised not to worry any more about me, or to think that what happened is somehow your fault."

The girl's dark eyes searched hers. "It is just that I feel you have not told me the whole truth about this ordeal, Meg. I think you are suffering more than you want to let me know."

Meg bit her lip. Her longtime friend knew her too well. She *was* suffering, but the cause of it was not anything she could tell Rosa or anyone. She missed Carson, more than she would have thought possible. She found herself searching the crowds for his tall form swinging toward her. She listened in empty rooms for his melodically deep voice. In bed at night she closed her eyes and imagined that she was back with him in their cabin that smelled of *ocote* and wood smoke from the big fireplace, their two bodies moving silkily against each other.

"Once and for all, Rosa dearest, I am just fine. It was an adventure, actually. I may be a little disoriented for a while, but that's the end of it."

The Mendoza bodyguards climbed up onto the wagon, and Johnny moved to Meg's side.

"They have to get started, *zorrita,* or they'll miss the train," he said gently.

"You just go on back to Mexico and have a beautiful wedding, Rosa. I'll be thinking of you, and before long I'm sure Papa will allow me another visit down there."

Rosa Maria shook her head with a little laugh. "Your father doesn't want to let you out of his sight, and I can't say that I blame him."

She leaned over and kissed Meg on the cheek. *"Vaya con Dios, mi querida amiga,"* she whispered, choking back tears.

Meg's eyes stayed dry until the wagon disappeared down the long lane to the road. Only then did the tears pool in her eyes.

It seemed that Rosa's leaving was the real end to her Mexican adventure. The fear, the fascinating glimpse of the infamous Villa and his remarkable wife, the vicious encounter with Aguirre—it was all over. And so, too, was her tempestuous romance with the American renegade, Carson. He had introduced her to feelings that she had not known existed. In just a few short days, he had stolen her heart and changed forever the way she would look at the world.

"Vaya con Dios, my love," she whispered to herself.

Johnny gave her a sharp look and noticed the beginning of tears. He put an arm around her shoulders and gave her a reassuring hug, then reached out and tweaked her nose gently. "You're a million miles away, Meg."

She smiled at him, a real smile this time.

"That's my girl," he said, taking her arm. "Now what can we do to make you forget about saying goodbye to your little friend? How about a swim?"

Ever since she could remember, Johnny had been around to take care of her, to tease her, to cheer her up when she was blue.

"You're on," she said softly, and, leaning over, gave him a kiss on the mouth.

Johnny's eyes widened in surprise. The smile left his face, and the hand that had been in his pocket tightened itself into a fist.

He cleared his throat. "All right then, let's get a move on."

* * *

"There seems to be no question about it, Miss Atherton. You are not legally married."

Meg sank back into the plush red velvet chair that sat to one side of her father's broad mahogany desk. She had spent the morning dreading this meeting with her father's solicitor, Hiram Lockhart, but she had never expected he would be bringing news like this.

"But a marriage performed by a Catholic priest is legal in this country," she said weakly. "We signed papers—"

"It doesn't matter. They were of absolutely no legal validity," Mr. Lockhart said briskly. He sported long sideburns all the way down to his chin—the kind that had gone out of fashion around the turn of the century—and they moved around in the most curious way when he talked. Usually his pronouncements made Meg want to giggle, but not today.

"Church weddings have not been legal in Mexico since Juarez's reform laws fifty years ago. Many people still go through them for the tradition, but it is the civil ceremony that makes the marriage a legal entity."

Charles Atherton watched the conversation between his daughter and his old friend with misgivings. He was relieved, of course, that there was no messy legal tie between Meg and this outlaw ruffian. But the girl had not been the same since she came back from Mexico almost a month ago. And she was reacting quite strangely to Hiram's explanation. Shouldn't she have been relieved, too, to have the matter over and done with?

He bit down hard on the polished stem of his pipe. Damnation, if he could just get his hands on the men who had taken his little girl! He had gone so far as consulting with his friend Colonel John Sutherland of the

Seventh Cavalry about the possibility of entering Mexico with a contingent of soldiers. The colonel had been sympathetic, understanding a father's distress over the mistreatment of his only child, but he had been adamant that no such mission was possible at the present time. His queries to Governor Ferguson's office had met with similar failure.

Ostensibly Villa was still considered friendly to the United States. The scattered reports of raids across the border, cattle and horses stolen, the occasional prostitute treated too roughly by men reported to be part of his band—none of it was enough evidence to justify breaking the sovereignty of Mexico's borders.

"We're monitoring the situation, Charles," the colonel had told him. "We have very good intelligence in the area. If we get a shred of real evidence that Villa is acting counter to the interests of the United States, we'll be after him like fleas on a dog."

If he couldn't seek revenge for his daughter's ordeal, he reflected as he listened to Hiram and Meg discussing the niceties of Mexican law, perhaps he could think of ways to distract her, make her forget the whole terrible experience.

"Hiram," he interrupted. "Are you and Martha busy this Saturday night?"

The lawyer and Meg both sent startled looks in his direction.

"I thought we'd have a little shindig here at the ranch. Kind of a welcome-home party for Meg."

Mr. Lockhart seemed to take the invitation as a dismissal, and appeared relieved as he stood, mopping his brow. His sideburns danced as he gave his head a little nod. "I'd be pleased to come, Charles."

Meg stood, too, and regarded her father with a puzzled look. "You haven't mentioned anything to me about a party, Papa."

Atherton pushed himself backward, listening to the reassuring creak of his old leather chair. "I was just thinking that a little merriment would do you good, Meg. Things have been kind of gloomy around here since you got back. You need to meet some young people, return to a normal life."

And stop mooning after some hard-bitten cowboy on the wrong side of the law, he said to himself. He knew his daughter too well to be convinced that her low spirits since she returned were due just to "disorientation." He didn't know what kind of hold this bandit had over her, but he was resolved to do his best to break it.

"I know you mean well, Papa, but I'm really not in a very good mood for socializing."

"Nonsense." He boomed out the word in the gruff voice that had always meant that his mind was made up. He turned back to the lawyer, who was listening to the exchange uncomfortably. "We'll count on you, Hiram—around six o'clock?"

Johnny's face was flushed and Meg suspected it was from more than the dancing. "How much of that punch have you had, Johnny?" she asked him as he whirled her past the furniture that had been piled up at one end of the big main room to make enough space for the dancing.

"Not a drop, Meg my sweet." He gave her a silly grin that only deepened Meg's frown.

Something had been different about Johnny since she had returned to the ranch. Or maybe it was she who was different. In any event, they hadn't been able to resume their carefree relationship of the past. He seemed nervous around her, almost angry at times.

At one point she had teasingly asked him if he had found a girl to spark in town and it was turning him into a grump. Instead of responding in kind to her teasing, as he always had in the past, he had reddened and turned away from her. She didn't bring up the subject again.

He certainly didn't appear to have any other girlfriend in mind at the dance tonight. He had been firmly planted by her side since the guests began arriving.

At first Meg was thankful for his presence. She had spoken the truth to her father when she said she didn't feel like socializing. It wasn't just her longing for Carson. It was also waiting for the questions, and the same snide looks she had experienced in Mexico. She had been glad to have Johnny next to her.

But now, surrounded by people who were, after all, old friends, she was beginning to relax enough to be a little embarrassed by Johnny's hovering presence.

"There's Lizzy Carpenter, Johnny—she's been sweet on you since we were sixteen. Why don't you go ask her to dance?"

"She steps on my feet," he grumbled. He hadn't lied when he told Meg that he hadn't sampled the punch. But he hadn't told her about the fifth of whiskey hidden behind the upturned sofa. He had made regular visits to it when she wasn't looking.

"What's the matter with you, Johnny?" Meg demanded.

Johnny looked intently into her honey-gold eyes. "Nothing that we can do anything about, *zorrita*, so let's just forget it."

"Tell me," she said, her voice full of concern.

He took both her hands and gave a shake of his long hair, his grin back in place. "It's nothing, Meg. Come on, this party's to cheer *you* up, right?"

"I don't know what it's for," she said irritably. "It wasn't exactly my idea. Papa has some notion that meeting new people is going to make me forget my little adventure south of the border."

Her lip threatened to tremble, as it seemed to do all too often these days. "Or maybe he thinks that now that my reputation has been ruined, I'm going to become an old maid. He practically begged his friend Colonel Sutherland to bring some eligible members of his officer corps out here tonight."

The dance had stopped and she leaned comfortably against her friend for a minute. "Oh, Johnny," she said, swiping angrily at her watery eyes. "It's downright humiliating."

It was a bad moment for the arrival of Martha Lockhart, Hiram's wife and the self-appointed town social director.

"Meg, you poor *baby!* What did those awful men do to you?" The next thing Meg knew she was being half smothered in Mrs. Lockhart's ample bosom.

"Hello, Mrs. Lockhart," she managed finally. "It's nice to see you."

"Well, thank you, my dear. But really, you must come sit down with me and tell me *everything.*"

Meg closed her eyes in despair, but before she could reply, Johnny's well-muscled arm went around her shoulders.

"Evening, Miz Lockhart," he said politely. "If you'll excuse us, Meg and I were just about to head out for a breath of air. It's getting too darn close in here."

Meg shot him a grateful look and let him lead her out the side door to the ranch house's wide flagstone veranda. It was edged by jacarandas in full bloom, making the night smell sweet. Against the wide black sky the stars were so thick they appeared to be rushing in on top of them.

"Meg, do you want to talk about what happened to you those weeks with Villa's band?" Johnny's voice was unusually serious.

Meg hesitated a long moment before replying. "Nothing happened that is going to have any effect on the rest of my life, Johnny. It's all over and done with, a memory I have to put behind me."

After all these years, Johnny knew her well. They had always shared each other's joys and pains. She tried to lighten her tone. "Maybe someday I'll take the memory out long enough to tell my grandchildren how I once met the infamous Pancho Villa."

"I think it's more important than you want to admit," he insisted.

They were both silent for several long minutes.

"It's important to *me,* Meg," he said finally. His arm tightened across her back. "Do you know how much you mean to me?"

"Of course I do, Johnny. You're my best friend— you've always been my best friend."

In the dim starlight she could see the tenseness of the muscles in his face. He looked as though he were about to tackle the wildest bronco on the ranch. "There comes a time when a man wants more than friendship, Meg."

Meg's long lashes fluttered. Though she supposed the declaration shouldn't have come as a surprise, it did. She had loved Johnny as long as she could remember. She couldn't imagine life without him. But her time with Carson had shown her very clearly just what Johnny meant by "more than friendship." And she couldn't think of Johnny in that way—not now, at least. Perhaps not ever.

She didn't know what to say to him. Her heart was already bruised from the loss of one love; she couldn't bear the thought of losing Johnny, too.

At her silence he dropped his arm from around her. "Oh, Meg, I know, I should be horsewhipped for talking to you like this just now. You're still trying to recover from whatever it was that went on in Villa's camp."

He took a couple nervous paces away from her, then back again. "It's just that—God almighty, Meg—when they told me you were missing, I thought I would lose my mind. They kept me hog-tied in my bunk for two days until I promised I wouldn't ride down across the border and go after Villa on my own."

Meg had heard a version of this story from John Hill, her father's foreman, but had discounted it as typical cowboy exaggeration. Had Johnny lain tied in his bunk thinking of her, while she lay in Carson's arms?

"I would have gone anyway," he said, "if we hadn't received your telegram from Chihuahua City."

"Oh, Johnny," she said with a sigh. She leaned against him and his arms went around her. "I'm so confused."

He caught the faint glimmer of a tear on her cheek and cursed himself for adding to her troubles. "Ah, Meg, honey, don't cry. Just forget I opened my danged fool mouth."

He hugged her to him tightly and rocked her back and forth a little as if she were a babe in need of comfort. "It'll be all right, little *zorrita*. Come on now, don't be sad. This is supposed to be a celebration."

To the tall lean man standing deadly still in the doorway to the veranda, the scene gave every appearance of a man gentling his lover. The newcomer watched in silence for a few moments more, then turned on his heel and reentered the party room.

"Captain Carson," a uniformed man called to him from across the room, "I want you to meet our host."

Trying to ignore the ringing that had started inside his head when he saw Meg in another man's arms, Carson obeyed his commanding officer's summons.

"Charles Atherton—Captain Timothy Carson." Colonel Sutherland made the introductions and watched with a calculating look in his eyes as the two men took each other's measure with a firm handshake.

"Welcome to our home, Captain."

"Thank you, sir," Carson said with a polite nod of his head. He wanted to hit someone.

"I'd like to introduce you to my daughter." He looked around the room. "I don't know where she's gotten herself off to."

"I'll look forward to the pleasure, sir." Another polite nod.

Sutherland looked confused at Carson's half-dazed responses. "Carson's one of our very best men," he said heartily to Atherton. "I've known him since he was a boy."

He clapped the younger man on the shoulder, but elicited no reaction. "Of course, I've told the lad that it's time he eased up a little on army work and started having some more fun, squiring the ladies and whatnot." He gave Atherton a conspiratorial wink.

"If you'll excuse me, gentlemen, I think I'll help myself to some punch." Mechanically Carson bowed to the two older men once more and turned around toward the refreshment table.

He had been a damn fool to come here. Meg was back in her own life now, where she belonged. And it was a life in which he could play no part.

Here she was—having parties and walking in the starlight with some beau—probably some gentrified banker or lawyer from town. He should have known that there was no way to continue what they had started up in the sierra. He'd just contact her decently through a lawyer, and they could arrange for a discreet divorce. Then they'd both be free to go on with the kind of lives they were suited for.

Still, he thought to himself, his insides churning as memories tumbled wildly through his mind, he'd be willing to bet that Meg's gentry beau's kisses didn't turn her to fire the way his own had.

But that was beside the point, he told himself roughly, swallowing a potent glass of punch in one gulp. He didn't belong here. Meg never wanted to see him again. The best thing he could do for her would be to leave now—let her keep on thinking of him as a renegade badman. Almost in a panic, he looked around for the nearest door. He was getting out of here.

The clearly audible gasp turned heads around the room. Carson spun around, and there was Meg, standing next to an attractive, long-haired man of about her age and height. Thoroughly familiar with every curve of her body, he saw immediately that she had lost some weight, and her skin looked whiter than it had under the mountain sun. But her beauty still sent a piercing stab through his stomach.

Meg swayed and grasped at Johnny's arm for support.

"What is it, lovey?" he asked her with concern.

Carson heard the endearment clearly from across the room. His face tightened.

Meg could not believe her eyes. It was like seeing a ghost—the face that had haunted her dreams for so many nights. But he was in *uniform*. What kind of trick was this?

"I'm all right, Johnny." Carson was moving across the room toward them, his diabolically handsome face set in stern lines, and his glacier eyes freezing her in her tracks.

"Hello, Meg."

It simply wasn't possible. She found her voice. "What's this all about, Carson?"

Her father and Colonel Sutherland had by now made their way through the gathering to join her. Sensing that things weren't proceeding as he had hoped, Sutherland jumped in.

"We've been wanting to introduce you, Meg. This young man is one of my officers, Captain Timothy Carson."

"One of your *officers?*" Meg asked incredulously.

Carson's expression had not altered; his eyes had not left Meg. She looked up at him directly, her expression changing from one of shock to one of rage.

Everyone seemed to be waiting for her to speak.

"Excuse me—Papa, Colonel, Johnny—I would like to have a few words alone with *Captain* Carson."

Before Carson could reply, Meg had grabbed his hand and was pulling him backward out to the veranda. Carson could practically see the steam rising from her as she fumed, and his mouth quirked up in a half smile. For the first time all evening, he began to feel good.

She turned on him in fury. "You slimy, wretched, lily-livered, despicable—"

He held up both hands in defense. "I get the idea, Meg," he said mildly, controlling a laugh.

"How could you do such a thing to me? All that time in the camp, when I was scared to death. And you led me to believe that you were as bad as they were."

Her brain was spinning as she tried to put together this entirely new picture of the man she had fallen in love with. He was an *army officer,* not an outlaw. But he had lied to her—frightened her—he had even *made love to her!*

"It's my job, Meg. I've done undercover work for the army for years now."

"Your job," she sputtered. "It was your job to hold me prisoner, to keep me for days, terrified and alone?"

Carson raised a hand in defense. "Meg, I've never seen you terrified. I was just doing my best to keep you from getting yourself in even more trouble."

"And what about that ridiculous wedding?" she went on, without paying any attention to his reply.

Carson's amusement was gone. She was right—he had used her badly. "It was all part of the assignment, Meg. I couldn't do anything to arouse Villa's suspicions or get him riled with me."

Her voice shook. "And making love to me, was that part of the assignment, too?"

He didn't have an answer. There was no excuse for what he had done to her. It hurt to watch as tears filled her beautiful eyes. "I'm sorry, Meg," he said finally in a low voice.

The tears spilled over and she brushed at them with an impatient hand.

"Sorry?" she raged. "You're not anywhere near as sorry as I am. I ought to go in and get my father right now and let him skin you alive."

He shrugged, feeling guilty and miserable. "If that's what you want, Meg."

"Oh!" She stamped her foot in fury. "What I want is to have you out of my life, to forget I ever met you. Do you understand?"

Her words only confirmed what he had been saying to himself all evening. She was through with him—never wanted to see him again. The hurt was so deep it surfaced as anger.

"If we were in the sierra you would probably tell me to go to hell. But we're back in *civilization* now, right? Your manners have gotten pretty again. I understand you just fine, Meg."

They glared at each other. Finally Carson nodded toward the door. "You'd better get back inside. Your boyfriend in there is no doubt wondering what's happened to you."

He took a step back from her, and Meg felt the distance between them as if it were a yawning canyon. She thought of how she had yearned for this man over the past few weeks. Her pride was wounded and her sense of fair play was outraged. How could she have been taken in so?

It had all been a sham—not just the wedding ceremony, but all of it—the nights in his arms, the passionate kisses. They were just part of his *job*. It had all been playacting.

"Get out of my house," she told him, her voice shaking with rage and despair.

"I'm going," he answered her bitterly. "And don't worry, Meg, you'll get your wish. I won't intrude in your life again."

She dropped her gaze for the barest moment, and when she looked up he had gone.

"Carson!" she called out desperately. There was no answer from the inky darkness.

"Do you mean to tell me, John, that *that* man is the son of a bitch American renegade who helped Villa kidnap my daughter?" Charles Atherton regarded his old friend with disbelief.

John Sutherland harrumphed low in his throat. "Listen to me, Charles. I know Carson—he's one of the sharpest men I've ever met. If I hadn't thought he was worthy of Meg, I'd never have brought him here tonight."

"John, the man *seduced* my daughter—put her through some kind of phony wedding ceremony, then took her to his bed. And you sit there bald-faced and tell me the bastard's worthy of her?" He slammed his hand down on his desk.

Atherton had not known what to make of Meg's strange reaction to the handsome young captain, but before he could go after her, Sutherland had requested to speak to him alone in his office. He could not believe the tale his old friend was now telling him.

"I probably would have left it alone, Charles, just let Meg go on thinking that the American she had met was one of the bandits. But when Carson came back from Mexico, there was something changed about him."

He sat forward in his chair, squarely facing down Atherton's rage. "Carson's been a loner all his life, lost both his parents as a kid. But when he told me the story of his marriage to Meg—I tell you, Charles, I think the man's in love with her."

Atherton sat back and closed his eyes. Meg had not once admitted that she had had any feelings for the man she supposedly married in the outlaw camp. But she, too, had come back changed from Mexico. Both Rosa Maria and Johnny had commented on it, and he had seen it himself.

"Did he tell you he's in love with Meg?" he asked Sutherland.

The colonel paused a minute, then shook his head. "Not in so many words. In fact, he put up a fuss about coming here tonight. But Carson's not a man who would easily admit something like that. I think he's always been afraid to get too close to anyone—afraid to lose everything, like he did with his folks. That's part of the reason he's been such a good soldier—he doesn't form attachments. He does his job and moves on. And he's absolutely fearless."

"Well, tarnation, John. What kind of man is that for my daughter?"

"Charles, we've been friends for a lot of years. Now tell me honestly. Can you see Meg settling for some tame, ordinary banker down in El Paso? She's got too much spirit—you've raised her that way." He waggled a finger at his friend and risked a small smile.

"Meg needs someone strong and independent like herself," he finished.

Atherton stared broodingly into space. "You were a lucky man to have all sons, John." He sighed. "I only want the best for Meg, but I wish to God I knew what that was."

Sutherland stood. "I just have a feeling about this, Charles. Give Carson a chance. You know how fond I am of Meg. If he does anything to hurt her, I will personally help you boot him all the way to the next county."

Atherton reached out to grasp the hand Sutherland extended. "You could have picked a better way to do this, John," he grumbled. "Meg was white as a sheet when she saw the fellow."

"Maybe I was wrong to bring him without warning." Sutherland himself was having doubts about the results of this surprise reunion he had planned. Trying to cover up his misgivings, he reached over to clap his friend on the shoulder. "I have a feeling Meg will know how to handle it, Charles."

Atherton sighed deeply, the furrows plowed by age into his tan face more shadowed than usual. "I hope you're right, John."

Chapter Eleven

By the next morning, neither man was very confident of Meg's ability to handle things. The night before, when they emerged from Atherton's office, Meg had been rushing red-eyed up the wide ranch house stairs, and Carson had disappeared completely.

At breakfast she ate sparsely and refused to discuss the matter. She received with cold politeness Sutherland's apologies for springing Carson's new identity on her unexpectedly.

The colonel left after breakfast to ride back to the fort, sharing a perplexed look with Atherton at Meg's frigid goodbye.

"Do you want to talk about this man, Meg?" her father asked as Sutherland rode away.

"No, I'd rather not, Papa."

She gave him a peck on the cheek and then disappeared again up to her room.

After three days of enduring her silence, Atherton was at his wit's end, and he cornered Johnny in the stables.

"Johnny, you've got to help me do something about Meg. She's been moping around since the night of the party."

Johnny stopped working on the saddle he was mending. "It's that army captain, isn't it?" He stood and effortlessly tossed the big saddle to one side. "Are you going to tell me what's going on with him, Mr. Atherton? Meg won't talk about it."

Atherton sighed. "Johnny, if I knew myself, I might be able to tell you. All I know is that she creeps around the house like death warmed over. She won't eat—I just don't know what to do with her."

Johnny jammed his fists into the pockets of his jeans. "I'll talk to her—I'll take her out riding."

"I don't know if she'll go with you," Atherton shouted after his young trainer as he started toward the house with determined strides.

"She'll go," the muscular young man called back over his shoulder.

He found her in the music room, languishing on a love seat, an unopened book on the floor beside her. He planted himself in front of her.

"You can come riding with me, Meg Atherton, or I will take you riding with me. Which will it be?"

Meg looked up at him, just a spark of interest beginning to glimmer in her gold eyes. "Doesn't sound like much of a choice to me."

"It's not," he said brusquely, dragging her to her feet. "Your father says you need some fresh air."

As always, the ride did wonders for Meg's spirits. And Johnny's presence cheered her. He was his old, brotherly self today, teasing her gently and carefully keeping the conversation on neutral topics.

"I'll race you to the old feed mill," he hollered as they rounded a familiar hill. Since old Mr. Bean had built a modern plant way up the river, the wooden structure had grown more dilapidated each year. It had been one of their favorite play areas.

She knew she had little chance to beat him, but she urged her smaller horse forward and managed to arrive less than a length behind.

She dismounted, breathless and laughing for the first time in three days. Johnny caught her horse's reins with one hand and grabbed her affectionately around the neck with the other.

"Too bad you're a girl or you might have beat me," he taunted. It was the teasing refrain from their childhood that had once made her madder than any other. He hadn't used it on her in years.

"Oh, you—" In a mock rage she struggled against him and used an old trick he had taught her, moving suddenly with all her weight against the outside of one of his legs. The move knocked them both off balance, and they went down laughing in a tangle of arms and legs.

"Oh, Johnny, you're just what I need—you always are." Meg flopped back in the dust with a child's disregard for the tidiness of her clothes.

Johnny pulled one booted foot out from underneath her and sat up slowly beside her. He looked off into the distance.

"Am I really, Meg?" he said softly. "Is it really me that you need?"

She looked up at his strong back, at the profile of his dear face. His words the other night at the party came back to her in a rush. "There comes a time when a man wants more than friendship," he had said.

She knew what she needed now—a friend—but what did Johnny need? All at once she knew she was being unfair to him by relying so on his friendship, while unable to offer him in return the things he was beginning to want from her.

The laughter left her face and her words faltered. "I just meant—"

He turned suddenly back to her, his brown eyes full of an unaccustomed bitterness. "I know what you meant, Meg. I know exactly, and there's not one damn thing I can do about it."

He smashed his hand against his bent knee.

"I'm sorry," Meg said brokenly.

Their eyes held, each mirroring the other's unhappiness. They both knew with inevitable certainty that their days of wrestling together on the ground like children were over. It was all over—they had each just lost a best friend.

Meg sat up and dusted off her hands. "Oh, Johnny, why do things have to change?"

He looked down at the ground. "I guess it's the people who change, Meg, whether we want it to happen or not."

He stood and offered her a hand to pull her up. He forced a smile. "But some things don't change, *zor-rita*. You still can't beat me in a fair horse race."

They both heard the third horse at the same moment. He was already almost on top of them, but Meg knew from experience that even then they wouldn't have heard him if he hadn't wanted them to. The man could move like a ghost.

Johnny dropped the hand he had been reaching toward Meg and turned to face the newcomer.

"Captain Carson, isn't it?" he asked in the tone of bulldog belligerence Meg had only heard him use on dishonest horse traders.

Carson regarded them both with hostility. He had seen them tumbling together on the ground. In another minute they might have been making love before his very eyes. The blood rushed through his head in hot pulses.

Damn Sutherland! The man might be a good army officer, but he knew nothing about women. He had practically ordered Carson back to the ranch.

"I want you to take this application for the railroad right-of-way over to Charles Atherton," he had told his young officer, not even bothering to pretend that the request was anything other than an excuse for sending Carson back to the Atherton ranch.

"And see if you can patch things up with your pretty little lady while you're there."

Carson had fumed and halfheartedly argued, but eventually agreed, since he had almost made up his mind to head back to Los Alamos even before Sutherland's interference. He couldn't get the beautiful vixen off his mind, and until he did, he wasn't much good to the army or anyone.

But now he knew he had made another mistake. It was no use. Though he couldn't seem to move on with his own life, Meg had definitely moved on with hers. The man with her didn't look much like a banker or an accountant today—more like an ordinary cowboy. But it hadn't mattered who he was when he was twisting on the ground with Meg in his arms. Carson had wanted to kill him.

"I don't believe I've had the pleasure," he said frostily to the solid young man glaring up at him.

Johnny's expression relaxed slightly. After a moment's hesitation he offered his hand to the man on the horse. "Juan Carlos Silvano, Captain. I'm Mr. Atherton's stockman and horse trainer."

Of course, Carson remembered, this was Johnny. "Just good friends" Meg had said—a typical female lie. The other night at the party and now today he had seen with his own eyes that they were certainly more than just friends. Had she gone directly from his own bed to her cowboy's?

Carson knew he was dealing with a sore ego. It had hurt more than he cared to admit to return to San Felipe to find her gone. He had ridden hard back from El Aguila after tracking down Villareal—the man had only delayed in Sonora to witness the birth of his child, not for any sinister reason—to find the little cabin he and Meg had shared empty. Meg had not even left him a note. She was simply gone. Nothing was left to give evidence of what they had felt for those few days together.

Carson was more than ever glad that he hadn't let her know the true extent of his feelings for her. He had almost slipped that night of the fireworks, had almost broken his own cardinal rule of never getting involved. But he had managed to restrain himself. And now the brief affair was over and done with. So what in hell was he doing here? He looked down to where she still sat on the dusty ground, her hair wild and tousled around her lovely flushed face.

"What are you doing here, Carson?" she asked angrily, echoing his thoughts.

He made her pulse race—still, dear God, even though she knew it was all over. As he sat so tall and graceful on his big horse, looking down at her with something akin to hatred in his ice-blue eyes, just looking at his darkly handsome face made her heart thunder.

He reached to his saddle horn and loosened a string that held together a small package wrapped in brown paper. In one swift movement he released it from its bindings and sent it sailing roughly down into her lap. The paper split open to reveal the exquisite Indian dress she had worn for their wedding ceremony.

"The old woman wanted you to have it," he said gruffly.

Tears burned her eyes. She ran her fingers gently over the embroidered design of a multicolored owl.

Johnny frowned up at the tall man on the horse. "See here, Carson," he said indignantly, but Meg stopped him with a lift of her hand.

"It's all right, Johnny, never mind." Clutching the half-wrapped dress, she stood and put her hand on Johnny's arm. "I think Captain Carson and I need to talk for a few minutes, Johnny. Would you mind?"

He looked doubtfully from Meg up to Carson. "Are you sure you're all right, *zorrita?*"

"I'm fine—really." She leaned over and gave him a kiss on the cheek, not noticing Carson wince as he watched her. "Thank you for bringing me out here today, my friend."

With a quick nod to her and a last, skeptical glance at Carson, Johnny got on his horse.

The man mounted like an Indian, Carson noted, without using the stirrups and with no visible effort. As he rode away down the trail his body and the horse's seemed to become one.

"He's a good rider, your friend." He turned back to Meg. "Or should I say, your lover?"

Meg gave a deep sigh. "Not that it's any of your business, Carson, but Johnny's not my lover. You're the only one who can claim that distinction,'' she added bitterly.

His first reaction was relief at her words—then anger. With a fluid move mirroring Johnny's mount, he was off his horse and had taken hold of both her shoulders.

"I'm not your lover either, Meg—I'm your *husband*." Before he could stop himself he crushed her against him and his lips met hers. The bright Indian dress tumbled to the ground unheeded.

"I'm your husband," he repeated against her mouth.

It was the same heat—instantaneous and devastating. Their bodies seemed to be forged together like molten metal, his manhood instantly hard and throbbing against her soft stomach. He lifted her off the ground so that the rigid part of him moved against the sensitive tops of her legs. His mouth was liquid magic, steaming pleasure into the core of her being.

For several moments they both surrendered to their drowning senses. He eased her down to the ground, and his hands began a feverish rediscovery of her body.

His eyes were hooded looking down at her, his breathing uneven. "God, I've missed you, Meg."

She lay flat, letting the coolness of the ground seep into her. She put both her hands on his, stopping their movement over her.

"You're not," she said, her voice hoarse.

He went very still. "Not what?"

"You're not my husband."

Carson looked down at her slender, fair hands, which no more than half covered his. "What are you talking about?"

Meg struggled to sit up and pushed at the strands of hair that had fallen down around her face.

"We're not married, Carson."

He pulled his hands away as if her skin had just burned him. "You may not want to admit it, Meg," he said, his anger beginning to mount anew, "but there's a parish record in San Felipe that says we are man and wife."

"I know." Her voice was still shaky. "But church marriages aren't legal in Mexico."

"What kind of nonsense is that? A wedding's a wedding, as far as I'm concerned."

"Well, not as far as the law's concerned."

She stood. "How about if we go in and sit down where we can discuss this like civilized people."

Carson's face had gone white, and the creases were deep around his mouth. He stood and nodded to her to lead the way.

The door of the old feed mill had long since been taken away to form part of someone's barn or stable. They walked through the wide opening and entered the mill. Even after the years of disuse the faint smell of sour grain still lingered. The sun filtering in through holes in the old roof made dappled patterns on the wood floor. Great tall mixing barrels stood like sentries along one entire length of the building. In a corner an abandoned pile of seed sacks showed evidence of having served as a nesting place for generations of field mice.

Both Meg and Carson felt their anger diminishing in the eerie silence of the cavernous structure.

"What is this place?" Carson asked in a hushed voice. Their footsteps echoed hollowly.

"It's an old feed mill. We used to play here all the time as children. Come on, I'll show you."

He followed her around one of the huge barrels to a small door that led to what seemed to be a supervisor's office, which was remarkably clean compared to the rest of the building. The room contained a long wooden bench and a sagging cot.

"This was our private clubhouse," Meg explained, motioning for Carson to have a seat on the bench.

He flicked his eyes briefly around the room, then turned them back to her. "All right, now, Meg. Let's start again."

She sat down at the far end of the bench and primly crossed her hands in her lap.

"Perhaps you'd explain to me once more how it is I'm not your husband."

"There's no question about it, Carson. My father's solicitor has thoroughly checked the legality of the matter." She avoided looking into his intense blue eyes. "The only marriages recognized as legal in Mexico are civil ceremonies," she went on. "What we did in the church was just for show."

Carson stood and began pacing the room. "I've never heard anything so ridiculous!"

Meg was torn between anger and a terrible urge to giggle. "You're pacing, Carson."

He stopped for a minute, then resumed his agitated walk. "I have a right to pace," he stormed at her. "In my book, a person's either married or not married, and you and I are married."

He marched over and sat down again on the bench beside her. "It's ridiculous!" he said again.

"Ridiculous?" she asked, her temper flaring. "I'll tell you what's ridiculous—being kidnapped in the middle of the night, dragged out of bed by a bunch of no-good ruffians, then held prisoner against my will for days, and finally being forced to go through a sham wedding ceremony and taken to bed by a lying, low-down, double-crossing—''

Carson had edged imperceptibly closer during her tirade. He watched as her eyes flared with golden fire. Suddenly his arms closed around her and he stopped her words with his expert lips.

''Damn,'' he whispered softly. ''Damn, but you're in my blood, woman.''

He lifted her into his lap and proceeded to strip the buttons down the front of her dress at the same time as he was thoroughly reacquainting himself with her exquisite mouth.

He pulled her out of her dress and rid her of her confining undergarments, freeing her white breasts, which grew taut and full beneath his slow hand.

Meg closed her eyes, the world spinning. It was as she had dreamed those long nights in her lonely bed, but this time it was real, and so much more intense.

''We're not married, Carson,'' she murmured as his head went down to take the tip of her breast in slow, delicious tugs.

''Shut up, Meg.'' He took her mouth again, tantalizing her with tiny nibbles then a sudden, scalding surge. She moaned as an unbearable ache started up her middle.

He stood, lifting her easily in his powerful arms, and took two long steps over to the old cot. Gently he eased her down, pulling off her remaining clothes as he did so. In a minute his were gone, too, and they regarded each other in the dusty light of the old office.

He's magnificent, she thought to herself as his well-muscled body came down on hers.

The touch of his skin all along hers sent little sparks shivering along her limbs. She moved restlessly underneath him. Involuntarily her hips worked against his.

"Shh...easy, sweetheart." Stroking back her hair, which had fallen out of its pins, he took a great shuddering breath then eased himself deep inside her. His fingers dug into her shoulders as he gripped her fiercely, struggling for control. Then he began—slow, hot, steady strokes, while his mouth made exquisite patterns on her body.

It couldn't last long for either of them. The explosion was too close to the surface, and it came with shattering force, leaving them weak and shaken, sharing deep, cleansing breaths.

"We're not married," Meg said weakly after a few moments.

"You could've fooled me." Carson gave a shaky chuckle. He teased her lips with his thumb, then planted a kiss on the tip of her nose.

Her eyes stayed closed. Her cheeks still carried the rosy flush of their lovemaking.

"If this is how you make love, ma'am, when you're *not* married," he teased gently, "I'm almost afraid to think what it would be like to be actually married to you."

The flush grew deeper on her cheeks. Her long lashes swept upward and her gold eyes looked into his. "It seems that I missed you, too, Carson," she said softly.

His throat closed, making any answer impossible. He carefully eased himself off her and nestled her in his arms. For a moment they lay quietly side by side on the tiny cot, sharing a special contentment in the afterglow of their passion. It was as though they were back in the sierra, all the deception and misunderstandings that had separated them forgotten.

But as reality returned, Carson's mood darkened. The words Meg had spoken returned to him in full force. They weren't married.

It was a blow he had not expected. Though he hadn't confided as much even to Colonel Sutherland, he had spent the past month adjusting his thinking to admit the possibility of settling down and sharing his life with another person. He had gone so far as to inquire about two different parcels of land up north of Fremont.

He looked at the delectable woman in his arms. Just having her there filled a void deep down inside him— one that had perhaps been empty since the day he had bidden his parents goodbye.

I'll be damned if I'll give her up, he said to himself. They'd gotten married once, they could damn well get married again.

The problem was, would she be willing? He knew she wanted him, the passion they had just shared left no doubt of that. But would she want to *marry* him—for real this time? A longtime loner with a reputation for being fast with women, horses and guns?

And what about her father? How much did he know about Meg's experiences in Mexico? Would he be willing to let his daughter marry the man who had seduced her? And what about the man Johnny, the "good friend" whom he had just seen with his own eyes with his arms around Meg?

"Tell me again about your friend, Johnny."

Meg decided that she rather liked Carson's tone of sheer male possessiveness.

"What about him?"

"Well, for starters, what were you two doing rolling around on the ground like two pigs on bath day?"

The incredible release of their recent lovemaking had left Meg in a benevolent mood. She chuckled. "You certainly haven't chosen the most flattering terms to describe it, Carson."

Carson's anger, too, had mellowed, but there was still an undertone of irritation in his voice. "I'm trying to describe it in terms that will keep me from wanting to string up your friend by his boot heels and put you bottom side up over my knee."

"I'd like to see you try either one," Meg said with mild indignation. "Johnny hasn't been bested in a fight since his own pa died, and as for me, I've had enough manhandling by bandits. Next time I defend myself."

Now it was Carson's turn to chuckle. Meg's feistiness when she got riled never ceased to delight him.

"Why did he call you *zorrita?*" he asked her, just now remembering the nickname that had sounded so much like an endearment on the horse trainer's lips. It had annoyed and puzzled Carson at the time.

Meg blushed. "Oh, it's just a pet name the hands have always used since I was a kid. It comes from my hair color, I guess."

Carson looked at her skeptically. "Little fox—more likely it comes from all the scrapes you just managed to get out of by the very tip of your beautiful little tail."

Her blush grew deeper at his description, and at the accuracy of his guess. The name had been bestowed on her for several reasons, the least of which was her red-gold hair.

"I must admit it's appropriate," Carson went on. "I've called you a vixen often enough myself in my head."

"I don't think the meaning is the same," she told him haughtily.

"I suspect you're right," he said, unoffended. "Now quit stalling and answer my question. What about you and Silvano?"

"The only answer you're going to get is the one I've already given you. Johnny and I are friends—best friends, if you like."

"I don't," he growled. "I saw him look at you, Meg, the night of the party. It wasn't a friendly look."

Meg struggled to keep her voice even. She wasn't ready to share Johnny's declaration of love with Carson. It wouldn't be fair to Johnny. It was something she would have to deal with by herself.

"I don't know what you saw, Carson, but Johnny and I are just friends—that's it."

They were silent for several moments. Unconsciously he had begun to hold her more and more closely, his arms tightening around her.

"Carson?" she whispered.

"Yes, love?"

"You don't have to squeeze me to death—I'm not running away anymore."

He relaxed his hold immediately, remembering remorsefully how he had bruised her arm in Mexico. "I'm sorry, Meg. I guess I'm just trying to make myself believe that this is real, that I really have you here in my arms again."

She pushed up and kissed him softly on the cheek. "I know. I've done my share of dreaming since I left Mexico. But this has to be the real thing," she said with a smile, running the palm of her hand up and down the soft hair of his chest. "My dreams were never this good."

He returned her smile. "They weren't, huh?"

Her body melted once again into his, soft curves tantalizing his lean hardness. To hell with her father, he said to himself—to hell with everyone. If Meg wasn't his wife now, she soon would be. He gave her a firm, definitive kiss.

"Maybe I'd be interested in hearing about some of those dreams."

Meg protested halfheartedly, her mind already dazed by the reawakening of her body. "I can't tell you about things like that, Carson."

"No?" he said softly, pulling her on top of him. "Then show me."

Chapter Twelve

The sky was turning to a spectacular pink by the time Meg and Carson rode back to the big ranch house. Their arrival caused no unusual stir, so Meg reasoned that Johnny must have told them she was with Carson. Her father would have had a search party out for her long ago if he had thought she was alone.

As they dismounted, he appeared on the open front porch of the house. He leaned against one of the wooden pillars, calmly smoking his pipe and waiting for them to approach.

Meg's stomach turned to jelly. How much had Colonel Sutherland told him about what had happened between her and Carson in the mountains? How much had he guessed himself? Now that Carson was back in her life again, now that she had experienced again the intensity of their passion, her father's opinion of him took on vital importance.

Of course, though Carson had been angry when she told him they weren't legally married, he had not said in so many words that he wanted a life together with her. Perhaps after he thought about it a while, he would be relieved. He would feel that his responsibility to her was over, and he could resume the free life he had always lived.

I couldn't bear to lose him again, she thought with a pang. I'll just have to make him see how happy we could be here together. And as for Papa, I'll just have to make him understand.

She took Carson's arm and mounted the wooden steps. "You remember Captain Carson, Papa?" Her voice was pitched a tone higher than usual.

Her father took one step down toward them and reached out his hand toward the younger man. His face was grim. "Captain," he acknowledged curtly.

For one of the few times in his life, Carson was tongue-tied. "It's a pleasure to see you again, sir," he managed finally.

Meg's worries receded somewhat as she witnessed with amusement Carson's rare discomfiture. "And you know by now, Papa, that Captain Carson is the man to whom I was supposedly married in the outlaws' camp."

Atherton nodded, his face foreboding. Carson looked slightly ill. Meg beamed.

"So, let's all go have some dinner, shall we?" she asked cheerily.

Her amusement didn't last—there was too much at stake. She wanted desperately for these two men, each so strong-willed in his own way, to like each other.

To her relief both men relaxed somewhat over dinner. While giving little information about his secret activities, Carson gave intelligent and perceptive answers to her father's questions about Villa and the current course of the chaotic and bloody Mexican revolution, which had now stretched on for six long years.

"Villa considered himself a friend of the United States until the disaster at Agua Prieta last fall," Carson explained to the older man.

"When President Wilson allowed Carranza to use American railroads to move his troops from Laredo and El Paso to Douglas, Arizona, and refused the same right to Villa, it spelled disaster for Villa's armies. He has never recovered. We calculate he may now have only one-tenth of the men he once controlled."

Carson paused a moment to send an inexplicably uncomfortable glance over to Meg.

"But those men still have the power to wreak tremendous havoc along the border," he continued. "General 'Black Jack' Pershing has been brought down here to monitor the situation. Fort Bliss has become almost a war zone, and Pershing just sent six troops of the Thirteenth Cavalry over to Columbus, New Mexico."

Meg looked up from her corn soup in alarm. Carson's look had made her uneasy. "But surely, Carson, Villa is now no more than a bandit. Can't his own government deal with him? Why does our army have to get involved?"

"President Carranza has chased Villa all over the sierra, but the man has control of the state of Chihuahua and support from most of the rest of northwestern Mexico. The people there protect him."

He turned to Meg and spoke earnestly, as if trying to convince her of something she didn't yet understand.

"Our army is involved because Villa insists on raiding across the border. We just got reports of his raid on the Wright ranch outside of El Paso. Wright was killed outright and his wife was—" He stumbled a moment on the words as he realized their particular implication for

Meg. "His wife was kidnapped by the outlaws for their own purposes."

Memories of that first dark night—hands grasping at her, the rawhide thongs around her body—came flooding over Meg. Her father, who had begun to relax as he grew interested in Carson's narration, now looked antagonistic as he watched his daughter's face grow pale.

Carson was chiding himself for being a fool. It had been a mistake to respond to Mr. Atherton's questions about Villa. He should have changed the subject from the beginning. But the discussion had seemed to be academic, just a matter of satisfying curiosity. And he had thought that it might be a good chance to ease Meg into the idea of his returning to Villa's camp. He knew he would have to tell her—and soon, the way things were heating up—but they had just now been able to get over all their misunderstandings. He needed some time to solidify his claim on her before he could risk her wrath again.

Meg, also, was regretting the course the conversation had taken. She had thought her father was beginning to let down his guard with Carson just a bit. Now he sat looking at him with thinly disguised hostility.

Simultaneously Meg and Carson each spoke to change the subject.

"Carson is wonderful with horses, Papa—"

"I've been admiring your stock, sir—"

They looked at each other and laughed. "Ladies first," Carson said, flashing her his most charming smile.

It'll be all right, he said to himself. I'll make her understand. We just need a little more time alone together.

With the topic changed to horses, all three were able to relax again, and even Meg marveled at the depth of Carson's knowledge of breeding and training. By the end of the meal, Carson was acting almost normally, and her father's face had settled into an expression of reserved judgment. When she told him that she had invited Carson to stay with them on the ranch for a few days, he raised an eyebrow slightly, but nodded his agreement.

It wasn't by any means a warm welcome, Carson reflected as Meg's father showed him to the back guest room, the one farthest away from his daughter's, but it was a start. If he could just behave himself and manage to keep his hands off Meg for a while longer, he was beginning to think he could win the old man over. No more scenes like this afternoon in the feed mill, he told himself sternly. Not until they got married, *legally* married, this time.

He firmly shut the thick bedroom door behind him. He didn't care if he didn't sleep all night. He was not going to leave this room.

The wooden window sash had always creaked. As quiet as Johnny had been on his clandestine visits to her, she had always known he was coming. So the familiar scraping didn't alarm her. He had never before visited her in the middle of the night, but she supposed he was worried about having left her with Carson this afternoon. It would be like Johnny to want to check and be sure that she was all right.

She sat up in bed as a shadowy form moved across the room.

"Johnny," she whispered softly. "You shouldn't be here at this time of—"

Before she could finish her sentence, the figure was upon her and she was pulled up into Carson's powerful arms. His lips took hers in a hungry kiss, then he pushed her roughly back onto the bed.

"You were expecting someone else?" he asked. His voice was low, but she could hear the tightly leashed fury.

She took a minute to catch her breath. "I wasn't expecting anyone," she said angrily, "including you."

He sat down beside her on the bed. "Why did you call out the name of that cowboy, then?" he asked, calmer now, but still suspicious.

She couldn't stay angry. Actually, his jealousy made her feel surprisingly happy. But she didn't want him angry. Now that he was here in her very own bed she could feel her heart slowly picking up its beat. And she could think of more interesting ways than anger for him to channel his strength.

"Oh, Carson, you ninny." She leaned over toward his face in the dark and felt her soft lips brush against the rasp of his cheek.

"Johnny has come to visit me through that window since we were children. It started when I had the chicken pox and Papa wouldn't let me out of my room for ten days. I nearly died of boredom."

His frown had disappeared and his eyes had begun to glow in the dim light as he watched how the light silk of her nightdress clung seductively to the lush curves of her breasts.

He reached underneath the sheet and ran a hand the length of her leg. "How does he keep you from being bored, Meg, your cowboy?"

He reached the curls at the apex of her legs and started a slow massage. Meg gave a little gasp. "One last time, Carson. Johnny and I are just good friends."

Then he was covering her with his lean body, his mouth working its way up her neck and along the fine line of her jaw. "That's good," he said with deceptive gentleness. "For a minute there I thought I was going to have to deprive your father of his favorite horse trainer."

The expert movement of his lips was beginning to cause whirling sensations in her middle. "What are you doing here, Carson?"

He had moved away from her and was efficiently removing his clothes. Even in the dark she could see his broad grin. "I brought you this," he said, reaching behind himself and producing a plump peach. "Thought you might be hungry."

His eyes danced lasciviously, and he made exaggerated slurping noises with his mouth.

"Oh, you—" She giggled, blushing. But her stomach did a flip-flop at the sight of his tongue moving slowly over his full lips.

"I would have thought you'd have had enough this afternoon." Her voice had become hoarse.

"I did this afternoon, but now it's evening."

She gave one last token of resistance. "My father—"

His mouth invaded hers. He tasted of peach. "Your father has spent the evening making regular patrols of the hall outside your room. I finally gave up and decided to outflank him." He nodded toward the window he had come through.

Meg smiled. "I'm glad," she whispered.

He put his head down against her long tangled hair and breathed deeply of its fresh, wild scent. "Oh, Meg sweetheart, I tried to stay away. I told myself I couldn't make love to you under your father's roof, but then I lay awake in my big, lonely bed and I thought of you lying here alone in yours. It just seemed to kind of go against the laws of nature,'' he ended ruefully.

He moved his rigid body against her as if to demonstrate exactly what laws of nature he was talking about.

Meg laughed happily. The now familiar tingling warmth was spreading deliciously through her body. ''Well, I suppose as long as you went to all this trouble to get here . . .'' she teased, reciprocating his moves.

He gave an almost animal growl, and at the same time made short work of her nightdress. The afternoon had taken the edge off his urgency, and he took the time to admire the gleam of the moonlight on her fair skin.

With skillful hands and a masterful mouth he covered every bit of her body that the moonlight could reach—and much that it couldn't.

Hot flushes of fever were hitting her by the time he rolled her over on top of him and guided her down over the center of his heat. He held her hips with his strong hands and helped her move frenetically up and down him as wave after intense wave overtook them both.

Then they were still, and they smiled at each other, rare and sweet matching smiles of harmonious completion.

''I love you, Meg.'' This time there were no fireworks to drown out the words.

Meg's heart rose into her throat. She couldn't speak, but leaned down to offer him her lips.

He took them in the gentlest of kisses, then settled her in his arms beside him. ''Did you hear me this time?'' he asked teasingly.

She shook her head. ''Say it again.''

"I love you, Meg Atherton. I think I've loved you since I first got a good look at you hiding all these beautiful curves under that ridiculous *sarape* that first night."

"So you *did* say you loved me on the night of the fireworks."

"It slipped out." He smiled down at her, but then grew more serious. "A lot of good it did me. You took the first chance you got to leave without so much as an *adios*.'

She smoothed her hand against the rough whiskers of his face in a contrite gesture. "I didn't know, Carson. I couldn't imagine that you could possibly be in love with me. Remember, I thought you were an outlaw." Her apology came to an abrupt end and was replaced with a playful but accusing swat.

"So does that mean if you still thought I was an outlaw you wouldn't marry me?"

She became very quiet. "Who said anything about marriage?"

"I did."

"But—I mean—" She stumbled over the words. She wanted it too badly. Was he just teasing her? "You haven't asked me to marry you."

He gave her a look of mock incredulity. "Do you think I would be here, in bed with you in the middle of a ranch full of fifty men, all at least as strong as your father and your horse trainer friend, if I didn't plan to make an honest woman of you?"

Meg felt light-headed with happiness. She beamed up at him. "So, it's just fear of what my father and his men will do to you that makes you offer," she teased. "Do you think a lady should accept a proposal as unromantic as that?"

He pinned her to the bed. "The lady had better accept, if she knows what's good for her," he growled.

And the lady did.

It was much later when Carson again brought up the subject of her abrupt departure from San Felipe.

"What made you decide to leave so suddenly with Luz, Meg? I nearly went out of my mind when I came back and found you had gone."

Some instinct made Meg hesitant to tell Carson about her encounter with Aguirre.

"You yourself said I needed to get out of there as soon as possible, Carson. You didn't seem to be making any progress toward getting me freed, so when Luz offered the opportunity, I took it."

Carson bit his lip in annoyance. He didn't like to be reminded at how helpless he had been to aid Meg in her predicament. "I had made up my mind to take you out of there when Villa sent me to El Aguila. I would have done it as soon as I got back."

"I couldn't wait, my darling." He smiled at her endearment, but his expression darkened at her next words. "Things had gotten to a point where I didn't feel safe any longer."

"What do you mean by that? What things?" he asked sharply, sitting up in the bed.

She still hesitated. Though she was reluctant to tell him about Aguirre's attack, she didn't want him to think that the decision to leave him had been made lightly. Finally she put aside her doubts and gave him a brief account of what Villa's loathsome lieutenant had tried to do to her on the riverbank that day.

She could sense the tenseness in his body, and his silence in the darkness was more lethal than words. "Carson?" she ventured timidly after a few moments.

He lay back down beside her and pulled her into his arms. "Yes, love, it's all right. I just—I'm—" He hugged her tightly against him.

"You did the right thing in leaving," he said finally. "I'm glad you're away from there, away from all of them. And that bastard will never hurt you again."

He kissed the top of her head. "I'll see to it personally," he muttered under his breath.

If her father noticed the dark circles of sleeplessness under their eyes the next morning, he made no comment. Nor did Henrietta mention, as she bustled around the table serving breakfast, that the larder had been raided of several pieces of fruit during the night.

The happy little cook had taken a liking to the handsome, dark-haired officer, and piled him up a plate that would have made a good-size breakfast for his entire platoon. Carson thanked her graciously and gave her a devastating smile that sent her through the swinging door to the kitchen humming gaily.

Following the meal, Atherton asked in a mild tone if he could have a few minutes of Captain Carson's time in his private office.

Meg looked on nervously as her father led the way down the hall, but just before they disappeared behind the heavy oak doors, Carson turned around and gave her a reassuring wink.

He wasn't really feeling all that confident, he thought to himself as he sat down in front of the powerful rancher's imposing carved desk. But he'd never been one to turn tail and run at the first sound of battle. He forced himself to sit straight in his chair.

"You have an impressive ranch, sir," he opened gamely.

The older man sat back in his big chair and regarded him thoughtfully. "That wouldn't happen to be the origin of your interest in my daughter, would it, Captain?" he asked bluntly.

So it *was* to be a battle, Carson reflected, working to control his temper. "If you think this ranch is the first thing that would interest a man in your daughter, Mr. Atherton, I would like to respectfully suggest that you get yourself a pair of good spectacles."

Atherton gave an unwilling chuckle. "I'm not saying that my daughter has no qualities of her own. But it has occasionally crossed her suitors' minds that she is my only heir. She will inherit a sizable ranch and considerable capital some day."

Carson rose to his feet, his face drained of color. "Sir, I am currently a guest under your roof, so I will not give complete vent to my feelings regarding your remarks. But suffice it to say that I don't give a goddamn if Meg inherits one bean from you or anyone else. I'm perfectly capable of taking care of her, and I intend to do so. I don't need or want your consent—or your money. I believe that makes continuation of this interview pointless."

He turned sharply toward the door, but Atherton's calmly authoritative voice stopped him. "Sit down, Captain Carson."

Carson's hand was already on the polished brass doorknob. He hesitated a moment, then turned slowly back to face the older man.

"Sit down, man," Atherton repeated. "Smooth down those feathers and sit down. We have a lot more to discuss, you and I."

Reluctantly Carson resumed his seat across from him, but remained silent, watching him with a resentful look in his blue eyes.

Atherton's face was just as severe. "Young man," he said, placing a heavy hand on the desk in front of him, "if you had told me a few months back that I would be calmly sitting across a desk from the man who had seduced my daughter—" he raised his hand to ward off Carson's attempted interruption "—instead of hogtying him to the nearest rail, or worse, I would have said you were crazy."

He sat back a moment and intently regarded the strong young man sitting before him. "But I want my daughter to be happy. And she hasn't been happy since she got back from that infernal trip to Mexico. Not until last night. Last night at dinner I had my daughter back again, with the sparkle in her eye and the bloom in her cheeks. And the only conclusion I can come to is that you were the one who put them there."

He allowed himself half a smile. "It's a hard thing for a father to admit, son. Maybe you'll go through that some day with a child of your own."

Carson let out the breath he had been holding. "I'll tell them to go talk to their grandfather about it," he said, his own expression relaxing.

Atherton's smile broadened. "Now wouldn't that be something?" he said, his eyes glazing for just a fraction of a moment.

A couple blinks and he was back to normal. "So, if you say you don't want my money, how do you intend to support these grandchildren of mine?"

"I've looked over a couple places north of here for horse breeding."

Atherton nodded. "We breed them here, and I have an excellent trainer."

"I've met him," Carson said dryly.

Atherton's eyebrows went up in a question. "Some say Johnny's the best in this part of the state."

"He's also in love with your daughter."

Atherton didn't reply, but sat for a few minutes considering Carson's words.

"Life's not always as neat as in the storybooks, is it, Captain?"

"No, sir."

"Well, all right, how are we going to work this? How soon can you get yourself out of that danged uniform and start in learning the business here?"

Carson shifted uncomfortably in his chair. "Are you offering me a job, Mr. Atherton?"

"Job, hell! I'm offering you my daughter, and my ranch along with her. I've been waiting years now to start turning over the reins to a son-in-law. Just never thought I'd find anyone strong enough to put up with all of Meg's antics."

Carson waited a long moment before replying. "I want your daughter, sir, and for Meg's sake, I want your ranch. But not before I've earned the right to it. I'll just start out like any other hand, if you don't mind."

Atherton gave a brisk nod of approval. "We'll work all that out," he said. "When can you start?"

Carson dropped his gaze from Atherton's light hazel eyes. They reminded him too much of Meg's. "Colonel Sutherland has promised me that he will accept the resignation of my commission the day I give it to him. But there's a problem."

"What kind of problem?"

"I have to go back."

Atherton's eyes widened. "Go back? Hellfire and brimstone, son, surely you don't mean back to Villa?"

Carson lifted his face and looked directly into the man's eyes. He could use this as a rehearsal, he reflected grimly. He knew that telling Meg of his plans would be one of the hardest things he had ever had to do.

"No other agent has ever gotten so close to him. Now that the raids across the border are picking up, there are rumors that he is planning a major strike against an American city. If that happens, the army is going to go after him, even if it means crossing the Mexican border."

He sat forward in his chair, wishing that it were Meg in front of him right now, listening to him with such calm understanding. "I have to go back. Lives are at stake, and I might be the only one in a position to get the information that can save them."

"Have you told Meg?"

Carson shook his head. "I've just managed to get her to forgive me for lying to her in Mexico. I thought I'd keep things peaceful for a day or two before I tackle that one."

He grinned ruefully, and Atherton gave him a sympathetic nod, rubbing his hand over his chin whiskers. "I don't envy you the task, Captain."

He stood. "I guess I'll have to forgive Sutherland for pulling that little surprise the other night, because I'm beginning to think he was right about you, Captain. I think you'll do."

It wasn't the heartiest praise in the world, but Atherton was a man of few words, and Carson had the feeling that this approval was not lightly given.

"Thank you, sir. I'll do my best to justify Sutherland's recommendation."

"You can start by calling me Charles," the older man said. He extended his hand and for the first time shook Carson's in a warm grip of male understanding.

"Now, you better go find Meg. She's probably as jumpy as a jackrabbit on an anthill waiting to hear what we're talking about in here."

He rounded the desk and clapped Carson on the shoulder. "That is, if she hasn't been eavesdropping outside the door the whole time."

Meg's intention had been to do just that, and she hurried to help Henrietta clear away the dishes so that she could carry out her plan.

Henrietta, unfortunately, was in a mood to talk.

"He's very handsome, your new man, Meg," she said with her bubbly, high-pitched voice.

Since his wife had died, Charles Atherton had had a series of cooks and housekeepers, never allowing any to stay long enough to really become part of the family. It was as if he couldn't bear to see any woman even partially take over the role his wife had played to such perfection. But now as he mellowed a bit with age, he seemed in no hurry to replace the good-natured Henrietta, who had lasted longer than any of the others.

"Yes, Henrietta, he is." Both women paused to gaze a moment down the hall to the closed doors of her father's office.

"Your papa, he likes him, too."

Meg reached over to hug the plump little woman. "Oh, I hope so, Henrietta," she whispered.

She shook herself out of her reverie. "And if you would just get on out of here, I could go listen at the door and find out," she said mischievously. Henrietta giggled and allowed Meg to push her gently back through the door into the kitchen.

She had just turned to tiptoe down the hall, when her plans were once more thwarted by the appearance of Johnny in the doorway of the dining room.

Immediately she gave up on her eavesdropping mission. She hadn't seen Johnny since he left her on the trail with Carson yesterday, and she knew she owed him an explanation.

"Good morning, Johnny," she greeted him. "I'm glad you came. I wanted to talk to you."

Johnny's usually sunny nature was not in evidence today. He looked as if he had not slept well. "Good morning, Meg," he answered dully.

"Sit down—have some potatoes." The big platter of fried potatoes and onions was the only dish left on the table, and she pushed it toward him.

He shook his head. "I'm not hungry, Meg. I just came to see you. Are you all right?" His dark brown eyes searched her face. They had always been able to see things there that no one else could.

After a moment he said, "It appears that you are."

A flush rose over her face. It had never been any use to hide anything from Johnny. "I'm in love, Johnny. I know it sounds crazy—you've probably heard by now that Carson was one of the band that kidnapped me— but I can't explain it. I've never felt this way before."

Johnny sat down next to her. The expression on his face was painful for Meg to see. "Are you *sure*, Meg? This man's not just your typical cowboy, he has that ruthless look of a man who lives by violence. How can you be in love with someone like that?"

She took both his hands in hers. Tears rose in her throat. "I don't *know*, Johnny, don't you see? It just happens. I wish it had been you."

A tear spilled over and rolled down her cheek. "I guess there's just no way to tell your heart to do the sensible thing. It goes where it will."

Johnny reached up and wiped away the tear with the back of his hand. "Don't cry, *zorrita*. I didn't come here to make you sad. I just need to know that you'll be all right."

"I'll be fine, Johnny," she told him firmly.

"Are you expecting to be able to make a man like Carson settle down to a normal life?" he asked, still dubious.

She didn't answer for a moment. "It's all come on so suddenly, Johnny, we haven't even had much of a chance to talk about it. But I think he's tired of the way he's been living. I think he's ready to settle down."

Johnny shook his head. "It's not as easy as you think to change a man, Meg. You know, some men will promise anything—they'll even believe their promises for a while—until they get everything they want from a woman." His voice was full of contempt for the kind of man he was describing. And he obviously thought Carson was one of them.

In her heart Meg knew that Carson was different. *His* promises were real. He was ready to put his adventurous life behind him and concentrate on building a marriage. Though she could understand Johnny's reservations, she was sure she was right.

Unfortunately, she thought to herself, Johnny's view of Carson was being colored by jealousy, and there simply wasn't anything she could do about that.

"Maybe he already has," Johnny said softly, watching the emotions pass across her face.

"Has what?"

"Gotten what he wanted from you." His normally warm, teasing voice was harsh with resentment.

"Oh, Johnny." She pulled her hands away from him, her tears falling in earnest now. "Don't hate me. I've already told you, I can't help it—it's beyond my control. Sometimes I feel like I'm out in the deepest part of the swimming hole, and there's no shore anywhere, nothing to hang on to."

His resentful tone vanished, and he leaned over to put an arm around her shoulders. "Don't Meg, it'll be all right. I hope that Carson turns out to be everything you think he is."

He picked up a napkin from the table and wiped her cheeks. He was her Johnny again, tender and concerned. "Just remember, I'm here, Meg. If your fancy gunman doesn't work out, you won't drown out in the middle of that swimming hole. I'll plunge right in and get you."

He gave her a heartbreaking smile. "It wouldn't be the first time, lovely," he teased, ruffling the top of her hair.

She grabbed his hand and held it for a minute against her cheek. "Sometimes I wish I were two people, Johnny," she said softly.

He grew serious again. "We can't be what we aren't, Meg, it never works. I just hope you're making the right decision. Your captain handles a horse and a gun like a man cut out for a life on the run."

"I know, Johnny. That's what I thought about him, too, for a long time. But I'm convinced now that he's different. You'll see.'' A bright smile erased the last sign of her tears. ''Beginning today, Captain Timothy Carson is a changed man.''

Chapter Thirteen

"This is the highest point on the ranch." From the top of the modest hill, endless gentle waves of Texas grasslands stretched out in front of them.

Meg plopped down in the middle of the long, sweet-smelling grass. "I've always loved it up here. I used to think I could see the whole world."

Carson smiled down at her. In the tousled young woman sprawled happily on the ground it was easy to see the spirited child who had sat on this hill looking out at her world. He sat down beside her.

"And some day," Meg went on, "we'll bring our children up here, all seven of them."

"Seven?" Carson's brows lifted in mock horror.

"Seven," Meg repeated firmly. Since her talk this morning with Johnny she had spent the day elaborating on her fantasies of settling down with Carson to a normal life. She knew she was right, and she had been even more sure of it when he had reported on his conversation with her father. Now that her father was willing to give his consent to their marriage, there were absolutely no obstacles left.

She gave a sigh of deep contentment and lay back. The grasses closed in around her, tickling her face. She giggled.

"Happy?" Carson asked softly.

"Mmm—very." She looked up at him, her big eyes solemn and beautiful. "I never thought I could be so happy, Carson. Tell me it's not all a dream."

He dropped a light kiss on her mouth, but didn't say anything. He sat with his chin propped on his bent knees, staring out over the grass sea.

"I only wish this *were* the whole world, Meg," he said finally.

Something in his tone made Meg sit up. They had had the most wonderful day. She had at last found a rider whose skill compared with Johnny's, and they had ridden to the far reaches of the ranch before stopping for a picnic lunch.

Then Carson had insisted on a nap after lunch.

"A nap?" Meg had asked.

"Yes—you know, a *siesta*—I picked up the custom in Mexico," he had told her with a wicked grin, pulling her down on the blankets and beginning to methodically rid her of her clothing.

"Carson, what are you doing? It's broad daylight and we're outside, and . . . and besides, they don't take off their clothes for a *siesta* in Mexico."

"I've improved a bit on their system," he had told her in a husky voice, his body moving over hers.

And afterward they *had* taken a nap. And awakened to the pleasant midafternoon hum of rustling grasses and buzzing insects.

Now it was almost time to head back for supper, and for the first time all day, Carson's relaxed, content expression was gone, and he looked again as he had in the sierra—watchful, careful, on guard.

"What is it, Carson?" Meg asked him sharply, a sense of foreboding adding an edge to her tone.

He drank in one more time the tranquillity of the vista in front of them, then turned to face her. The time had come.

"Meg," he said gently, "please believe me that I do want to be here with you, and climb this hill with our seven children tumbling along beside us, but we're going to have to postpone getting started with it all for a little while."

Meg's face looked small and white, surrounded by her loose cloud of hair.

"I have to go back to Villa's camp, Meg."

She stared at him, dumbfounded.

"The army needs information more than ever now, and there's not time to get another agent as close to Villa as I am." His explanation seemed to have no effect on her shocked expression.

"I don't have any choice." Though he felt wretched, his words sounded merely angry. He couldn't seem to make her understand what he was feeling. He knew he was hurting her, filling her again with all the doubts about him that their happiness together had begun to put to rest.

He made a move to take her in his arms, but she pulled away. Frustrated and feeling helpless, he stood and walked several paces.

Meg could see every muscle tighten in his back as he swung his arms back and forth as though fighting an imaginary swarm of insects.

Her brain felt like a steam engine had just rolled through it. He was leaving her, going back to Villa, and in all likelihood he would end up as dead as those informers she had seen shot before her very eyes.

And for what? To keep Villa from stealing any more U.S. army beef in his little raids across the border? It was just as Johnny had said. Carson was made for a life of danger. Two idyllic days of happiness and passion, and he was ready to throw it all away for another adventure. She couldn't believe it.

"The past two days have meant nothing to you?" she asked him bitterly.

Carson fought his irritation. He couldn't imagine how she could say such a thing after the intensity of what they had shared. But she had a right to be angry, he told himself. He had again let himself get intimately involved with her under what might be considered false pretenses.

He overrode his impatience to try one more time to make her understand. "Sweetheart, they have meant everything to me, and I want to have a lot more just like them. But many lives might depend on the work I am doing in Mexico, work that I started before I met you. I can't just leave it unfinished."

"And just how much longer do you think it will be before Villa discovers who you are? How long do you think you will live after that happens?"

Carson looked down at the ground. "If you like, Meg, I'll stay long enough for a wedding ceremony. We don't know—" He stumbled, trying to find the right words and knowing that he was saying it all wrong. "That is, there may be some—consequence—of our being together as much as we have."

She turned on him, furious now. "Well, that's very noble, Captain Carson, but thank you anyway. I'm perfectly capable of dealing with any consequence myself. You just go ahead and ride off and get yourself killed. I'll be fine."

She jumped to her feet and skirted his outstretched hand to make her way to her horse.

"I was hoping you would understand, Meg."

She mounted up and looked over at him. "I do understand, Carson. I finally understand all too clearly. It's just like Johnny said."

"And what do you mean by that?" he asked her, finally letting his anger surface. He grabbed her horse's bridle.

"He tried to warn me," she told him. Her contemptuous tone hurt him more than her earlier shock. "He says that you're a man made to be on the run. That once you'd gotten what you wanted from me, you would be gone."

He regarded her in silence for a moment, letting the cruel words settle into his brain. "If that's really what you think of me, Meg, then perhaps there's no point in continuing this discussion."

He dropped his hold on her horse and stepped back. She wheeled the animal around and sent it plunging at an irresponsible speed down the hill. She was halfway back to the ranch before she let up the pace. The poor animal was lathered and exhausted when she reached the stables.

In her hurt and fury she ignored the puzzled looks of the stable boy over her uncharacteristic poor treatment of her mount. Her eyes blinded with tears, she stalked around to the front of the house, only to be met by the extremely unwelcome sight of her father sitting on the front porch with Colonel Sutherland. She glared at both men and, without a word, went inside, slamming the screen door resoundingly.

Carson was just moments behind her, his horse also showing signs of fatigue. The two men on the porch stood as he approached.

"A lovers' quarrel, Captain?" Atherton asked mildly.

"I told her about my leaving," he answered angrily. "She didn't take it well."

"Apparently," the older man observed.

"It seems that the horse trainer you prize so highly has her convinced that once I leave she'll have seen the last of me."

Atherton squinted as he stared out at the sun sinking low on the horizon. "I'll talk to her," he said.

Carson shook his head. "Meg knows her own mind—you know that better than I do." He took a long look around at the prosperous, tidy ranch buildings, then brought his eyes back to the porch. "What are you doing here, Colonel?" he asked his commanding officer bluntly.

Sutherland looked concerned. "I'm sorry to say that I've come for you, Carson." He looked from his young officer over to Atherton and back. "I was hoping things would be working out for you better by now, but in any event, I have to ask you to come back with me. Things are heating up."

"What things?"

"We have good intelligence that Villa is planning to attack an American city. If there's any way to stop it from happening, we've got to give it a try."

Carson shrugged. "Well, there's nothing keeping me here," he said bitterly. "Let me fetch my gear and we can get going."

Atherton came down the steps toward Carson. "Stay to supper, son. Let's talk this out."

Carson stretched out his hand as the older man approached. "I thank you for your hospitality, Mr. Atherton, but I think we'll just head out right away. I've already been away from Villa's camp for too long."

He shook the older man's hand and then disappeared into the house. Atherton looked over at Sutherland and shook his head. "Young love," he snorted. "Is there anything in the world more painfully foolish?"

Sutherland gave a halfhearted smile. "I'm just sorry that I need him so badly right now, Charles."

Atherton regarded his friend soberly. "Tell me truthfully, John. What are the chances of his getting back out of that hornets' nest?"

Sutherland's own expression became grave. "Carson's good, he knows how to take care of himself. But at the same time—"

He stopped and his lips flattened together as he fought for control. "There are not many men who have gone up against Pancho Villa and lived to tell the tale."

Meg changed out of the dusty clothes she had worn on their ride and dressed with great care for supper in a green sprigged muslin dress and a matching hair ribbon that set off the reddish highlights and gave a becoming cast to her pink cheeks.

She was still angry, and more than a little hurt. Johnny's warnings ran over and over again in her head. But she had calmed down enough to decide she would hear Carson out. He had, after all, offered to marry her before he left, even if it hadn't exactly been the most romantic of proposals. Would a man running away commit himself in such a fashion? Unless, she reflected grimly, he had adopted Villa's bizarre view of matrimony.

And she had come to know something about Carson's sense of honor. He wouldn't leave a job unfinished, especially if it meant that lives could be lost. By the time she was ready to head downstairs her mood had mellowed considerably.

The dining room was empty when she pulled open the heavy sliding doors. Before she could stop to wonder where everyone was, her father came up behind her and gave her a little hug.

"Captain Carson's gone, Meg," he said gently.

Her face fell. "He left?" she asked, unbelieving.

Her father nodded. "He and Sutherland rode out about an hour ago. He told me he had explained to you that he will still be on assignment for the army, investigating Villa."

Meg swallowed hard. "Johnny was right about him," she said, her voice hard.

Her father sighed and pulled out the chair beside her place, motioning her to sit down.

"Listen, Meg, I know this isn't easy. You've been through a lot in the past couple months, and it seems fair that by now you should be able to settle back and enjoy yourself for a spell." He reached out and affectionately smoothed back a stray lock of her hair. "But you've never particularly been a person to take the easy route."

Stiffly Meg sat down in the chair next to his. She didn't speak.

"Carson seems to me to be a fine young man. He's honest and direct. And most importantly, the fellow seems to be deeply in love with you."

Meg started to protest, but her father gently stopped her words with an upraised finger, and continued on. "But if it's Carson you want, then you darn well better get used to having him part-time, because the next time the army needs a good man for some special mission, he's likely to be off again. You've just got to accept that part of him right along with all the other things about him that have been putting those pretty roses in your cheeks the past couple days.''

She considered her father's words a minute. ''Johnny said he was one of that kind of men who are just after one thing, and then they disappear.''

Atherton hid a smile. ''I don't think I'd take Johnny's words as gospel when it comes to Carson, Meg. The boy has been your protector for years, and more than a little sweet on you. It will be hard for him to let you go.''

Meg pushed away her plate. She couldn't imagine trying to get any food down. ''I'm so confused, Papa.''

''Well—'' he reached for the serving dish of fried chicken ''—starving to death won't make anything better. There's not much you can do now except wait—the perpetual woman's curse, I'm afraid.''

''Did Carson leave any message? Why didn't he come to say goodbye?''

Atherton raised an eyebrow. ''He seemed to think you'd been pretty clear in your dismissal, Meg.''

She banged the table with her tiny hand, unconsciously copying a favorite gesture of her father's. ''I've got to go after him, Papa.''

She stood up, determination replacing the sadness on her face. ''I can't let him go back across the border without talking to him.''

Her father jumped up and put out a restraining hand. ''Whoa, daughter. You're not going anywhere—it's already dark. And who's to say where he was heading?

You could ride all the way down to Fort Bliss and find
that he had gone somewhere else.''

For all her protests, her father was not to be budged.
Not at dinner that night, nor the entire next day, when
she alternated between rages and fits of despair. It was
not until all the emotion had drained from her and she
addressed him with the cold logic of a determined
woman that he finally relented and reluctantly agreed
to take her looking for Carson at the military fort. They
left the next day at dawn, which brought them into Fort
Bliss before midmorning.

Just a few minutes later they were being shown into
Colonel Sutherland's cramped office.

"Charles, Meg." The distinguished gray-haired officer was on his feet instantly. "What are you two doing here?"

Atherton shook his friend's hand and gave him a
long-suffering look, pleading for patience. "Meg wants
to talk to Captain Carson, John. It seems they have
some things to discuss before he heads back down to
Mexico."

Sutherland motioned them both to a chair, but his
face was troubled. "You're too late," he said soberly.
"He left immediately, the same night we got back here.
He wouldn't even stay the night to sleep."

Meg closed her eyes. He was gone—back to Villa, to
danger and perhaps to death. And she hadn't even said
goodbye.

Her father put a comforting hand on her arm. "Is
there any way to reach him at this point, John?" he
asked Sutherland.

The colonel shook his head. "I can't even reach him.
No one can until he decides to make contact with an-

other one of our agents down there. It would be too risky for him.''

Atherton nodded. ''Yes, I can see how it would be.'' He turned to his daughter. ''I guess that's all we can do, Meg. Like I told you, we'll have to go back to the ranch and wait for your young man to get his business taken care of.''

''At least stay to dinner, Charles. You've had a long ride for nothing.'' The colonel issued the invitation to his friend, but his eyes were on Meg's downcast face.

''Thank you, John. We'd be pleased to stay. Meg hasn't eaten enough to fill a thimble in the past two days, and it's a long trip home.'' He stood. ''We need to let you get back to work.''

''I'll get my orderly to give you a tour of the fort while you're waiting, and I'll meet you in the mess hall in about an hour,'' Sutherland told him. He walked over to the door and called to a young man with white-blond hair sitting at a desk in the outer office.

Meg listened in a daze to Sutherland's polite introductions of his aide, a Corporal Olsen. She couldn't believe that Carson was gone, perhaps truly now, forever.

The corporal was a pleasant young man, who exerted himself trying to bring some life to the face of the beautiful young woman Sutherland had asked him to entertain.

But Meg's responses were dispirited, and eventually the man confined himself to addressing his remarks to her father, who seemed to have a genuine interest in the everyday operations of the military fort.

''These men look like they're getting ready to head out,'' Atherton commented as they passed a group of thirty or so men on the parade grounds, some already mounted.

"Finally some action against that bastard, Villa," the young corporal said vehemently.

Meg's head came up. "What about Villa?" she asked him sharply.

The towheaded young man realized too late his indiscretion. "I'm sorry, miss, both for the language and the comment. I have no business talking about what those men are about to do."

"Please." Her face was now as animated as the young corporal could have wanted. "It's very important to me. What are those men going to do with Villa?"

The corporal backed a step away from her. "I—I think I had better take you back to the colonel, miss, sir. Maybe he'd be willing to answer your questions."

Sutherland was as reluctant as his corporal to talk about the Villa mission. "Villa specializes in leading the U.S. army on wild-goose chases," he told them. "This is most likely just another in the series."

"But if they know where Villa is, then Carson is there, too," she told the colonel, clutching the stiffly starched sleeve of his uniform. "And if they find Villa and there is fighting, how will they tell Carson from one of the bandits?"

She was using her most determined voice, which her father knew from past experience meant that she wouldn't be easily diverted. He watched Sutherland try for several minutes, then finally admit that one of his field commanders in El Paso had wired that he had set up a meeting with Villa at the Ziegler Hotel in El Paso.

Ostensibly, Villa had indicated that he wanted to discuss peace, but the army didn't trust him. They intended to go through with the meeting, but planned to surround the hotel and go into the meeting fully armed, ready to trap Villa and his men at the first sign of trouble. They could arrest Villa on the spot and charge him with being in the country with illegal weapons.

"And what about Carson?" Meg asked indignantly. "Does he know that Villa and his men are walking into a trap?"

Sutherland looked disturbed. "Carson has always been a man who could take care of himself in any situation, Meg. We've alerted the raiding party that an American agent may be among the men they encounter in the hotel."

"So that's it?" she asked in furious disbelief. "Too bad for Captain Carson if he gets caught in his own army's trap?"

"Meg, Carson knew exactly the risks he was facing by accepting this assignment," Sutherland told her severely.

Meg stood up and faced the old colonel. "I would never have believed you could be such a coldhearted—"

"Meg," her father remonstrated. "It's not John's fault. Someone has to protect the border from Villa's marauding. Remember, Carson volunteered to infiltrate Villa's camp. And he went back there of his own free will, in spite of your vehement opposition."

She sat back down again, silent but not placated. "When is this supposed meeting to take place?" she asked coldly.

"Don't get any ideas, Meg," her father jumped in immediately. "I know you—I can already see the wheels turning inside that pretty head. You are *not* going to get mixed up in this. Just forget it."

Sutherland added his stern admonitions to those of her father, and Meg had no choice but to sit quietly and let them think they had convinced her not to interfere.

Inwardly she was making quick calculations. How long did it take to ride to El Paso?

She continued planning all the way back to the ranch, but in the end, even she had to admit that it would be nearly impossible for her to ride back down to El Paso alone—that is, if she were going to arrive in one piece, and in time to do Carson any good. She would have to go, as she had so many times in the past, to Johnny.

He was out in the corral when they arrived back from the fort, and wandered over to take their horses as they dismounted. It was obvious from the sullen look on his face that he knew where they had gone.

"Did you have a good trip?" he asked Atherton, pointedly ignoring Meg.

Atherton looked from his trainer to Meg and sighed. "Meg wanted to speak with Captain Carson, but we were too late. He was gone by the time we got to the fort."

Johnny's face lightened a touch. "Too bad," he said unconvincingly.

In an uncharacteristic gesture, he gave his hand to help Meg as she jumped agilely off her horse. She took it without comment.

"I'll rub these boys down," he told them. "You two have probably had about enough for one day."

"Thank you, Johnny," Atherton replied heartily, relieved to see his favorite hand recovering his good spirits. "Come on, Meg, let's go see if we can talk Henrietta out of some of that lemonade she rations so carefully."

"You go, Papa. I'll just stay a minute and help Johnny with the horses."

Atherton gave both their faces a searching look, then decided that it was probably best if they talked things out between themselves.

"I'll wait for you inside, honey," he said finally, and walked away with the brisk stride that age had still not affected.

"So, Meg." Johnny kept his tone carefully neutral. "It appears that your adventurer is off on another adventure. I won't say I told you so."

He paused and fixed her with his dark, intense gaze. "But I won't say I'm sorry, either."

Meg bit her lip. Could she really ask her old friend to help her, knowing how he felt about Carson—and about her? She knew it wasn't fair to Johnny. But she had had plenty of time on the long ride home to review her options, and he was her only hope. It might be Carson's life at stake.

"Johnny, I need to talk to you." She pulled him along with her into the shadowy recesses of the horse barn. Her agitation transmitted itself to him, and he became instantly wary.

"What is it, Meg?" he asked.

"I need your help."

Johnny closed his eyes. He couldn't even begin to count the number of times those words had been the preface to another one of Meg's outlandish escapades.

"You need my help to do what?"

"To go to El Paso."

Johnny looked puzzled. "If you need to do some shopping, Meg, we can ride into town Thursday and take the train."

"It's not for shopping, Johnny. I need to go there to find Carson."

Johnny's dark face grew grim. "Get another errand boy, Meg," he said coldly, turning to leave.

She clutched at his arm. "No, Johnny, don't go. You don't understand."

In a few, disjointed words she told him about the ambush planned for Villa and the possible danger for Carson. She ended her account with her father's and Colonel Sutherland's refusal to do anything about the situation except wait for the outcome.

"Sounds to me like the only sensible thing to do," Johnny told her. "You can't seriously think that you can go riding up to Villa and stop the whole thing?"

"I'm not afraid of Villa," she replied. "It's our own army that's putting Carson in danger. I just want to get there in time to warn him."

Johnny shook his head firmly. "Not this time, Meg. You've talked me into a lot of crazy things in the past, but I'm a grown man now, and I know better. You must be out of your mind to think the two of us on our own could make any difference in what looks like the beginning of a border war."

"All I want to do is get to the hotel and wait there. When Villa or any of his men show up, I can tell them what's going to happen, and everyone can get away before any trouble starts."

"As easy as that," Johnny said dryly.

"As easy as that," Meg repeated with a smile. "Oh, Johnny, you're the only one I can turn to."

Her voice took on its most persuasive tone, Johnny noted with a sinking heart. He had never yet been able to resist her pleading.

"I don't know how you always manage to talk me into these things, *zorrita*."

She leaned over and gave him a kiss on the cheek. "I knew I could count on you."

"That's me, faithful Johnny. You can always count on me in a pinch." He couldn't disguise the bitterness in his voice.

Meg's smile faded. "Don't think I don't realize how much I'm asking of you. I know how you feel about Carson, and about me. I'll never forget this."

The bitterness disappeared from his voice, leaving only a trace of pain in his dark eyes. "I've never been able to refuse you anything, Meg lovey. You know that."

She patted his arm helplessly, sudden tears springing to her eyes. "I can't lose him, Johnny," she whispered brokenly.

He gave a deep sigh. "Well then, we'd better hightail it down to El Paso and see what we can do about getting him out of trouble."

Chapter Fourteen

Meg self-consciously rubbed her hands down her travel-stained clothes as she and Johnny walked into the sedate, wood-paneled lobby of the Ziegler Hotel. Johnny removed his Stetson and looked around uncomfortably. Neither had expected that the place would have such an air of old-world elegance.

"Well, *zorrita*, we're here. Now what?"

Meg made a quick study of the well-dressed ladies and gentlemen lounging in the room's plush chairs. She was virtually certain that none of them could be in any way connected with Villa's band.

"We'll ask," she said with more confidence than she was feeling. Ask what? she then wondered. She certainly couldn't walk up to the front desk and ask for Pancho Villa.

A snobbish-looking young man with wire-rimmed spectacles was standing behind the ornate, polished dark wood desk.

"Could you help me please, sir?" Meg asked him with her prettiest smile.

His spectacles slipped down his nose slightly as he took in the sight of the disheveled but beautiful young woman across from him.

"I'm looking for a party of gentlemen—*Mexican* gentlemen—who are to be holding a meeting here. Do you know anything about them?"

For a moment the waspish young man looked as though he had some doubts as to the propriety of her purpose there in the hotel. Meg groaned inwardly as she pictured herself being thrown out of the lobby in a most undignified fashion.

Before she could speak again, Johnny was at her elbow, his strength presenting an impressive contrast to the anemic-looking clerk.

"Miss *Atherton* is here to represent her father in a business dealing. Could you please inform us where this meeting is being held?" he told the slight young man haughtily.

The man's mouth opened slightly. "Yes, sir," he said hastily. There were few people in El Paso who were not familiar with the huge Atherton holdings.

The young man checked a large book on the counter in front of him. "There is a meeting scheduled for about thirty people—a Mr. Cordoba. Would that be your party?" he asked them, now the height of politeness.

Meg peered intently at the upside-down scrawlings in the book.

"Upstairs, Johnny," she said excitedly. She grabbed his hand and led the way across the lobby at a most unladylike pace, leaving the clerk staring after them in bewilderment.

Johnny had spent a good deal of the trip to El Paso trying to persuade Meg to stay put on the outskirts of town and let him go in alone to warn Carson. Of course, she would hear nothing of it, so he had spent the rest of the trip trying to figure out what he was going to say to her father about this latest adventure. This time it was a bit more serious than sneaking over to the Carpenter ranch to spy on her father's weekly poker game, or the time they had run through the back parlor at the Red Garter, the town fancy house.

He caught Meg by the waistband of her riding skirt. "Where do you think you're going so hellfire-bent for trouble, Meg?" Fear for her translated itself into anger in his voice. "Let's just slow down here and see what's waiting up there before we barge in on who knows what."

His words were sensible, and Meg stopped on the stairs to let him catch up to her. For a moment she had been so excited to think that she might soon be face-to-face with Carson that she forgot what she was doing. But the logic of what Johnny said was clear. She didn't want to break into a gathering of Villa's men if she could help it.

Cautiously she and Johnny rounded the top of the stairs and peered down the hall. The sound of raucous voices speaking Spanish drifted distinctly out of the open door of a room about halfway down the hall on the right-hand side.

"It's Villa, it's got to be," Meg whispered excitedly.

"Now what?" Johnny whispered back.

But Meg was already on her way down the hall. She had had enough of discretion. Carson was in that room, and any minute the hotel could be filling up with soldiers shooting to kill any man who looked like a bandit.

Drums throbbed in her ears as she approached the open door. A shaft of smoky light filtered out into the hall. She poked her head around the door and saw to her dismay that the room was already half-filled with soldiers. Army uniforms were everywhere, but so far no one was shooting.

Across the room Villa was, as usual, surrounded by a retinue of his men. Nearer her, to one side of the room, she spied the tall, distinctive form of Carson, lounging carelessly against a carved wooden bar.

Meg felt suddenly at a loss. Now that she was here, how was she to warn him? Sensing that time was short, she went with her instincts.

"Carson," she called to him in a stage whisper. "Hurry—it's a trap!"

Carson's dark head snapped up sharply, as did all those around him. Before she knew what was happening, guns appeared from under tables, inside jackets— it seemed they were everywhere. Several shots were fired before anyone seemed to know who was shooting at whom.

Carson ran to the door and grabbed Meg fiercely. "You little fool," he said furiously. "What in hell are you doing here?"

There was no time to reply. By now a cortege of men around Villa, guns blazing, were ushering him out of the room. Some of the soldiers had ducked behind the bar Carson had been leaning on. Others looked frantically about for cover.

Dragging Meg along behind him, Carson headed for the stairs at the far end of the hall. Johnny came up alongside them, looking concerned and puzzled.

They raced down the stairs. At the bottom, Carson led them through a tiny door that opened on a narrow alley in back of the hotel. None of the other participants in the shoot-out seemed to have found this exit. Villa and his men must have blasted their way right through the front lobby. That would have been quite a sight for all those stuffy old fogies, Meg thought to herself.

They raced to the end of the alley and around the corner to the hotel stables. Villa and his group had made it there ahead of them, and the poor stable boy was trying to fetch everyone's horse at once. Most of the bandits ignored him and were fetching their own mounts.

Villa spotted Carson. "Eh, *gringo,* so much for your parley. I told you it was of no use to trust the *bastardos.*"

Carson didn't take the time to answer him. He found his huge stallion in one of the stalls and led him out of the stable.

His face grim, he turned to Johnny. "Take her home, man, and for God's sake, see that she *stays* there this time."

He mounted and turned to leave without a word to Meg, but Villa's powerful brown horse blocked his way.

"Bring the girl, Carson," the outlaw leader told him harshly.

Carson shook his head. "No, she'll only slow us down. Let her go."

"We can at least salvage something worthwhile out of this wild-goose chase. Bring her."

Villa was a man used to being obeyed. He blinked a couple times in disbelief as Carson continued shaking his head, adamant in his refusal.

Finally his mouth turned up in a nasty grin. "The girl has made you soft, *gringo.* If you will not bring her, I will."

He skillfully brought up his horse against Meg and, reaching down with both hands, lifted her in front of him on his saddle. Watching Carson with ominous displeasure, he motioned for his men to move out. "Maybe I give her to Aguirre this time, *gringo*. She has made you soft."

He spit on the ground to emphasize his disgust, then, giving his well-trained mount the slightest nudge, rode away, leaving Carson staring furiously after him in a cloud of dust.

By now Johnny had found his own horse and had retrieved his rifle. As Villa rode off down the street with Meg, he hesitantly lifted the gun to his eye. Before he could even find the sights, Carson had swung his high-booted leg and kicked the gun savagely out of his hands.

"Don't be even more of an idiot than you already have been today, Silvano," he told the man furiously. "Shoot at Villa and you're as good as dead—and so is Meg."

"Are you just going to let him ride away with her? What kind of a man are you?" Johnny's anger equaled his rival's.

Carson looked down at the man with ill-concealed dislike. "I'll catch up to them in a minute. But first I want to know what in *hell* possessed you and Meg to show up at that meeting today?"

"We were there because Meg insisted. For some reason I'll be damned if I can fathom, she wanted to save your worthless hide. She was trying to warn you that the army was planning to ambush Villa."

Carson uttered a vile curse under his breath. "I set up that meeting in there today, Silvano, *with* the army. It was the first time we've been able to get Villa to agree to discuss terms with us."

He closed his eyes and shook his head in disbelief. "Now, who knows what Villa will think? And what's worse, Meg's his captive again, and I don't think he'll let his wife get away with freeing her this time."

Johnny's mouth had fallen open with astonishment as he began to understand what a monumental blunder he and Meg had made. "Do you want me to go with you?" he asked when he finally found his voice.

"No, thanks," Carson answered sarcastically. "I think you've done quite enough for one day."

He pulled on his horse's reins to turn him down the street in the direction Villa's men had headed, but Johnny grabbed them from the other side to stop him.

"Carson," he said, his voice firm again. "Just one thing. I want you to know that Meg did this because she was afraid you would be hurt."

Carson's pale eyes were unreadable.

"She did it for you," Johnny said, a tinge of bitterness creeping back into his tone. "I don't know if it means anything to you, but she's in love with you."

Carson stared down at the strong young man for a minute, gauging what it had cost him to make the admission. The hard expression on his face softened a little and he nodded. A current of understanding seemed to be transmitted between the two men.

"Thanks," he said finally.

"Just bring her back safely," Johnny told him grimly.

"I will—you have my promise."

Johnny let go of Carson's reins, and the big stallion bolted forward.

Carson thought hard as he spurred his horse to catch up with the riders in front of him. Villa was angry with him—he knew that. First there was the debacle at the hotel, which Villa would blame him for, then the refusal to obey his orders over Meg. The next few minutes would be an interesting test of wills for the two men. Being out of favor with Villa was dangerous.

Carson's knees gripped his horse more tightly in nervous haste. Damn Meg for a meddling fool, he cursed. He actually thought he had made an important step—getting the local army commander, a Major Endicott, to agree to meet with Villa instead of shooting first and asking questions later. The major had impressed Carson as a sensible, seasoned veteran, and if he and Villa had been able to reach an agreement, this whole border war might have been put to an end. Villa could go back and play soldier in his own backyard, and the U.S. army could concentrate on keeping the peace in the still-wild Southwest.

And most important, I could have been heading back to the Atherton ranch ready to start a real life with Meg and her father, he thought to himself resentfully. Instead, he was once again the bandit, and this time an out-of-favor bandit who had to risk Villa's wrath to try to save Meg's pretty neck.

They were just up ahead of him, and he still hadn't decided on any kind of strategy. Villa held Meg easily on the broad back of his horse, and she didn't seem to be putting up any kind of a fight. Not yet, at least, Carson reflected grimly. He had better see to it that she was out of Villa's way before she did.

"Mi Jefe," he called ahead to the bandit leader.

Villa pulled up his horse and waited for Carson to come up alongside him.

"Let me take the girl off your hands—she can be a spitfire when she wants to be."

From within the circle of Villa's arms Meg glared over at him.

"You don't think I can handle this little wisp of a woman, Carson?" Villa asked coldly.

"The woman hasn't been born that you can't handle, *Jefe*. I'm just trying to save you the trouble."

"I haven't decided yet whether I will give her back to you, Carson. I may keep her myself this time—to make up for the problems you caused me in El Paso."

Carson groaned inwardly, but kept his tone pleasant. "She's my wife, if you remember, *Jefe*. You were the one who had us get married." He avoided looking at Meg.

"Yes." Villa sat looking at his American friend through his penetrating dark eyes. "Still, I think I will keep her a while."

Without another word he wheeled his horse around and headed down the road. Carson gave an exasperated sigh, but had no other choice than to follow in his cloud of dust.

They rode hard through the hot, dry plains of northern Chihuahua, stopping to make camp only once before they reached Chihuahua City. Meg had been given her own horse to ride, but she had been kept apart from Carson. Villa refused to talk to him long enough to hear his pleas for her release.

Meg was too tired from the exhausting pace to be frightened. She had come out of this before, she reasoned, and she would again. She knew that Carson had been trying to get Villa to hand her over to him, but she was no longer sure that she wanted that to happen. Little by little she had put together the story of the fatal hotel meeting and was beginning to realize that she had made a terrible mistake.

It appeared that Carson had been about to patch things up between Villa and the army. And she had come along to ruin it. Who knew what Carson's reaction to her would be now?

It was night when they rode into Chihuahua City. Wide paved streets replaced dirt roads, and gradually the poor, wooden houses of the countryside gave way to imposing brick and stone mansions.

The group of riders came to a halt in front of a large gray stone house with an elegantly ornate facade— Villa's Chihuahua mansion. The house was immense, Meg remembered from her visit here before with Luz— room after room of high carved ceilings and floors with different patterns of colorful ceramic tiles. The furniture was an eclectic mixture from the crude rough-hewn wood of the countryside to the most baroque French design.

Luz was there to greet them, her eyes on Meg in gentle remonstrance.

"How did you end up amongst us again, Margarita?" she asked chidingly.

Meg was so tired she could hardly shake her head in reply. "It's a long story, Luz."

The little woman took a good look at Meg's drawn face and put her arm around her. "And one that can wait until tomorrow for the telling," she said firmly. She turned to her husband. "Francisco, *mi vida,* the girl is half-dead. I'm going to take her up to her room."

Villa, who had been careful not to take his sharp eyes off Meg since they left El Paso, nodded and meekly relinquished her to the care of his wife.

Most of Villa's men had gone on to their own lodgings in the city. There was no sign of Carson—he was evidently not among those who had entered the house.

After a final glance around for him, Meg turned and followed Luz down a long tiled hall to the back part of the house, where a large open patio was surrounded on all sides by two floors of small rooms. It resembled a hotel more than a house. Moonlight lit the few scrubby plants in the middle of the open area. Their footsteps echoed hollowly on the tiles as they made their way up a small corner stairway to the upper level, which appeared deserted.

Meg took just a minute to look over the second-floor balcony to the patio below, then followed Luz through a squeaking door into one of the bedrooms.

"Here you are, Margarita, a nice soft bed. It will feel good after so long in that hard saddle." She shook her head like a scolding mother. "I've told Francisco many times he rides too far, pushes too hard." She lifted her shoulders in a resigned little shrug and smiled. "But there is only so much you can tell a man."

With a few more kind words she said good-night and bustled off, leaving Meg to sink into the bed in an exhausted sleep.

No one woke Meg the next morning, and the sun was high above the patio outside her bedroom door when she emerged. The only person in sight was a young maid, who was on her hands and knees polishing the ceramic tiles of the floor.

"*La señora está en el comedor,*" she told Meg shyly. Meg thanked the girl and skirted carefully around her to make her way down the gleaming stairs to the dining room, which she remembered was in the front part of the house.

As she headed down the dark hall from the sun-bright patio, Luz appeared and greeted her warmly. "I'm glad to see you looking so much better today, *querida,*" she told her, giving her a glancing kiss on the cheek. "And I have a surprise for you—he's been waiting."

Meg's heart started speeding up even before Luz threw open the dining room doors to reveal Carson, seated casually at the far end of a long elegant dining table.

He leaned nonchalantly back in his chair and watched her with his icy eyes, his expression carefully noncommittal as she walked into the room.

He looked as if he hadn't slept. His hair was tousled and he hadn't yet rid himself of a couple days' growth of beard. Dear God, Meg thought to herself desperately, but I love this man. And I've caused him nothing but trouble. He said he didn't need any other person messing up his life—and he was right.

She nodded to him without speaking. He picked up a fork and made nervous little circles on the tablecloth, belying his casual posture.

"I'll leave you two to talk things out." Luz's cheery voice came from behind Meg. Then she was gone, closing the room's tall double doors behind her.

"So, Meg. This time you were going to take on both Pancho Villa *and* the U.S. army?" he asked her sardonically.

She searched his eyes for signs of the fury she had seen back in El Paso, but it was nowhere in evidence. Maybe he had gotten over his anger, she thought hopefully.

"I just didn't want you hurt, Carson," she told him gravely. "I realize now that it was the wrong thing to do."

"You got that right, lady." He slammed down the fork he had been toying with. Just looking at her, he said to himself, was like acid in his gut. Her big gold eyes glowed as they watched him. Her ripe young body standing so stiffly proud in front of him made him ache to take her in his arms.

"I'm sorry," she said simply.

He shook his head, stood and walked around the long table to where she was standing. He had to touch her.

She took a step back at his advance, and he stopped.

"The point is, Meg, what business did you have getting involved in the first place? You of all people should know what a dangerous man Villa can be." He tried to keep his mind on the issue at hand, but his eyes wandered to her waist, which was impossibly tiny in her long trim riding skirt.

The familiar kindling of his eyes made Meg at last sense her advantage. She closed her eyes briefly in relief. He wasn't angry. Or at least, his anger was mitigated by the undeniable attraction that still existed between them. Now all she had to do was keep his mind going in that direction instead of back to the debacle in El Paso.

She advanced the step she had retreated, which brought her inches from his stern face. "I did it for you, Carson," she said softly.

Pride be damned, she thought to herself.

"You're a bloody idiot, Meg." He further narrowed the gap between them. "And I'm crazy in love with you."

Then they were in each other's arms, mouths meeting desperately, as though they were drinking cool water after a long, parched thirst. Sensitive parts of their bodies became rigid and erect, and they rubbed against each other sensuously.

He didn't even need completion, Carson realized with surprise. It was enough to be holding her like this, feeling her all up and down the length of him, knowing that she belonged to him.

"She's in love with you," Johnny had said. Carson hugged her to him even more tightly, and for the first time since his parents had died so many years ago, tears stung behind his closed eyelids.

"Why did you leave without saying goodbye, Carson?" she asked him brokenly.

He took her mouth in a fierce kiss, then answered. "I thought you had made it pretty clear that you weren't interested in hooking up with a man who couldn't settle down to a normal life." His dark brows raised slightly as he waited for her reply, though there was no longer any doubt in his mind about what it would be.

"As you so aptly put it," she murmured in his ear, "I was a bloody idiot."

She nibbled gently on his earlobe, then swirled her tongue into his ear. He had done this to her once in their lovemaking, and it had caused odd tingles all down one side of her. She giggled, remembering. "Will you forgive me?"

He pulled away and took a deep breath. Now things were getting out of hand. He had to remember that he was in Pancho Villa's dining room, and both his status and Meg's in the outlaw's army were still unresolved.

"Forgive you for what? For running me off your father's ranch? Or for spoiling several weeks of planning at the El Paso meeting? Or—" his voice became severe "—or for submitting me to sexual tortures when you know we are in a place where I can't do anything about it?"

Meg looked contrite at the mention of her misguided interference in El Paso. "For all three, I guess," she whispered remorsefully.

Her perfect face looked too small for the billowing disarray of her hair. Carson wanted to bury himself in it and in her.

"I forgive you," he said huskily.

A discreet knock snapped both their heads around to the door. It was Luz, smiling and apologetic.

"Well, I'm glad to see that you're both looking a bit happier," she said serenely. "I'm sorry to interrupt, but my husband wants to see you both in the library."

Meg's eyes met Carson's. They each were carefully trying to conceal their misgivings. His strong hands grasped hers.

"Come on, little vixen," he said softly. "Let's go see what the big band bandit wants with us."

Chapter Fifteen

Carson deliberately kept his arm around Meg's waist as they entered the room Villa used as his office. It was crammed with boxes, papers, books, odds and ends of every description.

Villa's sharp eyes did not miss Carson's possessive hold on Meg. "We will talk about the girl in a moment, my friend," he said briskly, indicating that he wished them to be seated. "First, I want to hear your accounting of what exactly happened up in El Paso. I thought the American army *cabrones* had given their word to come to the meeting unarmed."

Carson sat down across from Villa. The truth was, he didn't know what had gone wrong, either. Perhaps it was Meg's interruption that had set off the shooting, but it was entirely possible that it would have erupted anyway. "Our men weren't supposed to have guns, either, *Jefe,* but those weren't exactly *tacos* they were pulling out from under the tables."

Villa chuckled appreciatively. "I always come prepared, Carson. That's why I'm still alive."

He shrugged. "I didn't really hold out much hope for this meeting anyway," he said philosophically. "You can't trust Americans.'' He looked over at Meg and smiled.

"They say I am a *bandido,* a thief." His smile disappeared and he pounded his fist on his desk for emphasis. "I have *never* stolen. I only take from those who have much to give to those who have little."

Carson, who had heard this homily from Villa before, sat back in his chair, resigned. Right about now he didn't care if Villa robbed the U.S. treasury—he just wanted to get matters straight about Meg.

"A poor man who takes food when he is hungry does not steal," Villa continued forcefully. "He is merely doing his duty to sustain himself. It is the rich who steal, because even though they have everything they need, they still deprive the poor of their miserable bread."

Meg listened thoughtfully. When she returned to Los Alamos after her kidnapping, she had been regaled on all sides by tales of the terrible deeds of this man and his band—cruel murders and ruthless rapes. But obviously there was more to this bandit-revolutionary than his detractors gave him credit for.

With an abrupt change of mood, Villa jumped up from his chair and went over to pick up a hat lying on a table atop a jumble of papers and maps.

"Have you seen my new hat? It's very nice—American." The flat-crowned, wide-brimmed hat was trimmed with a silver braided band and silver tinsel stars on the crown and under the brim. Villa pushed it back on his head in his customary fashion.

"What do you think, eh? Do I look like a fancy *gringo?*"

Though Carson was relieved to see Villa regain his good humor, he was anxious to get down to the business of their meeting. Villa still could hold the failure in

El Paso against him—against them both—with dire consequences. He had to find out the outlaw leader's intentions.

He racked his brain trying to think of the best approach. "You said we would talk about my wife," he said with slight emphasis on the last two words.

Villa regarded him with amusement. "Your wife—ah, yes. I don't believe you ever thanked me, Carson, for securing for you such a beautiful bride."

Carson was silent.

"Well," Villa continued, waving his hand back and forth. "No matter. To you, it has turned out to be a good thing that she is so very beautiful. But to me, it is turning out to be a good thing that she is also very *rich*. Or at least her father is."

His dark eyes gleamed. "And so we are able to have some good come out of our El Paso adventure after all, eh, *amigo?* Do you not think her very rich rancher father would be willing to make a large contribution to the army of Pancho Villa in order to have his daughter back safely?"

Carson cursed under his breath. "She's my wife now, *Jefe.*"

Villa's thick brows shot up. "So, do *you* want to pay me for her?"

"You know I don't have that kind of money."

"Just so. That is why we will send word to her father today. If he wants to see his daughter again..." The outlaw leader left the sentence hanging in the air.

"My father won't give in to your filthy—"

"Meg, shut up!" Carson barked at her furiously before she could finish her words.

Villa gave a little clap of approval. "Bravo, *amigo*. Finally you are learning how to deal with women. If you think you can keep her quiet and under control, I'll give her back to you until we get the money from her father. Deal?'' He stood, indicating that the meeting was at an end.

"Deal," Carson replied, extending his hand. "Thank you, *Jefe.*"

They turned to leave but Villa's voice stopped them. "Remember, Carson," he said firmly, "she is in your care. It would not go well for either of you if she were to turn up missing."

Carson nodded his agreement.

"And one more thing," the bandit called to them as they were leaving the room. "Keep her away from my wife!"

The big doors had barely closed behind them when Meg exploded. "How can you nonchalantly sit there and agree to something like that? Hold me for ransom, indeed!"

She tore her arm out of Carson's grasp and started down the long hall to the front of the house. "I'm getting out of here right now, and if you won't take me, I'll find someone who will."

She was furious—to hear herself discussed in there as though she were a stray steer that they were bickering over!

She had stalked halfway down the hall before Carson caught up with her and stopped her in the only way he considered prudent. Pinning her against the cold tile walls of the hall, he put his mouth over hers in a deep, hard kiss.

"Meg, sweetheart," he said ruefully, pulling away from her. "What is it that makes you so damn set on sticking that pretty little neck of yours in a noose?"

She slumped back against the tiles. "I won't stay here, Carson—not this time," she said weakly.

He pulled her into his arms again, gently this time. "Neither of us will stay here, darlin'. The army's going to have to figure out another way to get to Villa. I'm taking you out of here."

"Truly, Carson?"

"Truly, my little spitfire. But I'm not going to do it by marching out of the house in broad daylight. Villa's men surround this place. We'll go tonight—I'll come get you in your room after I see that everyone is down for the night."

"What about the ransom message to my father?"

"Let him go ahead and send it. You'll be back home before he even has a chance to worry."

He gave her a little kiss on the nose and released her. "Just one more day, Meg. All you have to do is stay in your room and not do anything foolish. Can you handle that?" he asked with a touch of affectionate sarcasm.

She nodded. "I promise to stay out of trouble," she said meekly.

Carson groaned. "Why does that worry me?" he asked under his breath. He looked down at her. "I'm going to go see about getting us some horses. I'll check back this afternoon and let you know what I've been able to set up to get us out of here tonight."

He gave her another quick kiss and then left, leaving her to walk slowly back up to her tiny bedroom.

The morning hours dragged as she waited for the long day to pass. She ate midday dinner with Luz in a small room off the kitchen. Villa was meeting with a number of his men in the big dining room.

Luz was apologetic and a little embarrassed when Meg told her about the ransom demand, but she made no offer to help Meg escape as she had the time before. The meal between the two friends was tense, and Meg regretted the restraint that had grown between them. She wished she could tell Luz goodbye, and thank her again for the support she had given her. But she knew she didn't dare give even a hint of Carson's intentions of returning for her that evening.

After the uncomfortable meal she started back toward her bedroom. She had almost reached the stairway when a door opened in front of her in the narrow hall, and suddenly she was face-to-face with Rodolfo Aguirre. She had not seen him among Villa's men on the ride from El Paso, and she had hoped to avoid him entirely until she and Carson could get away.

His teeth gleamed in his swarthy face as he looked her over with a nasty smile. "So, *gringa,* you couldn't stay away."

He sidled up against her and she closed her eyes, trying to rid herself of the memory of his big sweaty body on top of hers.

"Maybe you have realized that those pale-assed *gringos* are not enough man for a woman like you. You've come back to give Rodolfo another try, eh?"

She steeled herself not to shrink from him. "Go to hell, Aguirre," she spit. "Try putting your filthy hands on me one more time and I swear—"

"You swear what, little *gringa?*" he taunted, reaching toward her.

Meg had no idea what she would do; she only knew that the thought of his touching her again made her want to be sick. Fortunately, they were interrupted by the bustling little form of Luz coming down the hall toward them. The outlaw backed away from Meg and muttered a sullen greeting to his leader's wife.

"I believe my husband is asking for you, Rodolfo," she told him frostily.

Aguirre paused a moment, then appeared to decide to accept temporary retreat. He started to leave, then stopped and turned back with a question. "Where is that American lover of yours, *gringa?*"

Meg ignored his question and turned her back on him to continue down the hall.

Sharply he grabbed her arm and twisted her around facing him. "Answer me. Where's Carson? Has he been here today?"

"Why do you want to know?" she asked angrily, shooting a quick glance toward Luz, asking for her silence about her earlier meeting with him.

"Just give me the information I'm asking for." He turned to Luz. "Have you seen him, *señora?*"

Luz looked over at Meg. "Not recently, Rodolfo. Why do you ask?"

The big bandit's face brightened with a self-satisfied smile. "I told Villa from the beginning that I didn't trust the sneaky bastard. When I tell him what I found out up at Fort Bliss, he'll see that he should have listened to me. And we will all see the end of *Captain* Carson."

He chuckled wickedly and twisted Meg's chin in his big hand. "Which will leave you, my pretty one, free for me."

Before Luz could intervene with words of protest, he was gone, leaving Meg trembling and white.

He knew. Aguirre knew about Carson being in the army. Villa would kill him when he found out.

Meg looked over to Luz, who was watching her with frightened eyes. "Did you understand what Aguirre was talking about?" she asked in a small voice.

"Your Carson is trying to betray my husband?" Luz asked gravely.

Meg closed her eyes. "Please, Luz, it's not exactly like that. Carson was sent here by the U.S. army to find out more about what Villa plans to do—to keep him, if possible, from any more raids across the border. He doesn't want your husband hurt—he just wants to keep him out of the States."

Luz's brown eyes held hers intently for a few moments. Finally, the little Mexican woman nodded. "Francisco will kill him," she said soberly.

"Oh, God," Meg said desperately. "I have to find him—we have to get out of here now."

She pressed her hands to her eyes, trying desperately to think. How could she find Carson in a town the size of Chihuahua? And how could she even get away to find him—he had said there were guards surrounding the house.

She looked down at the kind little woman who had rescued her more than once from imminent danger. "You've got to help me, Luz. I don't like to ask, but you're my only hope."

Luz scarcely hesitated a moment. "What do you want me to do?"

"Do you have any idea where Villa's men spend their time here in the city, someplace where Carson might be?"

"There is a place—La Copa de Plata—a cantina. He might be there."

"You've got to take me, help me get out of the house. Please, my friend. I swear that if you help us, we will do nothing to cause your husband harm."

Luz considered her words for a moment. "Come, then. I will tell the guards I am taking you with me to the *mercado*."

She quickly and efficiently supplied Meg with a *rebozo* to go over her telltale pale hair, and loaded them both with big shopping baskets. The guards gave lazy shrugs of indifference to her explanations, and in no time at all they were standing in front of the trim red brick building that housed the town's most notorious bar.

Meg was breathing a little easier. If Aguirre had already told Villa what he knew about Carson, she reasoned, the guards would never have let them go so easily. She had to locate Carson quickly, then they could be out of town before Villa had a chance to act.

She and Luz mounted the wooden sidewalk. Cautiously, Meg tried to peer through the frosted glass windows of the Copa de Plata. To her immense relief, through one of the pale glass scrolls she could see Carson's familiar wavy black hair.

Borrowing a peso from Luz, she asked a grimy little boy who was selling baskets along the side of the road to run into the building for her and fetch him. The boy's big brown eyes grew round at the sight of the shiny coin, and he quickly disappeared through the tall cantina doors.

In a moment he was back, followed more slowly by Carson, who was looking around him with a perplexed look. When he saw Meg, his face settled into a frown, and he strode sternly across the street to where she and Luz were waiting for him.

"What are you doing here?" he asked, irritated. "How did you get out of the house?"

"Carson, we don't have time for questions. Aguirre knows that you are an army agent, and when we left he was about to tell Villa."

Carson swore fluently. "I knew the bastard was up to something when he disappeared in El Paso. He must have been checking me out then. Damn!"

"We have to get out of here now," Meg said firmly.

Carson glanced warily at Luz.

"Luz has agreed to help us," Meg told him, "as long as we promise not to do anything to harm her husband."

Carson studied the tiny woman for a moment, then nodded. "I never got the chance to thank you for helping Meg out before, *señora,* and now it appears we will owe you a double debt."

Luz gave him one of her splendidly serene smiles. "I am helping you because I think you are a good man, Carson. You can tell the army that Francisco is trying to help his people—he doesn't want trouble with the Americans."

Carson was not as positive about Villa's intentions as his wife, but he wasn't going to stand around to argue the point. If Villa now knew about his army connection, his game here was up. The sooner he got away, the better.

With Luz's help they secured two horses and enough food so that they wouldn't have to stop for supplies at least until they crossed the border.

While Carson was tying the packs onto their horses, Meg put her arms around Luz. She had the feeling that this time their parting would be a final one, and she wished there were some way she could thank Luz for everything she had done.

"You're quite sure you won't have trouble with Francisco over this, Luz?" she asked her friend.

"Do not worry, Margarita. Francisco is ruthless in his politics, but not with his women. If he finds out that I helped you, he will be angry, but he will not harm me."

"I'll never forget you, my friend," Meg told her, tears rising to her throat.

The Mexican woman smiled. "I think from now on you will remember to stay safely on your own side of the border, *querida*."

Meg returned her smile wanly. "I think so, too."

Carson was ready with the horses. With his swift, fluent Spanish he thanked Luz again for her help, then leaned over to give her a kiss on her soft brown cheek.

Meg gave the now blushing woman a final embrace, then let Carson boost her up on her horse. As they headed down the street, she turned to wave a final *adios* to the staunch little Mexican woman with the enigmatic smile.

"I don't know if we should risk the main road to Juarez," Carson told her, referring to the ramshackle town on the Mexican side of the border at El Paso. "Villa could be after us any time now. But it's a long, dry stretch if we try to skirt the road. Are you up to it?"

They had been riding for almost an hour and had left the bustle of Chihuahua City far behind.

Meg gave him a tired but gallant smile. "Now that I know we're leaving here for good, I'm up to anything," she told him.

Her game little face made his heart constrict inside his chest. In all his years of wandering alone, he had never known that a woman could be like this—a true help-mate, a person to share not just a bed, but thoughts, joys, even problems.

Of course, sharing a bed didn't sound too bad just now, he reflected wryly as he shifted uncomfortably in his saddle. He had been riding behind Meg, watching her graceful, straight back as she sat expertly on her horse. His eyes drifted regularly to her petite, rounded derriere. Perhaps when they got a little farther into the semidesert countryside north of the city they could afford to stop for a few minutes—

His thoughts were drifting pleasantly, and the group of riders was upon them before he even was aware of their approach. Meg's cry brought him sharply out of his reverie, but by then it was too late. And it didn't take the gloating words being shouted for him to know exactly who had apprehended them.

"You're mine now, American," Aguirre called to him exultantly. "And perhaps I will let you stay alive long enough to see your woman learn what it is to be in the arms of a real man."

There were at least thirty men with him. Even if Meg had not been with Carson, it would have been pointless to try to escape. The odds were simply too great. With a leaden heart he watched as Aguirre himself took hold of Meg's reins and started off with her back to the city—Chihuahua City—where the only justice and all the power were in the hands of Pancho Villa.

It was, undoubtedly, Aguirre's wish to taunt him with the knowledge that Meg was now at Aguirre's brutal mercy that was the reason he was still alive, Carson thought to himself as he lay, hands and feet bound, in the closet-size dark room where he had been thrown by

Villa's men. Villa's laws were strict and unyielding, and Carson knew that Aguirre could easily have shot him on sight and received nothing but the outlaw leader's thanks. Once a man betrayed the band, his death warrant was signed.

It was ironic that death, which he had courted so nonchalantly in the past, should rear its head now, just when the idea of a life with Meg had become so precious.

But his agony was not for himself. It was for Meg. What would that vicious son of a mongrel dog, Aguirre, do to her? He pulled savagely against the rawhide thongs binding him. In his entire life he had never felt so helpless.

In another room in the back of the same building—the livery stable where Villa kept his horses—Meg had so far been unharmed. Aguirre had left her under guard in there, telling her with a menacing sneer that he was going personally to Villa to tell him of their capture and ask for the privilege of killing Carson this very night.

"But we'll do it slowly, *gringa,*" he had told her with deadly relish. "So that you can have time for a prolonged leavetaking."

At least it meant that Carson was still alive, Meg thought to herself. But she had seen how thoroughly they had tied him up. She couldn't hold out any hope that he would be able to free himself and get them out of this mess.

She began to study the room for any possible means of escape. If she could get away from her guards and find Carson before Aguirre came back from Villa's, perhaps they had a chance.

The guards sat on either side of the door. Their guns were holstered, but their expressions were alert and wary. Aguirre had threatened to cut off valuable parts of their bodies if they let anything happen to the girl, and he was a man who was not past doing such a thing.

She had spent several minutes in close calculation of just how quickly she could spring over to one of the guards and get his gun out of his holster when the door banged open, almost knocking one of them out of his chair.

It was Aguirre. His sneer was gone and his face was a thundercloud.

"Lopez!" he barked to the guard nearest to him. "Tie the girl up and throw her in with the *gringo*. Villa wants to personally attend his execution tomorrow morning. In the meantime, I have to meet with our men. We ride for Columbus tomorrow."

Both guards got to their feet. "The girl is to be shot tomorrow, too?" the man called Lopez asked.

"No," Aguirre snarled. "She's mine. But she'll have to wait until after the raid."

He turned to Meg, his anger diminished as a leering smirk returned to his face. "Will you wait for me, my pretty one? Just spend the time thinking about how good we're going to be together."

Meg shrank from the touch of his big hand against her face, but Aguirre was too preoccupied to notice. Briskly he gave the guards their orders and started out the door.

"Tie her well, and guard them both with your lives," he said in a final stern warning. The two men nodded vigorously, and then he was gone.

The guard Lopez was a stubby little man whom Meg had met several times on her first visit to the outlaws' camp. She attempted a smile with him, but he appeared unmoved. Instructing his companion to keep watch over her, he walked across the room to the far wall to get a coil of rawhide that was hanging on a great iron hook.

Pulling a knife from his boot, he cut off a piece and walked toward Meg.

She had little difficulty forcing tears into her eyes. "Please," she whimpered affectingly, "not with rawhide."

She held out her delicate wrists limply toward the outlaw and fixed him with her wide-eyed gaze. "It cuts my skin so."

The short little man paused and looked down at the rawhide in his hands with uncertainty.

"I'm sorry, *señorita*," he mumbled almost shyly, "but I have to tie you."

"Yes, I know, but perhaps—" her lip trembled and a tear spilled down her cheek "—perhaps your bandanna?"

Lopez put up his hand to his neck self-consciously, then looked over to his companion, still stationed by the door. The other man shrugged.

"I guess that would work," Lopez said finally. He flung the rawhide up on its hook and unfastened a grimy-looking green bandanna from around his neck.

Meg looked down to hide her elation. This was one of the games she and Johnny had played when they were children. She knew exactly how to hold her hands as the bandit tied them so that she could be out of the bonds faster than a cricket could chirp.

The tenderhearted Lopez made the sport even easier, scarcely pulling as he fastened the bandanna around her wrists in a simple knot.

She followed along behind him meekly. So far, so good. Her hands were as good as free, and they were taking her to Carson. When she found out what kind of shape he was in, she could plan the next move.

Carson blinked rapidly as the shaft of light fell on him through the suddenly opened door. Two of his erstwhile companions in Villa's gang stood just outside the door, with Meg standing, head bowed, between them. She looked scared and intimidated, and it sent a shaft of anguish through him, even as he brightened just at the sight of her. In his pitch-black prison he had been beginning to despair of ever seeing her again.

One of the guards gave her a gentle push and she entered the tiny room. With both of them inside, there was scarcely room to move. Carson was seated with his back against the far wall, his hands tied behind his back and his legs bound together from ankle to knee. There was a kind of desperation in his eyes that Meg had never seen there before.

Once again the room was plunged into darkness as the door shut behind them. Meg fell to her knees beside Carson.

"Are you all right?" he asked her urgently. "They didn't—do anything to you?"

She groped with her hands in the darkness to find his face. "I'm fine, darlin'. Aguirre had to go meet with Villa, so he didn't have time to hurt me."

Carson slumped against the wall in relief. His imagination had been torturing him with scenes of Meg at Aguirre's mercy ever since they had been separated.

"I like it when you call me darlin'." His normally strong voice sounded weak.

Meg smiled in the dark. "Then I'll call you darlin' every day of our lives," she told him gently.

He gave a little snort. "Which might not be too long. We're still prisoners, and trussed up like roast pigs, to boot."

Meg had rid herself of the bandanna that had bound her hands almost as soon as the door had closed. It hadn't even presented a challenge after her years of practice with Johnny.

"Well, *one* of us is," she said in an amused voice, as her hands found him in the dark. They moved from the rough rasp of his chin to the solid muscles of his chest.

"They didn't tie you?" he asked in surprise.

"Of course they did. But the bandanna hasn't been made that can keep me tied. It's one of my varied talents."

She ran her hands down past his lean waist and rested them on the rock-hard bulges of his thighs. She could hear his swallow in the dark.

"You're amazing, love," he said with some difficulty. Inside he was fighting a battle with his pride. Here he was in one of the worst scrapes of his life, and this little scrap of womanhood who was so casually manhandling him was his only hope of salvation. And to make matters even more humiliating, the slow movement of her small hands over him in the dark was causing reactions in him entirely inappropriate to the dire nature of their current circumstances.

Her hands moved upward along his tight denim clad legs. Carson groaned. "See?" she said seductively. "My hands are free."

"They certainly are," Carson murmured, his groin turning to knots at her relentless approach.

She could feel the heat radiating from him, the tensing of his muscles. "Untie me, Meg," he whispered hoarsely.

Chapter Sixteen

"In a minute," Meg answered softly. "Don't be impatient."

She knew the timing was atrocious—by morning they might both be dead—but she couldn't help feeling a tremendous surge of excitement with the realization of her power over him. Always before, he had taken the lead in their lovemaking, had been the teacher, the authority. Now he was helpless before her—at her mercy, so to speak, and she intended to enjoy the sensation.

She moved closer to him, straddling his bound legs, and bringing the two hottest parts of their bodies together, though they were fully clothed.

Feeling her way in the dark, she began unbuttoning his shirt, pausing halfway to run her hands underneath the rough cotton to caress the silky hairs of his chest.

"Untie me, Meg, or I swear I'll—" He groaned again as her mouth unerringly found one of his hard nipples.

"Just relax, Carson darlin'. Lie back and enjoy it." She moved sinuously against him as she spoke, her split legs allowing her tender woman's center to rub against his now rigid shaft. Slow heat curled into her groin.

Her hands slid between their two bodies and unfastened his trousers giving her free access to his pulsing masculinity. He writhed against his bonds. His manhood in her hands seemed to have a life of its own.

"God, Meg!" It was half a curse, half a blessing.

His helplessness made her daring, and she bent her head to take him into her mouth, massaging the satiny skin of his shaft. His deep intake of breath and the sudden tensing of his body told her that she was bringing him close to fulfillment, and she instinctively knew his pride would not want it to happen that way.

Slowly she pulled away from him and reached down the length of his taut legs to the rawhide bonds. The outlaws' multiple knots came undone like magic in her practiced hands, and in seconds she had freed both his legs and his hands.

Fury fed his hunger, and with a growl he reached for her. His half-clothed body was about to explode in spite of their predicament, in spite of the fact that they were prisoners with guards outside the door, in spite of facing possible death in the morning. He had never wanted anything so urgently in his life as to enter her body and feel her closing around him.

"You're a witch, Meg," he murmured huskily in her ear as he deftly stripped her of her clothes. "You've bewitched me."

He didn't bother with his own garments, but entered her swiftly and with throbbing force. She tightened in his arms and clung to him, a sexy little whimper escaping from her lips.

Then the pitch-black room seemed to revolve in vortexes of liquid color as they climbed through endless spirals of sensation until they exploded together in great, tumultuous waves, then fell into blackness, still clinging to each other desperately.

"I ought to tan your beautiful little hide," Carson said weakly after several moments.

Meg grinned in the dark. "Don't try to tell me you didn't enjoy it." She moved her hand to rest over his still thudding heart.

"Enjoy it, hell. You darn near killed me. What were you trying to do, save Villa's men the trouble?"

His words wiped the smile off her face. How could she have forgotten where they were?

"At least now you know that I'm not always the one who needs the rescuing," she told him with just a touch of conceit.

He gave her a light swat on her bottom. "From where I'm sitting, nobody has rescued anybody. We're both still prisoners, and before long Villa's thugs will be coming back to deal with us."

Meg snuggled up against him. "We can't give up, Carson. There must be some way to escape."

He hugged her to him. "Did I say anything about giving up? I'm just taking a breather, trying to recover from being rescued by you."

Meg was glad he couldn't see her burning face in the dark. She didn't know what had come over her. Now that it was over, she couldn't believe she had been so bold. But it had been intensely exciting. She had the feeling that it was only the beginning of what she could experience with this dangerous and passionate man she had fallen in love with, if they could just get out of here.

"What are we going to do?" she asked him.

He gave her a final squeeze, then set her aside and began reassembling his clothes. "Get dressed, sweetheart. And while you do, tell me everything you can remember about what Aguirre and the guards said."

"They hardly said anything. Just that Villa himself would be back here in the morning to—" her voice faltered "—to supervise your execution."

Carson's voice was firm, reassuring. "Don't go soft on me now, vixen—that's my girl. Now what else?"

"There was something about a raid . . . they said they would be riding to a place called Columbus."

"Damnation." Carson swore furiously.

"What is it?"

"Columbus, New Mexico—it's one of the possible targets we knew Villa was considering for a definitive raid across the border—a whole town full of unsuspecting innocents just waiting for slaughter like lambs in a pen."

Meg sat back on her heels. "Good heavens! But I thought Villa had decided not to invade the States."

"I thought so, too," Carson answered her grimly. "But the mess up in El Paso—and perhaps even finding out the truth about me—must have changed his mind. If he hits Columbus, it means war. A border won't stop our army after that."

They sat together quietly. "We've got to figure a way out of here. Then we can send a telegram to the army warning them. They could intercept Villa at the border, before there's a chance for bloodshed." Meg's determined voice made Carson smile in spite of his worries. She never gave up, his feisty little vixen. He leaned over and gave her a kiss, sliding his lips along her cheek to find her mouth in the dark.

"You make it sound easy, sweetheart. But there are a couple problems. First, we have to get out of here. That's a bit of a long shot in itself. Then, supposing we do get out, there isn't a telegraph operator in all of Chihuahua who would send that kind of message—or any message at all, once the word gets out that Villa is looking for us.''

Meg refused to let her confidence be shaken. After the encounter they had just had, she felt full of energy and unaccountably happy, considering they were still prisoners. She had the unshakable feeling that together she and Carson could conquer the entire world if need be, much less Pancho Villa.

''Where is Columbus, anyway?'' she asked him.

''It's a couple miles north of the border into New Mexico, due west of El Paso.''

''Well then, we'll just ride there and warn them in person.''

''Meg, sweetheart, you're talking about a long hard ride from here through miles and miles of Chihuahua desert.''

''I've done it before, if you'll remember, Carson.''

Carson sighed. He definitely did remember the dreadful ride from El Paso to Chihuahua City with Meg as Villa's captive. It had been one of the most miserable times of his life, not knowing what the outlaw leader had planned for her. Why was it that since he had met her all he had tried to do was protect her—and all he had seemed to do was get her into worse and worse trouble?

''First things first,'' he said finally. ''Let's see what we can do about getting ourselves out of here.''

He stood up, his unbound legs tingling as they went back into an upright position. He stretched his hands along the wooden wall of the tiny room, trying to feel for anything that could be of use to them. His fingers touched what felt like a buggy harness, then some pulleys, a wagon sling, grappling hooks. Exploring farther his elation grew, and he gave a little cry of success.

It appeared that the room they were in was some sort of toolshed for the stable. The walls were literally covered with heavy barn implements. He would never have imagined that his former outlaw colleagues could be so foolish as to shut him in a room full of natural weapons. Of course, they had thought him bound and helpless, not counting on Meg's escape-artist abilities.

He lifted a heavy iron hayfork off its hook and hefted it with satisfaction. With such a weapon and the element of surprise on his side, he would have no trouble making short work of several guards.

"Do you think there were more than just the two of them set to guard us?" he asked Meg in an excited whisper.

"That's all I saw. What have you found?"

"Our ticket out of here, if luck is with us."

He reached down and helped her up to a standing position beside him. "Listen carefully," he told her tersely. "When I say 'now', I want you to scream like a wailing banshee—then get back as far as you can into the corner here."

"Don't you want me to help you with the guards?"

Carson gave an exasperated little sigh. "For once, Meg sweetheart, I want you to keep your lovely little neck out of this. I'll handle it."

"You wouldn't even be standing up if I hadn't untied you," Meg couldn't resist reminding him.

He sounded impatient now, anxious to get into action. "Yes, love, I'm aware of that. And I won't forget it."

His voice dropped in pitch. "Neither will I forget what you did before you untied me." The recent memory of her mouth on his body caused a hot flash to run through him, but he forced himself to ignore it, steeling himself to concentrate on the matter at hand.

"Are you ready?"

Meg's stomach had suddenly stiffened at the thought of what Carson was about to do—face two heavily armed men alone. Her hands felt like ice.

"I'm ready." To her disgust, her voice sounded weak and scared, and she cleared her throat, trying for a stronger, more confident tone. "Be careful, Carson."

"Just be sure you stay well back out of the way, Meg. I can't be worrying about where you are." He took a deep breath. "All right—this is it—*now!*"

The intensity of her scream splitting the blackness of the room startled them both, and Carson felt off balance for just a moment, but seconds later, when the wooden door of the room creaked cautiously open, he was ready.

He shoved back on the door with all his might, bowling over the guard on the other side. Without even looking at the first man, Carson gave a lightning glance around the outer room and spotted the second guard, his eyes widened in shock, as he was just getting out of a chair a few feet away.

Before the man was halfway up, Carson had reached him and sent him swiftly into unconsciousness with a quick, efficient blow to the side of his head. Then he whirled around in time to reach the guard behind the door, who had his gun half out of its holster. Reaching out his long arm, Carson crashed the heavy tool down on the man's back, stunning him enough to make him lose hold on the gun. Then he finished the job with a quick chop to the back of his neck. The outlaw slumped slowly to the ground, out cold.

Meg peered cautiously from the door of the tool-room. She swallowed back a sour taste in her throat. It was hard for her to believe that this lean, lethal-looking man who had just neatly dispatched two men with a hayfork and his two hands had used those same hands on her with such tenderness only a carson time ago.

She shuddered and looked around the dimly lit room. "Are there any others?" she asked softly.

"We won't wait around to find out."

As quietly as possible and watching all the time for signs of Villa's men, they found two horses and rode quickly down one of the dark streets of Chihuahua City.

This time they didn't stop at the outskirts. Neither spoke, each full of thoughts about their close escape, and the intensity that had overtaken them during their encounter in their small prison.

Meg was thinking that without a doubt the little *zorrita,* darling of the ranch hands and her father's pampered daughter, was gone. She was Carson's vixen now. Whether he was willing to settle down or whether she would have to follow him on his adventures, she was irrevocably his. Their marriage had perhaps not been legal, but she was his, for better or worse.

Carson's mind was running along the same lines. When they had taken Meg and shut him up by himself, he had spent the time letting his imagination torture him with scenes of what the outlaws might be doing to her, and blaming himself for her fate. He should have let her go that first day by the stream before she almost sliced his neck in two, he had told himself bitterly. He should never have gone through with the sham marriage, should absolutely never have laid a hand on her. And once she was safely back on her father's ranch—out of danger—he should definitely not have followed her there.

But Meg's actions during their moments together in the tiny prison had turned his self-recriminations to wonder. Here was a woman who had faced kidnapping, a brutal attack by that scum Aguirre, a deadly shoot-out, and was facing death or worse at the hands of the outlaws, and she coolly escaped her bonds, then began teasing him—hell, *torturing* him with pleasure.

He had never met anyone like her, and he no longer had any doubts. If that damn marriage they had gone through in Mexico was not legal, the first thing he was going to do after they settled this matter of the Columbus attack was find someone who would *make* it legal.

He looked over at Meg riding beside him. Even after the tension of the past days and an entire night without sleep, she rode like a champion, her back straight, her arms relaxed.

"I'm going to start calling you Timothy," she said suddenly.

He grinned, the name on her lips evoking vague childhood emotions of happiness and security. "How come?"

"It's not that I think you've become any more civilized," she said primly. "It's just that, well, if I'm going to be *Mrs.* Carson, it doesn't seem right that I go on calling you Carson."

He pondered her words for a moment, then said softly, "Are you sure you want to talk about being civilized, after what you just did to me back at the livery stable?"

Meg's inevitable blush spread up her face. "You must think I'm a hussy," she murmured.

He wanted to stop, tumble her down into his arms and show her in no uncertain terms exactly what he did think of her, but common sense prevailed. They needed to keep riding if they wanted to stay ahead of Villa's men and arrive at Columbus in time to warn its people about the raid.

They were camped for what they both hoped would be their last night on Mexican soil for a long time. To-morrow they would cross the border. It had been a long, arduous trip, but they were both cheered by the fact that there had been no sign of Villa. They must be still ahead of him.

Carson tiredly finished unsaddling the horses and staking them out for the night. The dry desert air was heavy with heat, even though the sun had disappeared more than an hour ago.

He had to admit he was exhausted. He had pushed himself and his horse about as hard as ever before in his life, and he kept waiting for Meg to show some signs of collapse. But it seemed that this last escape from Villa had given her boundless energy, and a kind of cheerful exuberance that no amount of fatigue could conquer.

It would have been easier, in a way, to have her just the tiniest bit tired, or depressed or intimidated. Hell, this vixen of his seemed to thrive on adversity. But it didn't change his mind about what he was about to tell her.

He sat down beside her on a grassy hillock where she was leaning back on her hands and contemplating the desert sky—a velvety blackness pierced with millions of tiny crystals.

"Have you ever seen anything so magnificent, Carson?" she asked him dreamily.

"How can you look so happy, Meg? Aren't you the least bit tired?" Carson's voice held just a tinge of irritation. He knew he was about to make the smile disappear from her lovely face.

"I'm just thinking. Tomorrow we reach Columbus and warn them about the raid, then we can telegraph home and maybe ask Papa to meet us in El Paso for the wedding. I do believe it's time you made an honest woman of me."

Her teasing tone splashed him with warmth, but he steeled himself for what he had to say. "Meg, when we reach the border tomorrow, I'm heading for Columbus, and you're going back to El Paso."

"What are you talking about, Carson?" She sat up sharply.

"I don't want you riding with me to Columbus. Villa could be there at any time—it's too dangerous for you."

"For me?" she asked him angrily. "And I suppose it's not too dangerous for you? You know very well that Villa will shoot you on sight."

"Then I'll just have to be sure he doesn't catch sight of me," he said mildly.

"Wrong—*we* have to be sure he never catches sight of *us.*"

Carson slammed his fist against his leg. "Now, listen here, Meg. There's no way—"

She refused to let him finish. "No, you listen to me, Carson. I've made my decision. You promised back in San Felipe that we would be together till death do us part, and as of now I'm holding you to that promise. If you're riding to Columbus, I am, too."

He knew that calm, firm tone from past experience, but he was not ready to give up just yet. "Don't be difficult, Meg. I can get there faster if I ride alone—and do a better job of helping those people if I don't have to be worrying about you all the time."

Meg gave an indignant humph and shoved a tiny finger at his chest. "Worrying about me? Let's just remember, Captain Carson, just exactly where you would be if I hadn't been able to free you back in Chihuahua—on the wrong end of Villa's firing squad, that's where."

Carson shook his head at her triumphant little smile. He had a desperate urge to wipe the smugness off her face with a kiss, and he knew right then that he had lost the argument.

"All right, Meg. I give up, on one condition. When we reach Columbus, you are to do exactly as I say, no heroics. You stay out of trouble, do you understand me?"

She looked up at him, her golden eyes wide with innocence. "Why, Carson," she said demurely, "when have you ever known me to get into trouble?"

This time Carson did not resist his urge. Easily lifting her into his lap with his strong arms, he bent over her and proceeded to very thoroughly banish any thoughts of Columbus or Villa from both their minds.

"I love you, Timothy Carson," she whispered after several long moments.

"I love you, too, vixen," he told her hoarsely. He eased her down to the ground and gently covered her with his hard body. The star-splashed jet-black sky closed in around them as they made love on the dry desert grass.

Chapter Seventeen

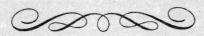

They were too late.

It was just a little past dawn, but the reddish glow they were watching was in the *western* sky, and it could only be blazing remains of the town of Columbus after the handiwork of Villa's men.

"They must have ridden through the night and attacked before dawn," Carson said grimly.

"How could they have gotten there ahead of us, Carson?" Meg's voice cracked with frustration. They both were thinking the same thing. While they had been blissfully making love under the stars last night, Villa and his men had passed them.

"If we had just kept on riding last night—" Meg said despairingly, voicing their mutual thoughts.

"We did our best, Meg. It's maybe one thing I've had a bit more opportunity to learn than you. You do your best and try your darnedest, and sometimes even that's just not enough."

Tears burned behind her eyelids. "We ought to go into town and see if we can help."

Carson nodded without speaking.

"It could be dangerous," she went on. "Villa's men might still be there."

"I hope they are," Carson said in a deadly soft voice. Without looking back at Meg, he spurred his horse forward through the chaparral toward the flaming town.

On the outskirts of town frightened citizens worked side by side with soldiers, setting up makeshift gun ports with sandbags.

Carson called out to a young corporal, who was briskly trying to direct the volunteers into some kind of organized effort. "Are Villa's men still here?" he asked the soldier.

The man took only a moment to glance over at Meg and Carson, then went back to his sandbagging, talking while he worked. "We think the worst is over. We know many of them have pulled out, but most of our able-bodied men are fighting the fires, so we're trying to set up a defense line here just in case."

"Where was the cavalry when Villa attacked?"

The man gave Carson a frustrated glance. "Well, sir, it appears this Villa fellow lives under some kind of lucky star. A lot of our men were over in El Paso for a polo match. Then there was a bunch stationed out at the Gibson ranch—they didn't get into town until dawn."

The man stopped piling the heavy bags for a moment and shook his head. Rivulets of sweat poured down his face. "We just never thought the bastard would really do it."

"Is the way clear to company headquarters?"

"As far as I know."

Carson got terse directions from the young soldier. As he went back to his task, Carson nodded his thanks, wished the man luck, then motioned to Meg to follow him. He wanted to get to the army headquarters, both to find out how he could best help, and to get Meg somewhere safe.

From the volume of black smoke billowing up against the vivid blue of the New Mexico sky, it was obvious that much of the town was in flames, and Carson carefully avoided the downtown area as he led Meg through back streets of the devastated town. They rode in silence, the occasional weak sounds of sporadic gunfire serving as grim reminders that the battle was not yet over.

As they passed the first side street that led to the main part of town, Meg pulled up her horse sharply. When Carson stopped and turned around, he saw that she was looking intently down the narrow street toward several neat shop fronts running along one side of it.

"What is it, Meg?" Carson asked with a touch of annoyance.

"I think that's Villa's horse," she said excitedly.

He followed the direction of her eyes. Sure enough, the remarkable white stallion was unmistakable. It was tied to a hitching post in front of what appeared to be a men's hat store.

Carson shook his head in amazement. "It is Villa's horse, and that's Aguirre's next to it, but where are the rest of his men? Surely he wouldn't stop here by himself."

Carson thought swiftly. He didn't like the idea of involving Meg in still another dangerous incident, but he had to check this out. He found it hard to believe that here of all places Villa would be without his usual entourage, but then, the only sure thing about Villa was that he was unpredictable.

The opportunity was too good to pass up. If they could walk in and capture Pancho Villa just like that, this whole border conflict would be over.

They tied their horses out of sight of the street. Carson doubled-checked his revolver to be sure it was fully loaded. Then, with some misgivings, he handed his rifle to Meg. He knew there was no way he could make her stay behind, and if she were going to be involved, she might as well have a way to protect herself. At least she had proven she was a good shot, he consoled himself.

The store was in a neat single-story whitewashed building, and they approached a tiny window to one side of it. The scene within Meg would not have credited if she hadn't seen it with her own eyes. There was Pancho Villa, in the middle of a daring border raid, preening himself in front of an elegant cheval mirror. On his head was a gray felt derby, looking ridiculously incongruous with his stained trail clothes.

Near him, half sitting on a table piled high with hats, was Rodolfo Aguirre, his expression a mixture of boredom and contempt as he watched his leader satisfying his untimely whim.

Carson leaned toward Meg and said in her ear, "I'll be damned, but it seems that Villa is taking advantage of his raid for some shopping."

Meg gave a half-hysterical giggle. She couldn't believe that they were just feet away from the leader who had caused all this destruction around them.

"I'm going to go in the front door," he whispered to her, pulling her to one side of the window. "Watch here from the window. Don't move until you see that I have them both covered—then you can come in."

With the stealth of a coyote stalking a chicken coop, he crouched low to pass under the window and headed toward the front of the building. Meg's knuckles grew white around the barrel of the rifle as she waited for some sound to indicate that he had entered the shop.

After several seconds that felt like hours, her impatience grew unbearable. Through the window she had glimpsed a door, partitioned off by a curtain at the rear of the store.

Quietly she made her way around to the back of the building. Just as she reached the tiny back door, she heard a commotion coming from inside the store. A gunshot sounded impossibly loud, causing her to jump reflexively. Then she heard a shout, followed by Carson's strong bass voice.

Unable to stand the suspense, she carefully opened the door.

"So, *gringo*, you shoot one of us, but the other one then will most certainly shoot you." It was Aguirre's hated voice, and from around the curtain Meg could see that the three men in the room seemed to be in some kind of a standoff, each with a drawn gun.

Taking a great gulp of air, she lifted the rifle and stepped firmly around the curtain. "Drop the guns, *señores*." Her schoolgirl Spanish made the words sound ludicrous as they came out of her mouth, but her hold on the rifle was firm and steady—and it was aimed with deadly accuracy at Aguirre's heart.

Carson scarcely had time to be once again piqued by having to accept help from his woman. Maybe I'm getting used to it, he thought to himself, as he shot her an admiring look, then carefully made his way over to Aguirre and pulled the pistol out of his hand.

The bandit's sharp eyes were on Meg. They held hatred and his usual perverted kind of lust, but there was a touch of admiration in them for the slender young woman in front of him.

"You don't deserve this woman, *gringo*," he said to Carson, then spit on the floor in a gesture of disgust.

Carson motioned for him to back up against one wall, which was covered to the ceiling with hats. With quick efficiency, he rid Villa of his pistol, then moved all the weapons well beyond the reach of the two men.

He was working from instinct, still in a state of disbelief that he had captured—with Meg's help—the most notorious outlaw in the Southwest. But now that the deed was done, he was beginning to have his doubts about the wisdom of his actions.

It would not be an easy task to get Villa and Aguirre safely turned over to the authorities. He was afraid to send Meg out into the still-battling city for help, and he certainly couldn't leave her here with the two men alone while he went.

"We'll have to tie them up, Meg."

Her insides were churning, but she nodded to him calmly. "Do you want me to do it?"

"Are you as good tying knots as you are untying them?" he asked her with a small encouraging smile.

"Yup," she answered simply.

He rummaged around behind a counter full of stickpins and hatbands until he found a coil of packaging twine and a knife. Without lowering his gun, he pulled off a generous length of twine, held it with his teeth and cut it.

When he had cut off a second piece, he slowly walked over to Meg and handed them to her.

"You always let a woman do your job for you, *gringo?*" Aguirre sneered. "What's the matter? Are you afraid to come near me yourself?"

Carson ignored him and addressed Meg. "Stay as far behind them as you can and still be sure you're tying them securely. Don't be tenderhearted—pull with all your strength."

Meg laid the rifle down on the countertop, tucked one length of twine in her skirt band and stretched out the other one, ready to use it.

"All right now," Carson said tersely to the two prisoners, who were both still standing with their hands in the air. "I want you to move your hands very slowly around behind your backs. If either of you makes a sudden move, I'll blow you straight to hell."

Villa looked almost sorrowful as he complied with Carson's orders. He fixed his magnetic eyes on his erstwhile American colleague. "Carson," he said with the melodic, authoritative tones Meg had come to know, "I once called you my friend. I have no desire to see you hurt. Let us go. We'll call it even. You stay here in your own country with the beautiful bride I found for you, and I go back to mine."

Carson shook his head, his sharp eyes watching carefully as the two men moved their arms behind their backs.

"I'm sorry, *Jefe.*" He still gave him the title of respect. He and Villa were on different sides of the conflict, but that didn't alter the fact that the man had proved his extraordinary leadership qualities time and time again.

"I told you from the beginning the man was a *hijo de puta,*" Aguirre growled at his leader. "I told you to let me get rid of him, but you wouldn't listen to me."

Villa looked over mildly at his lieutenant. "It seems, Rodolfo, that these days you find a great deal to complain about regarding my actions."

Aguirre looked disgruntled but made no reply. By now Meg had made her way around him, giving the man a wide berth as she did so. When she was directly behind him, she held out the twine and took a deep breath.

She was going to tie Aguirre first. He was the bigger man, and to her mind, the more dangerous one. She moved closer and reached out with the rope. The sight of his big, meaty hands, the backs covered thickly in coarse black hair, brought back a wave of memories. She remembered those same hands on her, squeezing her as his body twisted into hers. She swayed and hesitated a moment, trying to clear her mind.

It happened so fast that she could not be completely clear on the sequence of events. All she knew was that at the first touch of the rope against Aguirre's wrists, her world turned upside down and she was in front of him, struggling in his arms.

While his lieutenant was wrestling with her, Villa lunged for the rifle and turned swiftly to point it at Carson's head. His voice was very soft. "Now you, *mi amigo*—drop the gun."

Carson closed his eyes for a moment in frustration. He looked over at Meg, straining futilely against Aguirre's hold on her, then lowered his hand and let his revolver clatter to the floor.

"Aguirre, put down the girl and pick up his gun." The calm command was back in Villa's voice. He was in the position he was most familiar with—in control.

Aguirre was holding Meg's slight body painfully against him. One of his big arms was around her waist and the other around her neck, twisting it at an excruciating angle.

"First I'm going to break the neck of this bitch," he told Villa, his voice sounding crazed. "I swear I'm going to twist her head off like a chicken's, right in front of the eyes of her lover here."

"Rodolfo, I said to let the girl go." Villa's voice stayed calm.

Aguirre turned deranged eyes on his leader. "I told you to give her to me. She's been nothing but trouble since she first arrived at camp. Now I don't care what you say, she belongs to me."

Regardless of the rifle pointed at him, Carson had been about to make a lunge for the Mexican when he saw Meg's grimace of pain as the big man's arms closed around her, but he stopped himself as he saw that Villa's expression had become cold and calculating.

"I will only say it one more time, Rodolfo." The words were said with a kind of deadly quiet that sent a chill along Meg's arms, but the man holding her seemed too much caught up in his own rage to be affected.

"Who are you anyway to tell me I can't have her?" he raged at his leader. "The great Centaur of the North, stopping in the middle of a battle to try on hats like some kind of a friggin', sissified dandy."

Before the words were out of his mouth, even Aguirre knew he had gone too far, but by then it was too late.

To Meg's shocked ears, the shot seemed to come from somewhere else, distant from the scene taking place around her. She saw as if in slow motion the jerk of the rifle against Villa's sturdy shoulder, saw Carson's eyes widen in amazement, then watched as he lunged across the room in time to pull her from Aguirre's arms before the big bandit collapsed, lifeless, to the floor.

Before Carson could turn her head away from the sight, her gaze fixed in horror at the bright red fountain of blood bubbling up from a hole directly between Aguirre's eyes.

Feeling Carson's arms strongly around her made reality return. She shuddered, and Carson hugged her more tightly.

Over her head he looked directly at Villa, his gaze half admiration, half defiance. "Nice shot," he said nonchalantly.

A small smile quirked the corner of Villa's mouth. Then he turned his attention to Meg. "Are you all right, Margarita?" he asked, using his wife's name for her.

Meg pulled herself slightly away from Carson's embrace and turned to Villa. "Why did you do it?" she asked him in wonder.

Villa shrugged. "My Lucita—she likes you."

He looked down with an expression of mixed disgust and sadness at Aguirre's big body crumpled on the floor. "She never liked Rodolfo," he said almost to himself. "Lucita never liked Rodolfo."

From out on the street came the sound of several horses approaching. Villa smiled. "My men," he said to Carson. "You see, my friend, they were coming back for me. You didn't really believe that Pancho Villa would be so foolish as to let himself be captured like a bushy-tailed squirrel?"

He laughed at Carson's look of chagrin. "Ah, you Americans. You're such optimists."

"So now what, *Jefe?*"

Villa stood looking at the two handsome Americans standing side by side in each other's arms. "I should shoot you, Carson," he said matter-of-factly. "You tricked me. It has been many years since anyone has been able to trick Pancho Villa, and the ones who have tried are now fertilizing the barren soil of my country."

He looked over to Meg. Her golden eyes were pleading.

Was this how it all would end? she was asking herself. This Mexican bandit with the short stature and the immeasurable presence would pull a trigger and all their dreams of a life together would be shattered forever?

She could feel Carson's body tense next to her, and her own nerves tightened in response. Suddenly she jumped as Villa gave a quick flip of his hand, shifting the rifle upward and out of firing position.

"I never gave you a wedding present, Margarita," he said. His cheerful tone was completely incongruous with the tightness of her nerves and the presence of Aguirre's dead body at their feet.

"So, I give you your husband's life. It's my present to you." His teeth gleamed as he fixed her with one of his famous broad smiles.

She sagged against Carson and closed her eyes. "Thank you," she murmured weakly.

Now that the decision was made, Villa became all efficiency again. He ran a finger along the stock of Carson's rifle. "It's a good gun," he said briskly. "I'll take it with me."

Quickly he collected the other weapons that Carson had taken from them—both his and Aguirre's—and after a moment's thought, he picked up Carson's revolver and tucked it into his gun belt.

"Maybe you won't need this anymore, Carson. Now that I've found you a wife, you can settle down and raise chickens somewhere, eh?" He laughed, and both Meg and Carson found themselves joining in his mirth out of sheer relief.

"That's sounding better and better to me, *Jefe*," Carson told him with a smile. He leaned over and gave Meg a solid kiss.

Villa watched them, beaming. "Ah, marriage. It's a wonderful institution, no?"

One of Villa's men from outside began pounding on the door. "*Jefe*, is everything all right?" the man called.

Villa stretched awkwardly with his arms full of weapons to give them a little farewell salute. "I'm coming," he called to the man outside.

He started toward the door, then as an afterthought, reached down to pick up the gray derby where it had fallen on the floor in the initial scuffle. He tucked it under his arm, then left the room without so much as a glance at his former lieutenant dead on the floor.

Neither Meg nor Carson said a word for a few moments after the door closed behind the powerful little man.

"I don't believe it," Carson said finally.

Meg, too, was shaking her head. "What do you think made him change his mind about shooting you?"

"You got me. I guess it's like I've said before—the one thing that's for sure about Villa is that nothing's for sure about Villa."

"Well, I think he's a romantic."

Carson raised a skeptical eyebrow.

"I mean it," she said firmly. "I think that's why he let us go—because we're in love with each other, and because he takes credit for arranging the whole thing."

"Villa hasn't controlled an army of thousands of men by being romantic, Meg."

"Nevertheless." Her eyes became dreamy.

Carson laughed and pulled her up against him for a kiss. "Just what I've always wanted in life—a romantic vixen."

"So what do we do now, Carson?" Meg murmured after several long moments that had become as romantic as either of them could stand.

Carson tried to regain control with a deep breath. "I think we ought to take Villa's words to heart."

Meg looked puzzled.

"You know," he went on. "The ones about marriage being a great institution."

Chapter Eighteen

"Are you sure your father won't pull out his shot-gun when he finds us staying in the same room?"

Meg giggled and burrowed down farther under the covers against the naked warmth of Carson's body. She couldn't believe that her fearless lover, who had braved alone Villa's entire band, was nervous about the arrival of her dignified, usually mild-mannered father. He had mentioned it several times since their arrival in El Paso last night.

They had exchanged telegrams with the ranch while still in Columbus, and the plans were for her father and Johnny to join them here for a final—legal, this time—wedding ceremony.

There had been no real reason to stay in Columbus. There had not been much they could do to help the hapless residents of the small New Mexico town. Villa's marauders had raided it of much of its supplies of food, weapons and other staples and had left a city full of charred ruins as their calling card. Now the towns-people were pulling together to try to restore what the raiders had left.

Upon their arrival at army headquarters, Meg and Carson had agreed to say nothing about the big Mexi-can bandit lying shot through the head in a hat shop in town. Aguirre's body would be found and marked as just another casualty of the day, and the story of their last, bizarre encounter with Pancho Villa would remain untold.

Amazingly, only eighteen Americans had so far been counted among the dead. The raid had proven more costly to Villa—at least 120 dead *villistas* were found. The bitter people of Columbus buried them roughly in a mass grave.

Meg and Carson had ridden back to El Paso in a subdued mood, shaken by the destruction they had seen, and almost unable to believe that it was now finally over. They could begin their life together without the shadow of Villa hanging over them.

But being able to spend the night with each other in a good clean bed had done much to restore their spirits. The only flaw had been Carson's anxiety about his reception by her father.

"Don't be silly, Carson darlin'." Though he had awakened her at dawn with a slow and amorous kiss that had led to a pleasantly drowsy session of lovemaking, she could feel that he was again rigid against the softness of her belly. She smiled and slid her hand along the tense muscles of his thighs.

"After all, we're already married, sort of." With exquisite slowness she trailed her fingers into the thick hair of his groin.

"And as soon as Papa and Johnny get here, we're going to be married again."

Her hand finally closed around its target and Carson groaned low in his throat.

"What time do we have to go meet their train?" he asked, his voice tight, stopping her gentle manipulations with a firm hand.

Her long gold eyelashes swept upward. "I told you last night—not until noon, love." She rolled away from him, her body cooling against the chilly sheets. "But, of course, if you'd like to go downstairs first for a big, hearty breakfast..."

In an instant he was on top of her, his hands entwined in her soft hair and his mouth against hers in a compelling kiss that left her breathless.

"That happens to be exactly what I want, my little vixen," he said in a low growl, "a very hearty breakfast."

Accordingly, they arrived late and a little hungry—but extremely satisfied—at the big El Paso station. Carson began to get edgy again as the train steamed in. This father-in-law business was one thing that years with the army had never prepared him for.

Meg was the first to spot the gray head of her tall father walking along at some distance down the tracks. She gave a little cry and ran to meet him, knocking his valise out of his hand with the exuberance of her greeting.

"Meg dearest." He hugged her tightly and his usually firm voice cracked a little. "You can't know how worried we were about you."

Behind him came Johnny, waiting his turn for a vigorous embrace. With a swift glance at Carson, he leaned over and kissed her full on the mouth.

"The next time you have a yen to head south of the border, *zorrita,*" he told her sternly, "I have your father's permission to tie you to a hitching post."

"Ah, but you should know that it wouldn't do much good, Silvano," Carson interrupted and put a possessive arm firmly around Meg's shoulders. "Meg happens to be an expert with knots."

Johnny looked puzzled as Meg and Carson gave each other a small, secretive smile.

"But I'm all for keeping her at home for a while," Carson added. He reached out and gave Johnny's hand a hearty shake. "I'll help you do it. Maybe chains would work."

"Now, see here—" Meg was immensely pleased to see the warmth of the handshake between the two men, but she refused to be discussed like some kind of stray puppy.

"We're just kidding, love." Carson leaned over and gave her a kiss on the top of her head. "I don't think even your friend Johnny would claim to be able to keep you under control for long. Heaven knows, I don't."

Her father was looking on in amusement. "Well, I'm glad to see that you gentlemen have come to the same conclusion I came to some twenty years ago, the first time she learned to bat those great long eyelashes at me."

"Oh, Papa." The lashes swept downward.

Carson turned to shake his prospective father-in-law's hand.

"We're certainly glad to have you back safely, son," Atherton told him warmly. "Are your obligations with this whole Villa mess over with now?"

Carson nodded. "A punitive expedition has been authorized, and Pershing will be heading across the border any day now. It's in their hands now."

"Will they catch him?"

Carson smiled. "Who knows? Chihuahua's got more Villa supporters than mesquite bushes. And Villa knows the sierra like his own hand."

Johnny had been restlessly glancing back toward the coach car where they had disembarked. "I thought we were invited here for a wedding, not to talk about a bunch of outlaws,'' he said, sounding jittery.

Meg looked at him curiously. "What is it, Johnny?"

He grinned. "We have a surprise for you."

With a graceful lope he ran back to the stairway of the railroad car, just in time to take the arm of a radiant young woman descending from the train.

Rosa Maria! Meg gave an elated shout, and then suddenly the two girls were weeping happily in each other's arms as the three men stood by, beaming.

"What are you doing here?" Meg managed finally. She extricated herself from her friend's embrace, and turned a questioning look on her father, then Johnny.

Johnny was the one who answered. "When Rosita found out that you were again in Villa's hands she insisted on returning to the ranch to see if she could do anything to help." He gave the blushing young Mexican a tender look.

Rosita? Meg looked at her two friends. The glance Rosa was sending back to Johnny was unmistakable.

Then she looked over at Meg shyly. "I have told my father that I will not marry into the Lopez Negrete family, Meg. He may never forgive me but—" she gave a little shrug and her face lit up in her characteristic sweet smile "—I think he will someday. In the meantime, your father has offered to let me stay with you on the ranch, as long as it takes until I can make them change their minds."

Shooting Meg a look of impudence, Johnny boldly reached over and took Rosa Maria's delicate hand in his own callused, brown one. "We'll take good care of her, won't we, Meg?"

A lovely blush painted itself across Rosa Maria's pale skin. Meg could hardly believe what she was seeing. She distractedly introduced Rosa to Carson.

Carson knew what the girl meant to Meg, and he turned the full force of his charm on her. "How come I never found anything as beautiful as you when I was south of the border?" he asked her with an engaging grin.

Meg took the opportunity to pull a reluctant Johnny a little ways off from the rest. "What's going on between you and Rosa?" she demanded bluntly. While she had to admit to herself that she felt just the slightest twinge of sadness when she saw the admiring look in his eyes as he gazed over at her lovely friend, her overriding reaction was one of deep happiness. She could not have wished for a sweeter companion for him.

Johnny had the grace to look slightly abashed. "She was so miserable, Meg, when she arrived, after the row with her family. And then we both were worried sick about you."

He swallowed deeply and looked uncomfortably at Meg's unreadable face. "Neither one of us meant for it to happen, *zorrita*—we just were kind of *consoling* each other."

At last Meg relented and let her smile break through. "I couldn't be happier for you both, Johnny," she told him, giving him a big hug to confirm her words.

Then she turned to give another to Rosa Maria, and it seemed all at once that everyone was laughing and hugging everybody else.

Meg ended up in the strong arms that had by now become the most familiar and dearest to her.

"Happy, sweetheart?" he asked her softly.

As her father smiled at them benevolently, she nodded and turned her lips up for a soft kiss that was a chaste acknowledgment of all the deeper passion they shared.

"It *is* like in the storybooks, Carson," she told him mistily, dropping her head onto his solid shoulder.

"Happily ever after, my love," he agreed.

Author's Note

Six days following the March 1916 raid on Columbus, New Mexico, "Black Jack" Pershing and his punitive expedition of 6,600 men crossed the border into Mexico. For the next eleven months, they chased Villa all over the sierra without ever so much as catching sight of him. His raids on Glen Springs, Boquillas, Eagle Pass and Dryden caused further deaths and property damage, but the people of northern Mexico continued to support and protect him. Some say this was the United States army's first experience in fighting guerrilla war, the type that has continued to bedevil it throughout this century.

Villa's real name was Doroteo Arango. Born in Durango of an impoverished family, he planted cotton on the Lopez Negrete *hacienda* until the degenerate son, Leonardo, raped Villa's sister. After killing Leonardo he was forced to turn outlaw and sometime later named himself Francisco Villa after a dead revolutionary hero.

There is no documentation of Villa's having had any peculiar fondness for hats, but his fondness for women was legendary. Several women have made claims to be his legal wife, but Maria Luz Corral was the one who lived with him in his Chihuahua City mansion. After his death she supported herself by opening up the house as a museum, where she herself greeted visitors until her death in the late 1970s.

Luz and Villa are the only real characters in this fictional account, though the character of Aguirre was based on Rodolfo Fierro, a lieutenant of Villa's who was famous for his brutal executions.

The U.S. army did actually have agents assigned to scout intelligence on Villa. Some of these men disappeared without a trace, as did the American writer and journalist Ambrose Bierce, who had intended to chronicle Villa's exploits.

After the assassination of President Venustiano Carranza in 1920, Villa finally came to terms with the Mexican government, and he was given a ranch near Parral. But Villa still had many enemies, and on July 19, 1923, he was shot there in an ambush. Though his body was found with forty-seven bullet wounds in it, the people of Chihuahua continued to insist for many years that their bandit-revolutionary hero still rode the sierra.

* * * * *

**Now that you've been introduced to our
March Madness authors, be sure to look for
their upcoming titles:**

From Miranda Jarrett—

COLUMBINE—Wrongly convicted for murder, Lady Diana Grey
finds herself on her way to the American Colonies as an inden-
tured servant.

From Ana Seymour—

ANGEL OF THE LAKE—The warm-hearted story of a widower,
wracked with guilt, and the woman who teaches him to love.

From Kit Gardner—

THE DREAM—A stiff-necked boarding school teacher is defense-
less against the charm of a handsome, carefree lord who has set
his sights on her.

From Margaret Moore—

CHINA BLOSSOM—Raised as a pampered Chinese slave, a young
Englishwoman must adjust to 19th-century British society.

Four great stories that you won't want to miss!

MMANB

**HARLEQUIN PROUDLY PRESENTS A
DAZZLING CONCEPT IN ROMANCE FICTION**

 One small town,
twelve terrific love stories

JOIN US FOR A YEAR IN THE FUTURE OF TYLER

Each book set in Tyler is a self-contained love story; together,
the twelve novels stitch the fabric of the community.

LOSE YOUR HEART TO TYLER!

Join us for the second TYLER book, BRIGHT HOPES, by
Pat Warren, available in April.

*Former Olympic track star Pam Casals arrives in Tyler to
coach the high school team. Phys ed instructor Patrick
Kelsey is first resentful, then delighted. And rumors fly about
the dead body discovered at the lodge.*

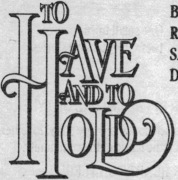